T0356122

The Light Through the Storm
By Margalit Ganor

Copyright © 2025 Margalit Ganor

Originally published 2022 in Israel by Valcal Software Ltd.

All rights reserved; Except for brief passages quoted in
newspaper, magazine, radio, television, or online reviews, no
parts of this book may be reproduced in any form or by any
means, electronic or mechanical, including photocopying
or recording, or by information storage or retrieval system,
without the permission, in writing from the publisher.

Published in the United States by Seventh Street Books,
an imprint of Start Science Fiction, LLC,
221 River Street, Ninth Floor, Hoboken, New Jersey, 07030.

Printed in the United States
Translation: Jerry Hyman
Cover design: eBookPro
Cover photo: Shutterstock
Text design: eBookPro

First Edition.

10 9 8 7 6 5 4 3 2 1

Trade paper ISBN: 978-1-64506-107-6
E-book ISBN: 978-1-64506-109-0

The Light Through the Storm:

A Heroic WW2 Historical Novel Based on a True Story

By Margalit Ganor

VIVA
EDITIONS

"Laugh, O laugh at all my visions,
I, the dreamer, tell you true;
Laugh for I believe in man still,
For I still believe in you."

Shaul Tchernichovsky, 1892
(Translated from Hebrew by Sholom J. Kahn)

To my parents, Machiku and Donia, of blessed memory
To my husband, Eli, of blessed memory
To my daughters, Osnat, Gili, and Liat
To my grandchildren, Shalev, Daniel, Yuval, and Yael

Prologue

Chernowitz, Bukowina, Romania, 1940

It was 7 p.m. and the curfew was in effect. It was forbidden to be out in the street. If caught, he would be shot on the spot. He looked around and saw no one. Machiku tightened the thin coat that was left after the Russians looted the house and he continued on his way.

A freezing wind blew. It was about to rain again. The click of his heels echoed on the beautiful stones that led from Herrengasse past the Opera House to his home at 17 General Mircescu Street. He wasn't concerned about the clicking of his shoes, rather about rescuing his family. His heart pounded as he approached their apartment. Avoiding the elevator lest anyone see him, he ran up the stairs, two at a time. He put the key in the door and entered quietly so as not to wake the child.

The house was cold. It had been a while since they'd lit the fireplace – due to lack of firewood. Donya came out to meet him, wrapped in a coat. He hugged her and led her into the kitchen. Then he addressed her in a self-assured tone, trying not to alarm her.

"Donika, we must go. Now," he told her.

She stared at him in amazement.

"Go? Where? Now, at night? The child is asleep and it's terribly cold."

"We have to go now," he repeated firmly.

"I don't understand," she said, her voice filled with anxiety. "We're not allowed out at night. Tell me what happened."

"We need to leave the apartment."

Chapter 1

Chernowitz, Romania, 1938

Until the age of forty-five, "Machiku" lived at home with his mother, Regina-Rivka. She pampered him and called him "my jewel." He admired her tremendously and valued her wisdom. One morning, when he was about to leave for the office, dressed in his fashionable three-piece suit, clean-shaven, wearing pleasing cologne, his pince-nez eyeglasses with a nose clip securely on the bridge of his nose, Regina came out of the kitchen to speak to him:

"Machiku," she said, looking serious, "I want to talk to you about something very important."

"What does Mom want to talk to me about right now, when I'm just about to go to work?" he wondered.

Machiku – Dr. Leon Schmelzer – was a well-known criminal lawyer with a splendid office located on the second floor of a large building. Its windows overlooked Herrengasse, one of the most famous streets in the city of Chernowitz, today known as Chernivtsi.

Beautiful Chernowitz, capital of the Bukovina Province in Romania, was part of the Austro-Hungarian Empire from 1848 until 1918. They called it "Little Vienna" in those days. A modern city, its houses were adorned with rounded moldings, its streets paved with stones. Horse-drawn carts for hire, *fiackers*, transported the populace from place to place. The city's multiculturalism influenced all aspects of life. A babel of languages was spoken on the streets: Romanian, German and Yiddish.

There was a dynamic Jewish community. Many Jewish organizations were established, newspapers and journals were plentiful. Writers, poets, journalists, notable men of science, were all an integral part of the society.

Machiku wasn't tall; he wore pince-nez clip-on glasses, and had a strong, energetic voice. Besides practicing law, he was politically active, one of the leaders of the Jewish community. He also served as director of the national branch of the JNF in Bukovina. A great many of both Jewish and non-Jewish citizens of Chernowitz knew him.

Machiku, a confirmed bachelor, sailor, and sportsman, would often leave town, taking one of the pretty Chernowitz girls on climbing treks in the mountains surrounding the city.

Now he entered the kitchen that was filled with the appetizing aroma of baking pastries. He sat down at the table, waiting to hear what his mother had to say. She served him a cup of steaming hot tea and one of the freshly baked *rugelach* right out of the oven.

Regina had never meddled in his affairs, although if he asked for advice, she was always ready to listen and offer it. Today, however, it was she who initiated the conversation. She sat opposite him and immediately got to the point.

"Machiku, my dear son," she began in her soft, pleasing voice, not admonishing, merely speaking as a loving mother, "you are already forty-five years old. How long will you continue to live as a bachelor, without a wife, without children to carry on your name?"

The ground beneath Machiku gave way. She had never broached this subject before and had always trusted him to make his own decisions. Several matchmakers had come to her with prospects for her son, but she sent them all away. She had never intervened in his personal life.

"Mamaleh, who do you want me to marry? One of the girls I take with me hiking in the mountains? None of them suits me," he said calmly so as not to hurt her feelings.

"I'm thinking of someone in particular. I believe she may even love you."

"What? Who?" Machiku pondered aloud, straightening the pince-nez spectacles on his nose.

"Miss Donya Blumenfeld, your secretary for the past ten years."

Machiku felt as if his mother had dropped a bomb. Miss Ida Donya Blumenfeld was already twenty-eight, but in his eyes, still an innocent young girl. She was the daughter of religiously devout parents. Her father, Zvi Hersch, was a grain trader, and her mother Yetti was a homemaker who had raised three daughters: the eldest, Nussia, then Ruzicka, who died at age sixteen, and finally Donya.

Donya was slender and lovely. Her auburn hair suited her smooth, fair complexion. Since she came from a religious home, her parents were very protective. She was always modestly and tastefully dressed, with no cleavage, God forbid, or sleeveless blouses. She wore dainty doll shoes and a small hat as was customary in those days. She had worked with Machiku for years, always striving to better herself. She had learned French, English, and bookkeeping.

Ten years ago she had come to the office of Machiku, who was sixteen years her senior. He trained her to run the office; she had learned to keep the accounts and speak with clients, sometimes even intimidating those who came in for a consultation with the criminal defense lawyer.

Machiku respected her intelligence and the speed with which she learned. She was modest and unassuming, always with a smile on her face at the right moment. He appreciated her ability to manage the office by herself while he was away on his travels. However … marry her? He was a man of the world and led a full, active life. She was young, quiet, and innocent. Their relationship had never crossed the line of politeness and appropriate behavior. There wasn't a hint of flirtation or frivolity between them. She addressed him by his full title, Dr. Schmelzer, and he called her Miss Blumenfeld. It had never occurred to him to think of her as a candidate for marriage.

He had already seen a great deal of the world; his life was rewarding and satisfying. Why would he even consider getting married? Still, his mother had brought up the subject and got him thinking. He cleared his throat. "She'll slap me in the face," he said. But Regina noticed a sparkle in his eyes.

"Go to her, my son. And if she's not convinced, bring her to me."

Machiku said goodbye to his mother and set off, deep in thought. What an idea. Marriage! With Miss Blumenfeld? It had never entered his mind. Should he give up his agreeable life as a bachelor? He always had plenty of women around him. How could he give up the good life and take on the responsibility of a family? That would completely change his life. The idea began to take hold.

As much as his mother's advice had surprised him, he began to envision himself walking arm in arm with the lovely young Donika. He imagined hearing a crying baby, and suddenly the idea to marry and start a family began to appeal to him. Moreover, the images that entered his mind aligned with two principles in which he believed. According to the first, things happen at a certain time and place because that is what God has determined. As for the second, things happen because they're preordained. One must accept them and look for the good in them.

However, how could he suddenly propose marriage to someone whom he had not flirted with even once, especially since he respected her peace of mind, her modesty, and her beauty?

Taking brisk steps, he strode from his mother's house on Turkengasse to his office, but instead of going in he entered the café near the square. He would not be able to look at Donya in the same way as before. Everything had changed. Now he saw her from a different perspective. He had to think it through, to calm the emotional turmoil that had overtaken him after the talk with his mother.

Machiku sat at a corner table and gazed out at the street. He could see the square, the Ringplatz, in all its splendor. Everywhere was evidence of the of the Habsburgs' construction style since the reign of Emperor Franz Joseph I. There was the magnificent city hall, with its splendid architecture and unique elegance, and the glorious opera house borne upon pillars topped by curving embellishments, all like the identical buildings in Vienna.

It was warm inside the café. People sat and chatted with each other, a plate of the café's special pastries set before them: apple strudel with the house whipped cream, Viennese Linzer Torte, and coffee and tea served in delicate porcelain cups, their edges trimmed with gold.

"Coffee and a blintz?" the waitress asked. She knew what he usually ordered.

"Just coffee today." She raised an eyebrow but said nothing.

Some of the customers acquainted with him tried to catch his eye to strike up a conversation, but he was engrossed in his own thoughts.

"He must be preparing for the trial of that criminal who attacked the old woman with an axe," someone said, and they left him alone.

Machiku sipped his coffee, and as usual made a quick decision, as fast as the speed of his sips. He paid the bill and left a tip for the waitress on the table, then stood up and made his way to the office.

In the reception area, absorbed in her work on the typewriter, sat his secretary.

"Miss Blumenfeld," he muttered, passing her as he entered his office, "could you please come into my room?"

As usual, Donya brought her notebook and pencil, ready to transcribe her employer's letters and instructions. She was wearing a floral mid-length dress, elegant and modest, with dainty doll shoes on her feet. It would never have occurred to her what awaited. She entered the room.

"Miss Blumenfeld," Machiku began abruptly without prior preparation, and said, "Would you agree to marry me?"

She froze as if hit by a lightning bolt. Her face turned crimson. The notebook fell from her hands. Dumbstruck. Could her esteemed employer have possibly fathomed the feelings she often had about him, the ones she was always careful to put out of her mind? She didn't know how to describe her emotions, nor did she dare utter the word "love."

She had never gone out alone with a man, not even as a casual acquaintance. Although her parents and friends had tried to arrange matches for her, she refused all offers. Dr. Schmelzer? She didn't dare call him by his first name, Leon, not even to herself. He was a wealthy, well-known lawyer, and she his simple secretary. They had always kept a proper distance out of mutual respect and their age difference. She looked to him as a father figure, and suddenly he's asking her to be his wife? Thoughts raced through her mind. She felt as if a huge dam had burst open and flooded her to the point where she almost fainted.

"Dr. Schmelzer, are you mocking me? What have I done that you speak to me like this?" she asked, leaning on the chair near her for support, trying to keep her knees from knocking.

"I'm serious," Machiku replied resolutely. "Would you do me the honor of marrying me?"

Donya turned pale, not believing what she was hearing. Machiku noticed.

"If you don't believe that I'm sincere, come with me to my mother's and she will confirm what I have said."

Donya knew Regina well, as Machiku's mother had often invited Donya to their home for Friday night dinner and on the holidays. Donya respected her intelligence and kind-heartedness. "What did Regina have to do with all this?" she wondered.

"Come, we'll go to her now," continued Machiku.

Donya was muddled, feeling helpless. He took her arm in his and rushed ahead, determined.

They left the office and walked arm in arm towards his mother's house. Donya trembled at the physical contact between them. She had never walked in such a manner with any man. Brought up in an observant home, she followed a clear code of conduct concerning any connection with the opposite sex.

It had happened so quickly, with no forewarning. One moment she was the loyal secretary of the learned lawyer Dr. Leon Schmelzer, and the next she was Machiku's intended bride, on her way to meet her future mother-in-law.

"Maybe...we should...go to my parents' house first?" she offered, her voice cracking.

"Yes, it's very important that we do so."

Donya now believed that he was serious, although she had not yet come to grips with the powerful feelings that threatened to overwhelm her. The intimacy with which he had behaved shook her, body and soul.

They changed their route and continued until they approached Donya's parents' house, located opposite the Great Synagogue. Quite by chance, it was exactly at that moment that her parents stood on their small front balcony watching the passers-by on the street.

"Hersch! Come and see with whom Donya is walking arm in arm?" the astonished Yetti, Donya's mother, exclaimed, horrified.

"Our Donya with a strange man?" Her father was shocked. "This is hard to believe."

"Who is it?" Yetti said, alarmed, widening her eyes to try to discern who the man was.

"*Donika mit a bocher?* Donika with a man? Who is he? How did this happen?"

The couple came nearer until they saw their daughter was walking arm in arm with her employer, Dr. Schmelzer.

"What disrespect! How dare he?" Hersch snorted.

"Maybe something happened? Maybe she was hurt and he's helping her, God forbid?"

The couple went up to the first floor, to Donya's parents' apartment, and knocked on the door. The flustered parents opened it, first taking a sharp look at their daughter to make sure she was well and unharmed.

"Thank God, you're all right," Yetti hugged her.

"Of course I'm all right, Mama. Why would you think otherwise?" Donya asked.

"Because we never imagined our daughter would allow herself to walk down the street arm in arm with a man!" bellowed Hersch. "You have shamed us in public!"

"I'm sorry," Dr. Schmelzer interjected. "I know that this is highly unusual, but I permitted myself to link my arm with your daughter's because I have come to ask you for her hand in marriage."

Hersch and Yetti were in shock. The room was silent. Donya's heart was pounding so hard she thought everyone could hear it. Yetti knew that Dr. Schmelzer was a lawyer from a good family, yet even when a matchmaker offers a match, the couple is obliged to ask permission to venture out in public together. Hersch thought this behavior was unexpected and unacceptable.

Donya overcame her parents' bewilderment. In an instantaneous decision, she went to them, hugging first her mother, and then her father. It was important that they support her and accept him as their son-in-law – despite the age difference and the complete surprise.

"My dear *maideleh*, my girl," said her mother, grasping what her daughter's embrace meant. "May it be for a blessing."

Hersch hesitated, but then reached out to take Leon's hand. "She's a rare gem. Take good care of her," he said guardedly.

"If this is to be, let us raise a glass to God Who has joined these two together." Machiku was swept away by the excitement. Thus far, he had acted quickly as was his custom, but now that her parents had given their consent, he became fully conscious of what he had embarked upon. He was about to bind himself for life to this lovely, delicate young woman in the presence of her mother and father.

"What about Regina? Does she know?" Yetti asked.

"I believe that in her heart she knows that Donya was meant to be my wife. We'll go now to tell her and the rest of the family."

Machiku looked into Yetti's blue-gray eyes, searching them for approval. It had all been done in an unusual way, but Yetti caressed Donya, and Hersch touched her shoulder as if to say, "Go, my daughter, with my blessing."

Machiku bowed as was the Viennese custom and shook Hersch's hand. The couple set out for Regina's house.

Through the window, she saw them approaching arm in arm. "Thank you, *Riboino Shel Oilam*. Oh, thank you, God!" murmured Regina in Yiddish.

Chapter 2

Regina, née Huttman, came to the house of Yossel Schmelzer at age twenty. He was twenty-five years her senior. She was a girl from a poor home, and he a *gvir*, a wealthy, respected man of high standing.

When he reached marriageable age, the matchmaker brought Yossel to the Huttman family home. He was tall and burly, with a long beard. As was the Hasidic custom, he wore a festive white cotton robe with a black coat on top, boots, and a black hat.

The Huttman apartment was on the ground floor of a building in a Chernowitz suburb where low-income families lived. The streets weren't paved. In the rain, the residents had to struggle with the mud; when it snowed, they sank up to their knees in it.

"We have come to speak with regard to your eldest daughter," announced the matchmaker.

Huttman seated them on the chairs around the dining room table. The room was simply furnished. In the corner was a wooden table covered with a plaid tablecloth on which they dined. Opposite were a bed and a dark cupboard containing prayer books, a bottle of *schnapps*, and tiny, azure-tinted glasses. Through the door, the kitchenette could be seen, with large pots piled up to save space. Huttman brought out the schnapps and poured it into the glasses.

"Yossel Schmelzer is a highly regarded gvir," said the matchmaker to Huttman, waving his arms to emphasize the importance of the groom as if he weren't present in the room with them.

Yossel was used to having his own opinions and making decisions without others doing it for him. However, in those days it was impossible to initiate a relationship or start a family without the services of a matchmaker.

"His family originates from the city of Vermeiza in Germany, and later settled in Stupca-Bukovina," boasted the matchmaker. "The Empress Maria Theresa, who had a special relationship with the Jews, declared the area to be a place where Jews could settle and even engage in agriculture as early as 1775. Yossel's father entered the cattle trade, which brought the family a large fortune. They probably also dealt with smelting metals. Schmelzer, for 'smelting,' would testify to that occupation."

Yossel confirmed these details of his family with a little nod. His eyes darted back and forth as he waited to see the girl chosen for him. The matchmaker went on to describe Yossel's home.

"As a young man, Yossel moved from Stupca to Chernowitz, where he built a large, two-story house on Turkengasse.

Downstairs were four shops. On the second floor were five apartments. In addition, he established two sugar beet alcohol distilleries on the east bank of the Prut River in the town of Sadegura, several kilometers from here.

"A man after my own heart," said Huttman, who barely made a living and whose beautiful, modest daughters were his most precious possession.

"Most importantly, is he also an observant Jew?"

"Very pious," the matchmaker promised. "He's observant in all things, great and small."

They continued to extol the history of his family while Yossel stared at the dilapidated walls and waited for his intended bride to be summoned into the room.

The eldest daughter entered. Yossel glanced at the lovely young woman. It seemed to him that she would bear healthy children and be a good wife. With a nod, he confirmed to the matchmaker and to the excited father that he liked the girl. The match was concluded on the spot with a handshake, raising a glass for a toast, and writing down the terms.

A year later the young bride died in childbirth, her newborn baby with her.

After the period of mourning, the matchmaker suggested that Yossel return to the Huttman house since there were more good, pious girls there. So, they did. They met again with Mr.

Huttman and wrote down terms for Yossel's marriage to the second eldest daughter.

Thirteen children were born to Yossel and this wife. The firstborn was a son, followed by twelve daughters. When his daughters were in their twenties, their mother passed away. Yossel was once again left a widower. He was already forty-five years old, but his masculine vitality was still vigorous, enabling him to fulfill the commandment "Be fruitful and multiply."

Immediately after the week-long mourning ended, the matchmaker again came to Yossel.

"There is one more daughter left in the Huttman house, a widow," he reminded the gvir. They went again to the Huttman house and while they were waiting for Mr. Huttman to join them, Yossel spoke to the matchmaker in confidence.

"The third daughter is too old, I don't want her," he said, "I want her young daughter, she is single."

"But she's very poor and only twenty years old, younger than your own daughters!"

"She's the one I want." Yossel insisted.

"But you don't know her; you know nothing about her."

"I know enough. I didn't know any more about my other wives."

"She's too young. How will she get along with your children who are much older than she is?" insisted the matchmaker.

"Every summer this girl came to my house to play with my daughters. I want her!" Yossel insisted.

If that was what the gvir wanted, what matchmaker would forfeit concluding such a match?

That is how Regina – beautiful, intelligent, and young – came into the home of the gvir. Her stepdaughters, whose mother had passed away, still lived in their father's home. They tried to make Regina's life miserable. There were three kitchens in Gvir Yossel's house: one for dairy, one for meat dishes, and the third for Passover. Regina learned how to function in each of them. One Friday, as the Shabbat meat meal was cooking in the pots, when Regina turned away from the wood-burning stove for a moment, one of Yossel's daughters poured some milk on the work surface designated for the meat meal.

This of course spoiled the food since according to Jewish dietary law it is forbidden to mix meat and milk at the same meal.

The Sabbath dinner was thrown out, and that daughter was quickly married off to get her out of the house.

Chapter 3

Despite the difficulties, young Regina was able to conceive easily. She and Yossel had three children: Wolf (Bubbi), the eldest; Leon (Machiku), about two and a half years later; and then a daughter, Lottie.

Leon was a clever, playful boy who enjoyed a close relationship with his mother. He called her "Mammu" and she called him Machiku. Being quick and agile, he was also called "hamster" – after the little animal that people like to raise at home. Every Sabbath, when he went to the synagogue with his father Yossel, Romanian boys would tease him because he was very short.

"Hey, little runt. When are you going to grow?"

"Oh hey, Tiny, how can you see anything down there on the floor?"

"Peanut, even if you stood up on a chair nobody would see you."

"What did you do, walk under a ladder, and now you won't grow anymore?"

"You swallowed a flowerpot and forgot to water it?"

These were older Romanian boys and there was no point in confronting them. Machiku held back from responding to the insults; instead, he was proud that his father let him hold his prayer book. After all, he wasn't that small if Dad trusts him to hold his book. When he returned home, he told Mammu Regina with tears in his eyes what the gentile boys had said.

"You did well not to get into a confrontation with them," his mother said as she stroked his head. "When a big wave comes at you, my son, lower your head and the wave will pass."

When Bubbi, the eldest, was six years old, Yossel, as was customary with a gvir, hired a *melamed*, a tutor, named Mendel. He was a young *yeshiva bocher*, a Torah student, with long side curls, a goatee, and a black hat. Every day he would come to the house and teach Bubbi Torah stories from the Bible. Regina wanted to encourage her eldest son to learn and the teacher to teach, so she baked cookies every day to welcome the guest and make her son happy. When the melamed opened the door of the house, snowflakes would often fly in, but then he would be welcomed with the delicious aroma of fresh pastries.

"Good day!" said the melamed in greeting.

"Come, Bubbi. The melamed has arrived!" cried Regina.

"In a minute," Bubbi muttered. He didn't like the melamed with the sing-song voice, and was afraid of the ruler that would land on his hand whenever he hesitated to answer.

Machiku, then almost four years old, also wanted to study Torah, but the melamed was there only for his older brother. Cleverly, he took advantage of his brother's delay. He ran and hid under the big dining room table. Regina, not noticing, came in with a plate of cookies for the teacher and his student. Machiku reached out a nimble hand and grabbed a cookie. It was very pleasant for him under the table, where he could feel the warmth of from the fireplace. From time to time, he heard the sound of a crackling twig and saw sparks flying up the chimney.

Bubbi finally sat down at the table and the lesson began. The teacher told him the Biblical story of Rachel, Leah, and their father Laban, who cheated Jacob. Machiku sat under the table and listened; he very much wanted to take part in the lesson. After all, he could already read the Torah in Hebrew and translate it into Yiddish.

"What does 'served for seven years' mean?" asked the teacher. Bubbi didn't answer. The melamed's ruler smacked his hand; there was a snapping sound, followed by a yelp.

"Read!" The teacher commanded. He didn't like teaching, but he was poor and hungry, and Regina Schmeltzer always had hot food and sweets for him. Bubbi recovered and read the verses the melamed had asked him to.

"And what is 'y'fat to-ar' (fine-looking)?" asked the teacher.

"Y'fat to-ar" means a woman with a lovely figure!" Machiku burst out enthusiastically from under the table.

Just then Regina came in from the kitchen, adjusting her apron.

"He interrupted!" The teacher complained, pulling the trembling Machiku out from under the table.

"I want to learn, too," Machiku murmured, trying not to cry.

"You're younger! Only I'm allowed!" Bubbi boasted. Actually, he had no desire at all to study Torah, but if Machiku wanted to, as the elder son, he could not yield his privileged place.

"From now on Machiku will also learn!" declared Mammu Regina. How could she deny her beloved young son?

That is how Machiku joined the daily lessons. He never once felt the melamed's ruler on the back of his hand.

As the brothers grew older, they began to go to school together. Little Machiku had a hard time carrying all his books. He would tie them together with a rope and lug them on his back. Bubbi had a better system. So as not to carry all the weight of the books, he would tear out the pages they had studied that day. He could even jump puddles, his books were so light.

"Machiku," he would mock his little brother, "you're stupid. Who carries all their books in a bag?"

Machiku wanted to hit him, but his brother was bigger and stronger. He remembered the words of Mammu Regina and lowered his head until the wave passed.

Chapter 4

When he was a young man, Yossel Schmelzer founded an ultra-Orthodox religious party and became its representative in Chernowitz. At age thirty he was a deputy in the city council. He observed all the commandments, but he knew how to adapt to the times. He allowed his daughters to go ice skating and attend college. He also set aside a substantial dowry for each of them.

One day, the leaders of Chernowitz announced that Emperor Franz Joseph was coming to visit. The townspeople quickly began planting flowers along the emperor's planned route and swept the sidewalks near their homes. At the schools, the children made little flags to wave before the emperor.

The town elders planned a reception at the Opera House with the Corinthian columns in the town square. They decorated the hall with distinctive paintings. On the plaza outside the building, hundreds of people could gather.

All the important citizens of the city were invited, particularly the men. The wealthy women ordered long dresses in the latest fashion, and seamstresses worked feverishly to finish the dresses in time.

The big day arrived. The emperor's entourage entered the city with the royal carriage pulled by a team of horses. Trumpets heralded the arrival of the honored guest. The carriage stopped in front of the Opera House, the coachman opened its door, and the emperor slowly descended. He sported a red and blue vest adorned with medals. On his feet he wore boots brushed to a gleaming shine.

The city elders led the emperor to the hall of the Opera House. The men stood straight in black tailored suits and bow ties and the women shone forth in a variety of jewelry and colorful dresses. They all applauded.

The emperor raised his hand for silence. His entourage gave him a glass of wine and everyone else raised their glasses.

"*Gesundheit*! Cheers!" the emperor exclaimed, drinking the wine from his glass. "Did everyone come to the reception?" he thundered. The crowd nodded their heads.

"Gvir Yossel Schmelzer didn't come." A hesitant voice was suddenly heard from the far end of the hall.

"What? I ordered everyone to attend!" The emperor was angry.

"He's very devout and was afraid he would have to raise a glass of non-kosher wine," stammered the mayor.

"If the man does not come to me, I shall go to him!" said the emperor to the stunned crowd. Although he was known for his generous support of the Jewish community in Chernowitz, his behavior was nonetheless unexpected.

The mayor and his deputies immediately nodded, organized the journey for the emperor and his entourage, and they all began marching from the Opera House to Yossel's house on Turkengasse.

Yossel heard the commotion in the street and peered out his window. When he saw the emperor's entourage approaching, his heart stopped. He went out of his house, approached the emperor, and bowed to him, slightly; a deep bow was reserved only for God. He took a bottle of kosher wine, poured some into the two goblets he had brought out with him, and together with the emperor raised his glass in a private, kosher, toast.

"I greatly value your people, your loyalty to me, and your religion. As a token of my esteem, I hereby present you with the amber mouthpiece I use for smoking," said the emperor and handed the valuable item to Yossel.

Yossel humbly accepted the mouthpiece. He turned it over in his hands, examining it from every possible angle. Such a gift from the emperor was hardly an everyday occurrence.

* * *

Due to his many business affairs, Yossel was often away from home. Sometimes he would stay overnight at the distillery or go to hear a lecture on the Torah by the Rabbi of Sadigura. On

Friday evening, when he returned home, he would go to the synagogue with the boys. After prayers, they would all return home together, which filled him with pride. There, Regina had a proper feast ready for the family. To fulfill the *mitzvah* of hospitality, Yossel would always invite a yeshiva student or a poor melamed to join them at the meal.

Before and after eating, they would sing Shabbat hymns. The singing that emanated from the house sent the spirit of the Sabbath Queen out to the entire street.

When World War I broke out and the emperor's rule was jeopardized, Yossel's two sons enlisted in the Austrian army. Machiku fought for more than two years; he was a young officer with the rank of lieutenant. He was wounded and awarded a silver medal for courage and heroism in battle. His older brother, Bubbi, was taken prisoner by the Italians. However, the military service of Yossel's sons didn't do him any good, as during the war, Mongolian units of the Russian army sacked his factories and set them on fire. Yossel took the rest of his family and fled to Vienna, where he died of starvation due to the scarcity of food – or possibly because of the hunger he imposed upon himself to avoid having to eat food that wasn't kosher enough for him.

Only about six months after Yossel died, the news of his father's death reached Machiku at the front.

After the war, the family returned to Chernowitz. Regina, now a widow, took over the rehabilitation of the family and the rebuilding of its assets.

Chapter 5

Theodor Herzl died in 1904, when Machiku was ten years old. The whole city was in mourning, and the streets were filled with notices of his death.

"Who is Herzl?" asked Machiku. "Why all those signs with his name? Was he a famous rabbi?"

"He was an important man for Jews," his friend explained. The friend's father was active in the Zionist movement. "Herzl wanted the Jews to leave Europe and go to establish their own state in Zion – the biblical name for Eretz Israel, which is now called Palestine."

"That's really interesting," Machiku said. "I never heard of Herzl at home. His name wasn't mentioned anywhere, not in *heder*, the Jewish elementary school, or at the synagogue."

Machiku was raised in a religious Hasidic home. It was forbidden to write on *Shabbat*. He prayed every morning and evening, and his father would eventually take him to the *mikveh*, the ritual bath, even though there was a bathtub in their house.

His curiosity about Herzl and his teachings only began in earnest in high school. His teachers taught him Herzl's speech at the First Zionist Congress, as well as the one by Max Nordau, another well-known Zionist. The class also read books by the historian Zvi Graetz.

Following his discharge from the army, Machiku began studying law at the university. While there, he joined Emunah, an academic association whose slogan was, "For Judaism and Jewish Science." Members of the association would meet and hold discussions revolving around their personal and national identity. Machiku became a central figure of the group and one of its chairpersons.

At one of the association's tumultuous meetings there was a great debate over a change in their identity cards. Many association members were in favor of "German" written in the language category.

"For years we have listed German as our culture," said Max Heller. "Since the days of the Kaiser we have been praying for the welfare of the emperor and his wife. The prayer is in all the Rosh Hashanah and Yom Kippur prayer books."

"After all, the Austrian emperor has allowed Bukovina to flourish as a separate, autonomous province," argued Leon Gruber.

"We live in the 'Land of the Crown' with self-government, and for us as Jews this is a kind of 'Golden Age,'" shouted Moshe Goldman.

"Chernowitz is 'Jerusalem on the Prut River' or 'Little Jerusalem,'" Joseph Czerniak declared in a loud voice as if reciting an epic poem. "All of Bukovina has become the second 'Land of Canaan,' the 'Eldorado' of Austria!"

"German is the language of the educated. Do you want to change that?"

The argument became heated. It seemed that they might even come to blows.

"We need to register 'Jew' as our nationality, and Yiddish as our language!" objected Machiku, who spoke Yiddish at home.

"But we don't understand a word of Yiddish, only German!"

This debate was Machiku's first battle for national aspirations. He didn't foresee how much grief would come from the registration of nationality on the ID card.

The Zionist movement had gained a foothold among many of the townspeople, including Machiku. He often appeared at the assemblies, traveling from town to town, speaking in support of the Zionist Movement. Thanks to this, he was elected a member of the Zionist Organization's Executive Committee in Bukovina, and had a very close relationship with the chairman, Dr. Mayer Ebner.

Dr. Ebner not only devoted himself to defending the personal and civil equality of Jews as individuals, but he also put forward his position on their rights as a national minority group. He argued that they should follow "Jewish policy" in the Diaspora in parallel with the development of Eretz Israel. He fought for equal political and civil rights for Jews in Bukovina and in the territories annexed to Romania.

In 1924 Chairman Ebner called Machiku and informed him, "An important guest is about to arrive in our area."

"Who is it?" Machiku wondered.

"His name is Menachem Mendel Ussishkin, one of the leaders of the Jewish National Fund, the JNF. He's coming to urge Zionist leaders to contribute funds for the purchase of land for Jews in Eretz Israel," he said, showing Machiku a photograph of Ussishkin. It showed a tall, thin, bald man in an elegant suit. He held up the letter that described, in German, the details of the visit planned by the heads of the JNF. They read it together and discussed the itinerary.

The guest was scheduled to leave Kishinev on the high-speed train in the coming week. They wanted to arrange festive receptions in his honor at every stop along the way.

"Who'll take part?" asked Machiku.

"Hundreds of members from twenty-six different Zionist organizations. It's essential that there be as many people as possible. Also, it's important that we recruit about two hundred noteworthy people to work on increasing the donations. That's the whole purpose of this visit."

"Preparations will begin in Kishinev and we'll be kept informed."

"Fine," said Machiku. "I'll make sure to take care of Ussishkin's visit and accompany him to the designated meetings."

Machiku, who meanwhile had finished his studies and was a certified lawyer, began to formulate the trip's details. He was young, but industrious and thorough, and feared no one. He knew how to present himself with dignity before important figures, just as he knew how to get along with the common folk. And so, he corresponded with all the dignitaries who would meet with the guest, outlining his journey in Bukovina. He also made sure to publicize the visit to all the synagogues in the city and sent press releases to the important Jewish newspapers.

Machiku consulted with his mother about everything. Some might say that he was too reliant on her, but he appreciated her intelligence and said she possessed great wisdom. She supported him all through his high school studies and at the university, as well as his Zionist activities. It was therefore only natural that his mother also be involved in his preparations for Ussishkin's visit to the city.

Regina took Machiku to a tailor to make a dark, three-piece suit. When Machiku tried on the custom-made suit, his mother looked it over from head to toe to be sure it was just right. Wearing the suit, his hair combed with brilliantine, and the pince-nez glasses clipped to his nose, he looked elegant as befitting a high-level Zionist activist.

"I'm so proud of you, Machiku," she said.

"Thank you, Mammu. I hope our visitor will reach out to the people of Bukovina, and that they will open their hearts and wallets, fulfilling the commandment of settling the Land of Israel," Leon replied. "Despite what is written about it in the Bible – a land of 'Milk and Honey' – it is full of deserts and swamps. We Jews must buy land there and tame the wilderness."

Regina looked at her son with pride. Small in stature, but with a thunderous voice. He had the iron will to succeed in whatever he did.

The long-awaited day arrived. On May 11, 1924, Ussishkin arrived in Chernowitz. He was greeted with the honor reserved for noblemen and kings. When the train entered the city, the Hazamir Men's Choir opened with the song "Mishmar Hayarden." Members of the Maccabi, Hashomer, and Blue and White movements were present. Everyone wore their organization's official attire. There were salutations for fifteen minutes, and from there everyone moved to the reception held in the magnificent hall of the "Jewish House."

All the important members of the community, the heads of the JNF, the Zionist leaders, including Mayer Ebner and Machiku, gathered in his honor, and they all posed with him in a group photo, wearing suits and bow ties.

Mayer Ebner introduced Dr. Leon Schmelzer, Machiku, to Ussishkin. Together they began discussing the events of the week.

"The next two days are for working sessions with JNF activists," said Machiku. "On Friday and Saturday we'll hold prayer services with the Orthodox of the city and the Hazamir Choir will again take part. On Sunday there'll be a national conference during which we'll hear reports on fundraising progress for the JNF."

Economically, these were hard times. In the first house they visited, the hosts were overflowing with esteem for their guest. Ussishkin was given the best room in the house, but the bathroom was outside in the yard. It was cold, and the hosts didn't know what to do. How could they allow their distinguished guest to leave a warm bed and go out to the yard in the middle of the night to relieve himself? They came up with a solution and tied a bucket outside the window of Ussishkin's room, an improvised toilet for the honored guest.

Despite the inconveniences, Ussishkin clearly saw that the young Jewish lawyer accompanying him was a born leader. On Sunday evening, a huge farewell party was held for Ussishkin. All the important people from Bukovina were invited, among them fundraisers, opinion makers, and the wealthy.

At the end of the week, Ussishkin surprised Machiku with this: "Eretz Israel is our ancestral land," began Ussishkin. "Dr. Schmelzer, from now on you will chair the JNF in Bukovina. You will see to it that many make the journey there and donate their money for redemption of the land."

"Yes, sir!" Machiku modestly accepted the appointment. He was not only moved by it, he also understood the core of Ussishkin's remarks. In one sentence, Ussishkin had grasped the differences in opinion among the Jews of Europe: contribution or immigration, the division of the land between Jews and Arabs, or Jewish settlement in all of it

In 1925, Machiku was invited to be among the guests of honor at the inauguration of the Hebrew University of Jerusalem. He returned from the visit to Palestine full of enthusiasm. When he entered the house with his suitcase, he was greeted by the aroma of freshly baked pastries in the oven, and he hurried to the warm, cozy kitchen where his mother awaited him. He put down the suitcase and hugged her. As always, only when he was in her arms did he feel content. Regina returned his embrace warmly and lovingly.

"How I missed you, *yingele*, my son," said Regina, beaming with joy at his return. "Sit down, tell me where you were and what you saw there."

"Mammu, you won't believe what's happening now in the Land of Israel, Palestine. People are rebuilding everything. I was with the leaders of the JNF. The JNF buys land for people to come from Europe and settle on it. This will be the new homeland for all Jewish people. I also attended the inauguration of a new Jewish university on Mount Scopus in Jerusalem."

"I understand you're excited about Eretz Israel, but will this new home be better than the one we have here?" Regina said, cooling his enthusiasm. "What do we lack? You're young and building your career as a lawyer. You have your own law office. You're involved in all JNF matters here in Chernowitz and throughout Romania. Many eyes are upon you."

"True. I work hard to make things good for our family and for us as Jews."

"Do you remember that Emperor Franz Josef came to Bukovina and promised to always preserve the Jews and their culture?"

"Yes, and of course in our prayer books there is a special prayer for the welfare of the emperor and empress."

"Well, then you're contributing here no less than if you were there."

"Nevertheless, I have begun to think about moving there."

Regina hesitated for a moment. She knew her "jewel" well. The more you try to dissuade him, the more he will stand his ground.

"Do you think that would be good for you?" she asked, smiling.

"Yes, it could be very good."

"Well, even I have heard of the terrible diseases there, like the malaria that people are dying from. And the conflict with the Arabs and other populations who also claim that it is their land."

"Yes, there are diseases in Palestine," he replied, "but they believe that they're creating something new. You know that Herzl thrilled all the participants at the Zionist Congress with the idea of a national home for Jews from all over the world. Maybe after I settle there, you'll come too?"

"I won't leave," Regina said. "I grew up here, gave birth to you here, and I don't know the language there. It is a land of desert, and the heat will be too much for me. You can go because you're young. I'll stay here."

Machiku was silent. He would not go anywhere without his beloved Mammu. She was getting older. She had taught him everything, from childhood to adulthood. It was her good advice that led to his success, and she supported him in time of need. How could he desert her? He was a son who takes care of his mother. Although he wanted to move to Palestine, they needed him there. Here he had money, friends, a social life, sports, and trips to the mountains, everything a young man needs. Apart from that, he still had much to contribute where he was. The JNF had always stressed that before immigrating to Eretz Israel he must send many wealthy Jews to buy land. There will be opportunities to immigrate later. Perhaps it wasn't yet time to leave Chernowitz. Yes, he would stay where he has everything and help others go.

Machiku remained in Chernowitz, continuing to travel back and forth to Palestine. He was confident in the future and happy with his decision.

He visited the Land of Israel, "Eretz" as it was called, eight times, and he continued his involvement in the life of the Jewish community.

Important guests from the JNF and the Zionist Organization always made sure to pass through Chernowitz. It was the heart of Jewish activity in Bukovina and an important collection center for donations to Palestine and its settlement.

In 1927, Dr. Chaim Weizmann, later the first President of the State of Israel, also paid a visit to Chernowitz. Machiku was among the hosts and even participated in the group photo, standing in the center right behind Weizmann.

Chapter 6

Machiku met Ida-Donya Blumenfeld while involved in Zionist activities and invited her to manage his law office and be his secretary.

Donya Blumenfeld was born in Gura-Humora, Bukovina, on December 10, 1910.

Hersch Zvi Blumenfeld, her father, was born in Suceava, Bukovina, to a rigidly Orthodox family that resisted advancements in the spirit of the times. The children studied only in heder and at the synagogue. Hersch wanted more modernity, but it was forbidden to talk about it at home. He was a mischievous boy. One of his pranks on Passover night was talked about for generations. Houses were built low in those days. There was a storage space, a "*boydem*" between the ceiling and the roof of the house. Hersch hid a small foal there, and when they opened the door for Elijah the prophet, he led the young horse into the house.

Donya's mother, Yetti, née Strenkler, was born in Buczac, Galicia. Her parents, Frima and Israel, were also religiously observant and spoke only Yiddish at home. But Yetti's three brothers attended university while she herself went to an external high school, earning a high school diploma. She studied German literature and writers and poets such as Goethe, Heine, and Schiller.

Together, Hersch and Yetti built a warm home, full of love and giving.

"I had a wonderful childhood that influenced my whole life," Donya said. "On winter evenings we would gather around the stove. My mother would tell stories and sing songs. My father would play the violin. His playing was a secret we were forbidden to tell his parents about."

Once a week, usually on Thursdays, Hersch opened the door to people who had heard of his charity without asking for anything in return.

Friday nights were sacred. Before Yetti lit the Shabbat candles and Hersch was about to leave for the synagogue, she would say, "Herschel, don't forget to bring home a guest from the synagogue for Shabbat." The guest was given the most honored place at the table so he could recite the blessing over the *challah*. He would stay with the family throughout Shabbat and then go on his way.

The happiest holiday was Purim. Yetti lit the special baking oven to bake challah, the length of the oven, for the Purim meal. The front door was always open, an invitation to guests. Anyone could come in to speak their mind. They all got a slice of challah, a little money, and some sweets. There were masks and songs, too, but the main thing was giving to others wholeheartedly.

Donya remembered that they would visit their grandparents on both sides of the family on the holidays. She remembered her parents' home as "*yontifdik*," meaning full of holiday spirit.

World War I broke out in 1914, when Donya was four years old. The family traveled to Vienna, escaping the Russian invasion. There, her mother and brothers reunited with Yetti's family. Hersch was conscripted into the army and Yetti took care of the family. The two older girls went to school while Donya stayed home. She was an energetic girl and wanted to work to keep busy. One day her mother saw her with a backpack over her shoulder.

"Where are you going, Donika?" she asked.

"I need to work. Since you won't give me anything to do, I'm going to find a job in someone else's house."

When her grandmother heard this, she said, "The girl is right."

* * *

Hersch sometimes received a furlough of a few days and came to visit in Vienna.

When the war ended in 1918, the family returned home. The girls went back to school and Hersch resumed his grain trade business. Even though it was unusual for girls to study, Yanke'leh the *melamed* came twice a week to teach them Bible and the Commentaries like the boys studied in heder. The girls were hard-working, so the teacher had no reason to hit them with the small stick, "*kanchik*," as he did other pupils.

Donya met with anti-Semitism for the first time in her life at age fourteen. A law was passed that Jewish children could not attend high school as full-time students but only as external students, so she studied management and accounting as an external student.

During that same period, Donya was also introduced to Zionism. One of her teachers at school taught the Hebrew language and "Auto-Emancipation," a pamphlet written by the Russian-Polish Jewish doctor and activist Leo Pinsker.

The ability to recite the article by heart was a condition for admission to the WIZO youth group. Donya passed the exam and was accepted. The group cooperated with the JNF, the organization that collected money to buy land and support the Jews in Palestine. They circulated blue and white donation boxes at weddings, holiday celebrations, and at funerals. All these occasions were suitable for spreading the word and learning about the possibilities of *aliyah* – immigration to Eretz Israel.

The family moved to Chernowitz in 1927, when Donya was seventeen. She was more and more attracted to Zionist activity, becoming involved in raising funds for the JNF, in discussions about Zionism, and about what was happening in Palestine.

It was during her Zionist activities when she first got to know Machiku and went to work for him, eventually becoming the manager of his law office.

When Machiku proposed marriage to Donya in 1938, there were about fifty thousand Jews in Chernowitz, one-third of the population. They were divided into various religious and cultural subgroups: commoners and educated people in the liberal professions such as commerce, law and medicine. Bukovina had many districts, and most of the Jews who settled in them were engaged in agriculture.

Hitler was sole ruler of Germany by that time and the news had reached Bukovina. Like others, Machiku heard about what was happening to the Jews in Germany.

"This is just talk, exaggeration," he said. "The Germans, after all, are a cultured people." He closed his mind to the Nazi rise in power and what the Jews in Germany and elsewhere were suffering. Life in Chernowitz had been good. Like an ostrich, he buried his head in the sand; despite his intelligence, he didn't realize the deadly signs of Hitler's rule. He and his good friend, Dr. Mayer Ebner, spoke at length on the subject. When Ebner asked him about immigrating to Eretz Israel, Machiku could not foresee that this would be his last opportunity to take action and go there.

Instead, he began preparing for his marriage to Donya.

Many weddings were held in Chernowitz, including modest celebrations in the center of the Jewish community. Machiku knew a great many people in the city, but he was concerned about inviting a large number of guests. Lots of acquaintances would anticipate an invitation to the wedding of the sworn bachelor who was about to change his life.

"You know, Donika," he said to his fiancée, "I don't want a huge wedding. Everyone will expect me to have elegant clothing made for them."

"I don't understand," Donya wondered. "What do you think they will expect?"

"That I pay their expenses for the wedding – clothes, meals, and more."

"Why would they do that?"

"Because I am 'the Gvir'" replied Machiku. "They would all line up to get something."

"I have never known you to be tight-fisted. You have always been generous with members of the community."

"It isn't the money," he said.

"A wedding is a happy occasion. People will have expectations. Is that what bothers you?"

Machiku choked up and said nothing. Not being able to express his feelings in words was rare for him. Donika, like every young bride, wanted to stand under the wedding canopy surrounded by her family, with her father on one side, mother on the other, lifting the veil and giving her daughter a sip of wine from the bridal cup. He didn't want to burden her with his worries.

Donika was also lost in thought. She pictured herself in a white bridal gown dancing in a circle with her sister Nussia and all the girls she knew from the WIZO social gatherings. They would dance around her in a chair while the men whirled in Hassidic dances in the other room.

She sighed softly. They were two separate worlds about to become one. Each was learning about the other and how to live as a couple and make decisions together.

Each was engrossed in their own thoughts, and neither could foresee the great variety of decisions they would have to make in the future. They were absorbed in the present, where the most important thing was their wedding.

Machiku gathered his thoughts.

"What if we don't have the wedding in Chernowitz?"

"But…where will we have it?" Donya was horrified.

"You and I will just drive somewhere and get married." He shocked her with this suggestion.

Donika stared at him and didn't know what to say. It seemed unthinkable. The bride and groom soar away on fairy tale wings, marry in secret, and live happily ever after. When they discussed office matters, she consistently came up with good ideas. She always knew what to suggest. This time she was taken by surprise and began to stammer.

"What about our parents? Won't they be at the wedding?" The question finally came out clearly.

"Leave it to me. Let me think about it." With that, Machiku ended the discussion on the topic.

Donya sank deep into thought. It was hard for her to imagine going somewhere by themselves to get married, without her family and her girlfriends. In addition, none of the relatives would be informed. Donya found it difficult even to see herself alone with him as her husband. She had not yet called him by any name other than Dr. Schmelzer!

'Machiku', 'Machiku', she said to herself repeatedly, trying to get used to the pet name of the man who would be her husband.

However, Machiku was a practical man who didn't delve into musing about things. "I'll look into it and we'll talk again. In the meantime, we'll keep our thoughts to ourselves. All right?"

She nodded. Machiku looked into her eyes. He saw in them the end of her girlhood, her faith in him, and her hopes. She would no longer be Miss Blumenfeld for him. She was going to be Donya, Donika Schmelzer.

Chapter 7

They sat in the train, traveling from Chernowitz to Bucharest, the capital of Romania. Machiku gazed out the window as they passed through villages with low stone houses, green fields ripe with grain.

He thought about the circumstances of the trip, about his sudden transition from years of bachelorhood to a life with family responsibilities. He was content with his decision to be married in another city, but he thought of Donya's parents' reaction. And especially Mammu's. How would she feel not being at his wedding? How will he feel?

He looked over at Donya, who sat by the window. It felt as though he was seeing her for the first time. She was young, slender, and lovely. Her red hair encircled her round, sculpted face and smooth white skin. He felt excitement, and a cloud of light and joy enveloped him. This sweet girl would be his life partner. She will be with him from now on, in his home and in his heart.

Donya opened her eyes. She smiled shyly and blushed when she realized he was looking at her intensely.

The rattling of the train was the only sound they heard in the carriage.

"How do you feel?" he asked.

"I'm still dizzy. My head is spinning like I haven't quite woken up."

"Are you worried or frightened?"

"A little of everything" she paused. She wasn't used to revealing her feelings to him.

"You're not alone, Donya. From now on I'm with you, by your side. Together, we're embarking on a new path," he said gently, aware of her concerns.

"I know everything has changed for you. I'm no longer your employer. Slowly you'll learn that I know how to be a loyal companion, standing by your side at all times."

She had never been alone with a strange man, although he was no stranger. She had been his secretary and trusted assistant for ten years. However, all that was about to change. They were going to Bucharest for their wedding. She will be this man's wife. It's a happy thought, but also scary. What will my life be like with him? Donya had a hard time breaking free from feeling she was so much younger; he was sixteen years her senior – he her boss, she, his secretary.

"When we return to Chernowitz we'll move into in the new apartment I bought for us," Machiku continued, as if reading her mind. "I know how creative you are. You have a magic touch. You can furnish and decorate the apartment. You know, there is even an elevator in the building." He spoke warmly to her, seeking to allay her fears.

"It's not the apartment and furniture that trouble me, Machiku," she thought to herself. "I'll be there alone with you. I have no idea what living with a man will be like. I'll live with you, in the same house. It's hard for me to even imagine" she said, blushing with embarrassment.

So far, she had not told anyone what they were about to do. She hadn't shared her feelings with her mother or her sister Nussia. She could certainly not talk about it with Regina. The religious home she grew up in had not prepared her for this. There were definite rules concerning what was allowed and what was forbidden. In addition, in the haste of making their wedding plans, she had not even received guidance or advice from the rabbi's wife, as all her friends did.

"It's hard for me that my parents aren't here with us," she said softly.

"We're making a bold move, but the right one," Machiku replied confidently. "I wanted us to get married modestly and quietly without having to have suits made for all the townspeople." He refrained from touching her shoulder, careful not to put too much pressure on her. Yet he was forced to admit to himself that the plan was unusual in its audacity. He secretly wondered whether it was modesty or close-fistedness that motivated him.

Perhaps, God forbid, it was his unwillingness to publicize the rich and sought-after bachelor marries his secretary.

"I know, and I agreed to it, but still, it's hard for me," she confessed. "I so need Mom and Dad by my side on this day."

Like every young girl, Donya had secretly dreamed of a long white dress hand-made for her by Mrs. Landau, the seamstress. She pictured the *klezmers*, the musicians who would entertain the guests. She thought about the good deed of providing a festive meal for the poor, and her mother and Regina leading her to the canopy. The cantor sings the seven blessings and the bride walks around the groom seven times. She hears "*Mazel Tov!*" from all the guests and she's crying with happiness and excitement. In her wildest imagination, she didn't see herself traveling alone with a man to be married in another city.

But he was so sure he wanted to do it that way, that she accepted it as a *fait accompli*. She was saddened by these circumstances. She didn't understand his motives, and he didn't elaborate. Her mother, Yetti, would never forgive him for preventing her from attending her daughter's wedding. It was neither acceptable nor understandable.

The train rumbled swiftly through forests and tall trees as it approached the destination where they would be married.

The conductor coming through the carriages brought her back to reality.

"Tickets, please," he exclaimed.

"Here you are, sir." Leon hurriedly showed him the tickets.

The conductor examined the tickets carefully, nodded, tipped his hat, and moved on to the next car. Donya breathed a sigh of relief. This was her day. Many Chernowitz girls would give everything to be in her place. Still, it was difficult for her to transition from a young girl working for an authoritative figure for so many years. She didn't dare reveal, even to herself, that she loved him, and the term "a man's wife" made her dizzy.

Machiku gazed at her, smiling, and gratitude filled his heart. For him, this day embodied what is written in the Torah, in the Book of Genesis: "Therefore shall a man leave his father and his mother, and shall cleave unto his wife: and they shall be one flesh."

On that day, July 4, 1938, Donya and Machiku were married in Bucharest.

***

They didn't speak until they arrived at the hotel where Machiku had booked a room.

She was in a dark blue tailored dress that came down to her knees, befitting a modest and elegant young woman. The dress accentuated her young, shapely figure.

He wore a three-piece suit and bow tie. They were serious, thoughtful, immersed in the experience, not giggling like newlyweds. On that bright summer day, everything was different. He's now the husband and she's the wife; she's *his* wife. They certified their new bond witnessed by people who didn't know who or what they were.

"Let's rest a bit and go out in the evening," Machiku quietly suggested.

"Go out where?" Donya asked.

"We'll go dancing. There are great ballrooms here with good music. You'll experience something not found in Chernowitz," he enthused. As usual, he had already checked on everything and decided that this activity would help dispel the strangeness between them.

"I have nothing to wear. I didn't know" Donya murmured. She had been to ballrooms before. She had gone a few times with friends from WIZO whom her parents knew and approved of. The girls danced with each other. This was the little freedom that her strict father Hersch allowed her.

She had, of course, modest dresses with her that revealed nothing, their length to the middle of her shin. Her beautiful feet were in doll shoes, the height of fashion at the time. Her generous salary would have allowed her buy whatever she wanted. But she didn't think she would need her beautiful dresses and hadn't brought them to Bucharest.

"You can wear your wedding dress. It's beautiful and looks like a dress more for fun than for a wedding ceremony."

Donya went into the bathroom to freshen up, closing the door behind her. She needed privacy and calm after the excitement at the wedding. "I wanted a long white dress with a train that young girls would carry," she thought. "Yet I agreed to travel with you and get married in Bucharest without the ceremony in a beautiful wedding dress and festive dance music."

"At least we'll have the dancing," she thought further, trying to drive annoying thoughts out of her mind and get ready to have fun. What a shame that her parents and family weren't with her. She couldn't share with them the joy and excitement. A terrible thought crossed her mind; she felt like an orphan, but she immediately banished it.

When she came out of the bathroom, perfumed and dressed, she captured his admiring look.

"I like it very much," he dared to say, aware of her shyness.

"I won't take the hat with the lace. I don't need a hat to dance. It was only for the wedding."

"Yes, yes. You're right." He tried to slip into small talk as if they were discussing putting a fresh ink ribbon into her typewriter.

They left the hotel room arm in arm, a gesture that would become their hallmark in the future. It bore witness to a supportive, comforting closeness.

From the quiet of the hotel, they were swept into the music of the ballroom. Just as they entered, the musicians played "Jimmy," a popular dance of the period. The graceful Donya turned and moved to the melody as if enchanted. Machiku, also an excellent dancer, was drawn after her. They were so engrossed in their dance they didn't notice that the dance floor was slowly emptying. They were left alone, dancing a waltz in front of the large, enthusiastically applauding crowd gathered around them.

The music changed. The lights dimmed. The sounds of a sensual tango filled the ballroom. Couple after couple took to the dance floor. The men were in evening attire, wearing suits, white shirts, and bow ties. The women wore knee-length dresses with low-heeled shoes on their feet.

They danced close together, as if they were in their own world. They felt each other's warmth. The row of mirrors on in the surrounding walls reflected the dancing couples who suddenly looked to Donya like a colony of penguins at the North Pole. She smiled and felt a serenity engulfing her. She was no longer alone. She has a partner who knows the dance steps, a prince who knows how to lead. She won't wake up at midnight like Cinderella, lost between dream and reality.

***

The next morning, they went down to the park next to the hotel. It was a pleasant summer day. They sat close together on the bench. After all, they were now husband and wife. Children frolicked in the park, and young mothers pushed baby strollers with high wheels. Water that sprayed from a fountain in the center of the park rose high in the air in a semicircle. In the air was the faint scent of freshly mowed grass and birds chirping in the treetops. Total peace enveloped them as if the world had stopped spinning to welcome the newlyweds.

Donya felt Machiku's body heat close to her. He cupped her hand in his to say, "We are together now." They still had to get used to their new status. No more boss and secretary, but husband and wife. For now, they were in their own world, relaxing before returning to the hustle and bustle awaiting them in Chernowitz.

"What are you thinking about?" he asked her, smiling contentedly.

"Nothing, really." Donya laughed softly. "Just wondering if all this is real. Maybe I'll wake up and find out it was all a dream."

"It sounds like a good dream. I hope it will continue and get better," he said as the smile on his face widened.

Donya was troubled. A thought crept into her head like a thief in the night. "What will I do now?" she wondered. "I won't be in the office anymore. I'll have to say goodbye to everything I'm used to. How will my mother and father and my sister Nussia relate to me?" They hadn't talked about that yet. They hadn't spoken about a lot of things. They were busy dealing with the impending wedding but not their future together. Walls of silence do not fall in a single day. Their trust in each other had to be built gradually. They both knew it. But Machiku didn't tell her that he already planned their return to Chernowitz. Mammu Regina would surely be happy to see that everything went well. He would return to the office and continue as usual. They'll have to look for a new secretary because it would be impossible for Donya to continue in her role as it was before their marriage.

A group of children running after a ball came near them. Donya looked at them. They were all five or six years old, fair-haired, and of various heights. They ran joyfully on the grass after the ball, which rolled underneath the bench where she and Machiku were sitting.

The children stopped in front of the couple, gaped and giggled. Machiku reached down under the bench and handed them the ball. The tallest child thanked him.

A young woman, most likely the boy's mother, approached. "They're just kids. They didn't mean to disturb you," she apologized.

"They're cute," said Donya. "Is the tall one yours?"

"Yes, Alexandru. He's six."

"It's a nice day to play with a ball," Machiku smiled at the young mother.

"You're not from here, are you?" the woman asked. People didn't usually sit in the park in the middle of a workday.

"That's right," Machiku confirmed. "We came here from Chernowitz to get married."

"Well then, congratulations!" The young woman replied and hurried after her son, who had continued running with his friends.

The children playing conjured up thoughts about children of their own. So far, the question of how many they would want hadn't come up even once. It was clear to Machiku that it was time to have children. He was in his forties and perhaps, God forbid, for him the train may have already left the station. Donya hadn't yet given her opinion on the subject, but she found it hard to picture herself as a mother and was fearful. Only yesterday she was dancing in a fancy ballroom like a sixteen-year-old. She had no experience in the marital partnership. The responsibility of motherhood was heavy upon her, as was the fear of childbirth. She had heard from friends who had been through it that it wasn't easy, not at all.

They continued sitting in the center of the blooming park, each engrossed in their own thoughts, coming nearer to each other and then moving away, like the squirrels at their feet looking for breadcrumbs. Soon they'll get their belongings from the hotel and board the train back to Chernowitz.

Chapter 8

The train back to Chernowitz slowed down upon entering the city. Nothing seemed the same to Donya. It was as if they were coming from another planet. It was familiar, yet strange. Perhaps it was she who was the stranger.

A hired carriage took them to their new apartment at 17 General Mircescu Street. The modern structure stood out from the old buildings of the city. It even had an elevator.

Machiku was elated. He had bought the most beautiful apartment he could find. In the stairwell he pressed the elevator button for the third floor. When he opened the apartment door he paused momentarily, wondering if Donya wanted him to carry her over the threshold. He wasn't sure and dismissed the thought. She seemed to read his mind.

"The right foot," Donya giggled. "We should start out on the right foot." They smiled. It was good to be lighthearted together. Machiku entered first and held the door for her. She stepped over the threshold – right foot first.

"Come on, I'll show you around the apartment," Machiku said, taking her hand.

Donya felt her heart pounding and was sure Machiku could hear it. It was the first time she had seen the new apartment. A single girl from a devout family was forbidden to enter her home before the marriage. Still holding her hand, Machiku led her from room to room. The place was only partially furnished. There was a bedroom, a study with a heavy round desk, and a kitchen with an oven. Most of the shelves were empty. He left the honor of stacking them with utensils and food products to his young wife. Machiku was glad he could offer her such a comfortable apartment.

"My life has been very different until now," he thought. Suddenly everything had meaning and purpose. Suddenly there is someone by my side. Together we'll build a family. No longer merely Regina's son. I'm starting a family of my own. And it came at such a good time, when I am established and well off.

The living room windows faced the main street. People were hurrying to their businesses, and children returning from school. Women from the villages sat on the street corners offering their wares to passers-by: eggs straight from the chicken coop, milk from that very morning, and small bunches of beautiful violets.

Machiku let go of Donya's hand. He opened an envelope and pulled out a *mezuzah*. Putting on a *kippah*, he attached the mezuzah to the door post with a prayer, as was the Jewish commandment in the Bible: "Blessed are You, Lord, our

God, King of the universe, who has sanctified us with Your commandments and commanded us to affix a mezuzah."

"Amen," said Donika as tears welled up in her eyes.

He put his arm around her.

"Now we'll go to the parents and raise a toast with them," he said.

She nodded, fearing what was to come.

He took a bottle of fine wine with them and they set off.

As was her habit, Mammu Regina was looking out the window so she could see if anyone was approaching. The dining table was already set with the finest Shabbat silver cutlery and the best dinnerware. There were festive white plates ornamented with small pink and green flowers alongside starched cloth napkins. The two families were gathered in the house, waiting impatiently. Everyone was dressed up in honor of the new couple coming into the family fold. Donya's parents and her sister; Bubbi, Machiku's brother with his wife; and his sister Lottie with her husband.

When Machiku and Donya entered, everyone rose. Regina hugged them first, close to her heart. She noticed how pale Donya was from the excitement. It made Regina recall when she was a young bride arriving for the first time at her husband Yossel's family home.

The atmosphere was charged. The tension was palpable on everyone's faces. Yetti moved her napkin and cutlery around on the tablecloth. Hersch touched his mustache as if trying to curl it. Bubbi and his wife Clara exchanged meaningful looks. "What an event! What a bride and groom!" The meal should have been one of joy and laughter, but only the clicking of knives and forks on Regina's porcelain plates was heard. The special meal was dampened by thoughts of the unusual wedding that had taken place without the presence of family members. No one ventured to express their feelings out loud.

At last, Hersch and Yetti approached their daughter, who was now Donya Schmelzer, and hugged her. Yetti had been glaring at Machiku all the while, thinking, "How could you keep us away from our daughter's wedding?" Donya went to her sister Nussia and her brother-in-law, Lemel. Machiku kissed his sister-in-law Clara's hand. Afterwards, he turned to Bubbi and patted him on the shoulder.

"It's like the Shabbat dinner for the bride and groom that we didn't celebrate before the wedding, as was the custom," Donya thought, and smiled her shy smile. Although she knew everyone from the years she worked in Machiku's office, it had all changed. She was now part of the family of the Gvir Schmelzer.

Bubbi observed the couple. How lucky my brother is, he thought to himself. He has it all – money, status, and the special love of Mammu Regina. Now he also has a beautiful young wife, the aging reprobate. Bubbi's wife, Clara, scrutinized her new sister-in-law. Her gaze lingered particularly on her stomach. "She must be pregnant. That's why they ran off to get married in Bucharest," she whispered to her husband in a venomous, superior tone that no one else heard.

***

Life entered its new phase: Machiku returned to the office, and Donya found other pursuits. She hadn't had a vacation in a long time. Now she could see old friends, cook enjoyable dinners at home, and visit her parents. Sometimes, in the mornings, she even allowed herself to sit in a café on Main Street. It was sheer pleasure. Chernowitz was known for the wonderful cafés with Viennese-type pastries.

Her greatest pleasure was meeting acquaintances who kissed her with "Greetings, dear lady, Mrs. Dr. Schmelzer." Even though she herself wasn't a "Dr.," according to the Austrian culture she was entitled to the great honor of receiving her husband's title,

Machiku wished to introduce his new bride to all his friends and associates. He bought her fine velvet and silk fabrics, and sent her to a seamstress, whom he told not to skimp on the materials.

"I don't need so many clothes," protested Donya, who was used to living modestly. "What am I going to do with all these colorful petticoats? After all a nice beige one is enough."

Nonetheless, her wardrobe soon filled up with everyday dresses, fancy gowns, and even a genuine fur coat that Machiku bought for her in a moment of contentment. He also bought her jewelry and genuine pearls to suit any grand occasion. They were invited to dinners, went to the opera, and to splendid cafés. Machiku relished in presenting her to his associates and friends. They lived like a prince and a princess in a fairy tale.

Chapter 9

Machiku made his way home on a rainy autumn evening. The leaves on the city's trees had turned yellow and fell to the ground with a light rustle. The houses were tinted red and yellow in a spectacular sunset. Large drops of rain spattered on the surface of the river, submerging into the water.

Donya was awaiting him, dressed in the latest fashion. She wore a lovely, pleated skirt, a silk blouse, and a scarf specially knitted for her to protect against the autumn chill. The blush on her cheeks was the color of a ripe, red apple.

Machiku sensed that she wasn't her usual self.

"Good evening, Machiku," she greeted him, taking his arm. She led him to the dinner table. It was set with their finest porcelain dishes, silver cutlery, crystal glasses, and starched folded napkins beside them.

"Red or white wine?" she asked.

"Since when do we have wine at dinner?" wondered Machiku.

"You could also have champagne. I bought it especially."

"Is this a celebration? Did I forget someone's birthday?"

She blushed, gazing into his eyes.

"I was at the doctor's today."

"What's the matter? Are you sick?" Machiku was suddenly alarmed.

"Heaven forbid, I'm fine. But I have something to tell you," she hinted.

Machiku looked at her carefully and it slowly dawned on him.

"A baby? Are we going to have a child? A real baby?"

"Yes," Donya confirmed. "That's what the doctor said."

Machiku leaped to his feet. He picked her up out of the chair and they whirled around in a make-believe waltz. The intensity of his joy was something Donya could never have imagined. He was laughing and crying at the same time.

She had gone through a difficult morning. After the doctor's examination, she sat at her favorite café, thinking. Machiku and their parents would surely be glad to hear she was expecting a baby. She was happy, too. It is a mitzvah to rejoice at the future birth of a child. However, Donya's joy was mixed with apprehension. What would it be like – pregnancy, childbirth, and raising a child? What if there is a lot of pain? What will happen if the birth does not go well, God forbid? Will they have a son or a daughter? Never mind! She forced herself to banish all the worries. They were about to become a family of three;

that was the important thing. She would go home right away to share the good news with her husband.

Caught up in his overwhelming joy, she gave in to his guiding hand and together they danced a glorious waltz of expectant parenthood.

***

One morning, Machiku and Donya were at the kitchen table, he with his newspaper and morning coffee, and she with a cup of hot tea. They loved this quiet time together before starting the day.

His face suddenly darkened as he read the newspaper.

"Donya, the Jews are now facing danger on two fronts – in Palestine and in Europe. They're connected, in fact."

"What's happening in Palestine?"

"Besides coping with disease and famine, it's the Arabs. They're constantly rioting against the Jews. Many have been harassed and some have been killed. The British, who have the mandate there, are failing to stop these attacks. The recurring issue in the newspapers is that Jews must try to establish a national home in Palestine, a state alongside the Arabs."

"Endless arguments are going on between Zionist leaders, including Ben-Gurion and Weizmann." He added, "They're trying to determine whether and how this goal should be pursued. They want to involve the United States and Britain in giving the Jewish people the right to immigrate and establish a Jewish homeland in Israel."

"But there are some positive results in the struggle, aren't there?" Donya asked.

Machiku was closely involved in the Zionist movement's debates regarding the establishment of a Jewish home in Palestine. The prevailing opinion in Chernowitz was to support the Jews in Palestine. They would encourage them, send them money, but not go to live there; rather, they would continue to live the good life in Chernowitz. The British, who ruled in Palestine, made it easier for them to choose not to immigrate. They issued the "White Paper," which set an extremely small quota for entry permits.

The news horrified Machiku. There was a rising tide of hatred against the Jews in Europe and the Arabs in Palestine were attacking them. Many Jews from Poland had fled and reached the border with Chernowitz. There they were arrested, and only through bribes paid by activists in the Zionist Organization were they allowed to enter.

"An absolute monster is lurking out there, with us as his target," he said.

"What do you mean?" Donya asked him, the anxiety in her voice quite evident. She stroked her belly. The fetus had already begun moving. She loved the small movements, like the bubbles that children make in the water.

"The German devil raises its head higher and higher. In November was "Kristallnacht," when the Nazis smashed all the windows of Jewish businesses in Germany. They've started abusing and expelling Jews, and now they've annexed Austria. This monster Hitler wants to conquer the world. A second world war."

"You shouldn't mention monsters in the presence of a pregnant woman," she said with a slight smile, and then her expression became somber.

"I'm sure nothing will happen to our child. God is protecting us," Machiku tried to reassure her, and possibly himself.

"But if there's war, how will we cope and take care of a little baby?" Donya said with great alarm.

"Since I was a decorated officer in the Austrian army and was wounded in the war, I'm sure that I'll have privileges with the Germans."

He looked at her lovingly and gently placed his hand on her belly. He felt an occasional flutter, like tiny ripples. Donya laid her hand on his. She so loved to feel his protection.

At that moment, neither of them knew what the future would hold.

Chapter 10

Donya awoke in the middle of the night with mild abdominal pains. The evening before they had been to dinner at Regina's, whose meals were sumptuous, to say the least. "Maybe I ate too much," she thought and rolled over on her side. But at six in the morning, the pain intensified. Machiku woke up and saw that she was very pale.

"What is it? You don't feel well?"

"My stomach hurts. Maybe I ate something last night that didn't agree with me."

He sat down on the bed and looked closely at her in the grayish morning light that peeked through the window.

"Maybe the pain isn't from food. Maybe it's the baby, Donya." He had no experience with newborns coming into the world, but something about her appearance and behavior told him the time had come.

"Let's get dressed and go to the hospital. They'll examine you and we'll know what's happening."

They dressed quickly and went downstairs. There were no carriages on the street at that early hour. In any case, they agreed it was better for Donya not to be shaken around in a carriage. They decided to walk to the Jewish hospital, which wasn't far from their house.

When they arrived, they stopped for a moment to catch their breath. Machiku looked at his wife. "God will be with you, and we'll return home with a new addition to the family," he reassured her.

"The pain is getting worse. It stops, then starts again," Donya grimaced.

"That's what Dr. Weiser told us would happen. They're apparently labor pains. We'd better go in." Machiku hurried her along.

Donya fell silent. She knew the birth was approaching, but when she heard him say it aloud, she trembled with nervousness. It was time. It was really going to happen.

They rushed into the hospital and were greeted with pale green walls and long corridors. High windows let in the daylight.

At the entrance to the reception counter, a tall, fair-haired nurse approached. "Do you need help?"

"Yes," Machiku replied quickly, "I think my wife is about to have the baby. She's in pain and it's hard for her to breathe."

"I'll check her right away," the nurse said, leading Donya into a room. She told her to lie on the examination table and put her feet up in the obstetrics stirrups. The nurse examined her abdomen and the condition of the fetus. It was an unpleasant test and Donya's pain was worse.

"Yes, you're in labor," announced the nurse. "I'll call for a doctor," she added and hurried out of the room.

Machiku was anxious but tried to look confident. He recalled a story about his father Yossel's first wife, who died in childbirth with the baby. "Dear God," he silently prayed, "protect the baby and my Donika."

It was a long while before Dr. Weiser entered the room. He examined Donya and confirmed what the nurse had said.

"This is a first child, and the process is only at the beginning," he explained, "I don't think it'll be so fast."

They were transferred to a private room, befitting their social status. Machiku sat at Donya's bedside and held her hand. Hours passed. Occasionally she moaned. He moistened her forehead with a gentle hand, trying to comfort her as the pain intensified.

"A little longer, just a little longer," he whispered to her, smoothing the pillows under her head.

A nurse peeked in occasionally to see what was going on. The doctor also came and went. Machiku didn't leave her side for even a minute, nor did he send word to the family to tell them his wife was about to give birth. Evening fell, and darkness spread over the city, the hospital, and its environs.

At night Dr. Weiser entered the room, observed the pregnant woman lying before him and made a clicking sound with his lips.

"It's taking too long," he asserted. "If the birth doesn't progress, I'll have to operate."

"Can we wait a little longer?" asked Machiku. He had heard of cases like this. It wasn't a simple procedure. Great skill was needed to ensure that mother and baby were not harmed.

"Mr. Schmelzer, here I am the expert. I have a duty to take care of your wife and the fetus in her womb," Dr. Weiser stressed.

"Of course, sir," Machiku nodded unquestioningly. They trusted Dr. Weiser. They had chosen him as their personal physician and Machiku had paid him a good amount of money. He wouldn't interfere with his decision. He was determined not to go home without Donika. She was exhausted. It had been eighteen hours. Machiku, too, was tired and his eyes closed involuntarily, though not for long. The nurse entered, woke Donya and prepared her for passage to the delivery room.

Machiku accompanied the nurse and his wife to the door of the delivery room. It wasn't customary in those days for a husband to be present at the birth, so he remained outside.

Inside, the doctor and nurse readied Donya for surgery. Just then a strong contraction gripped her.

"Doctor, I think the baby is coming!" exclaimed the nurse. "The head is coming out with plenty of black hair!"

Dr. Weiser looked. He grumbled at what he saw. The head did protrude, but the umbilical cord was wrapped around the newborn's neck. He had to make a quick decision. If he delayed, the baby could suffocate and die.

With a sure hand, without a word, he took a scalpel and cut the umbilical cord.

The baby came out with the very next contraction.

Dr. Weiser took the newborn in his arms, smacked it lightly on the buttocks and the sound of crying was heard.

"Mazal tov! You have a baby girl!" He announced to Donya, who was exhausted from the long hours of labor.

Donya looked up at him with a tired and grateful look.

Dr. Weiser examined the newborn and saw that it was healthy and whole. He handed the child to the nurse and hurried out of the delivery room to give the news to Machiku.

"Mr. Schmelzer," he called out to Machiku, who was pacing back and forth in the corridor, "you have a fine, healthy daughter."

Machiku grabbed the doctor's hands and shook them firmly.

"How is my wife? How is the baby?" he asked eagerly.

"Your wife is well, resting from her efforts. Your daughter was born with a lock of black hair on her head," the doctor said. "For a moment she frightened me, because it was an unusual birth. She came out with the umbilical cord wrapped around her neck."

"*Riboino shel oilam!* My God!" cried the startled Machiku.

"It's behind us now," the doctor reassured him. "I didn't tell your wife. Wait until she gets over the pain and can hold her baby in her arms."

Machiku said goodbye to the doctor and was left alone in the hallway.

He sighed in relief. God had heard him in his hour of need.

Dear God," he murmured, "we thank you for saving Donya and the baby. Thank you for this gift." He made the "*Shehecheyanu*" blessing, the prayer of gratitude. He wasn't sure it was the appropriate prayer for the circumstances, but it voiced his feelings at this moment. His own father Yossel had not been privileged to return home after the first birth with the mother and baby.

Machiku glanced at his watch. One o'clock in the morning. The baby girl was healthy and Donya had weathered the difficult birth successfully. He could relax and breathe.

Now he must inform the family.

He tiptoed quietly into the delivery room. Donya was asleep, her chest rising and falling, her breath coming softly from her mouth. He approached her carefully, so as not to wake her. Machiku kissed her on the forehead and then left to go to the family to tell them that all was well. A new addition had arrived.

Three days later they came home with the baby, a sweet, round little girl with a strand of black hair on her head.

Leon gazed at his daughter affectionately.

"What thick hair she has," he said to Donya. "It's as if we snatched her from a wagon of gypsies."

"Why did you suddenly think of dirty gypsies on street corners?" Donya scolded. "You have black hair, and she gets it from you."

"We have to think of a name," said Machiku.

"That won't be a problem," Donya replied. "She has a grandmother and a great-grandmother. God willing, as is the custom, we'll name her after one of them."

Leon shook his head.

"I want a Hebrew name for her so when we go to Palestine we won't have to change it."

"Oh, Palestine is a far-off dream," Donya dismissed the idea. "Besides, you told me that the authorities don't allow the use of

Hebrew names. Let's call her Pearl, after Grandma Pearl."

"Pearl isn't Hebrew."

Donya shook her head at him. "Well, what is Hebrew for Pearl?"

They didn't quarrel – perish the thought – but merely discussed the issue. He listened to her reasoning, and she to his wisdom and authority.

"P'nina."

"That doesn't seem suitable for Palestine either," Donya pouted.

"Here they don't allow us to give children Hebrew names, except for ones from the Bible or the name of a grandparent who died."

"I know!" Machiku's eyes lit up. "Pearl is also 'Margalit' in Hebrew, a precious stone. It's a special name and perfect for our little treasure!" He exclaimed happily.

Thus, they decided to name their daughter Margalit, and were happy with the choice. However, when they went to register her in the town hall, they met with opposition from the officials.

What Machiku's persuasive powers could not do was resolved with some cash.

Their daughter was born on June 27, 1939. She was registered in Chernowitz with her Hebrew name – Margalit.

Chapter 11

On September 1, 1939, two months after Margalit was born, the German army invaded Poland. World War II had begun. In Chernowitz they were aware of it, but the war had not yet reached their gates. Already, however, there was a curfew from eight in the evening, assaults on Jewish students by anti-Semites and, especially, anguish and fear of what was to come.

The Schmelzer family was occupied with the new baby. Donya and Machiku dressed her in fur outfits with matching hats purchased from Leibowitz, the city's most prestigious maker of infant wear. Grandmothers Regina and Yetti vied with each other for the privilege of taking Margalit out in an expensive baby pram that resembled the town carriages.

Regina would ride with her in a hired carriage to show her off. Sometimes she chose the fashionable Herrengasse to greet acquaintances.

"What a smile," everyone remarked as they made cooing sounds at Margalit. Regina would smile and think to herself, "What a pity Yossel didn't get to know his little granddaughter."

Yetti settled for walking the baby in her stroller to City Hall Square and the Opera House. "Now Donya and Machiku are in Chernowitz," she thought. "No more running off as they did at their wedding." She would be an active grandmother and participate in raising her granddaughter.

Yetti was skilled with her hands and a marvel at embroidery, Gobelin-style, like that done by queens and nobles in French and British palaces. She made the baby a special square pillow. On one side she sewed black satin fabric, and on the other she embroidered tiny stitches in brown, gold, and turquoise. Thin twine was woven around the pillow, with a loop in each of the four corners. Baby Margalit adored the special pillow and would not go to sleep without it. When it was put in front of her, she would lay her head on it, put a little finger in her mouth, caress the satin cloth with her tiny hand, and fall asleep.

As was the custom for well-established gentry, the young couple hired a nanny for their daughter. They showered the baby girl with rattles, dolls, and little rubber toys that beeped when you squeezed them. Machiku was a proud father. He observed everything his daughter did, even every smile or moan from an upset stomach. Donya, too, reveled in the baby's development. They kept a detailed baby journal to chart her growth and gave her the affectionate nickname "Litti" – little Margalit.

***

The war cast a shadow on Machiku's contentment and filled him with dread. Deep in his heart he regretted not having immigrated to Palestine before the war. He now understood the

Biblical verse when God said to Moses, "For you shall see the Land before you, but you shall not go there, into the Land that I am giving to the people of Israel." He excused his decision with various arguments: "I didn't immigrate because the leaders of the Zionist organization and the JNF delegated to me the task of raising funds and sending as many Jews as possible to Palestine."

He told himself, "Every time I gave a speech, I felt that the wings of angels were upon me. It was a mitzvah mission, to fulfill Herzl's vision of the Jewish state in my own way."

He was sent to Palestine several times for conferences or the opening of a new institution. Each time he would return home full of the praise that had been lavished upon him, but with the awareness that he could not leave his mother. He could not part from Mammu Regina in Chernowitz and immigrate to Israel without her.

In addition, what he saw in Palestine and what he heard about it was not always encouraging. There were Arab riots against the Jews. The British also often hounded the Jews and always ruled against them. The physical situation in the country was difficult. Hard manual labor was needed to cultivate the land, and it depleted peoples' strength. Many of them fell ill and died. "A land that devours its inhabitants," as was written in the Bible.

And so he remained in Chernowitz and married Donya. When their daughter Margalit was born, the possibility of immigrating to Israel again came to mind – but then it was too late.

Chapter 12

One morning in July 1940, Machiku rose early as usual to go to the office. His spirits were heavy. A grim atmosphere gripped the city. The war had been raging in Europe for almost a year. Food was rationed, but Machiku obtained supplies with his connections and bribes when needed. Fear was everywhere, as if a giant tiger were poised, waiting to leap and devour its prey. The Soviets were advancing toward Ukraine and Belarus. Refugees expelled from their homes by the Red Army passed through Chernowitz. They told horrific tales of Soviet attacks that left death and destruction all around. They raped and slaughtered the innocent, and people were robbed and their property looted.

"Good morning to you, Anton," Machiku touched the brim of his hat to his friend.

"It's anything but good," muttered Anton. "This morning our Romanian army commander handed over the keys to the Russians."

"My God," said Machiku. "What does that mean?"

"There's an agreement between the Germany's Ribbentrop and

Russia's Molotov in which the Russians will take control of northern Bukovina, including Chernowitz. But the Soviets, as you know, are brutal. They'll rob and kill us to establish a new 'order.'"

As they were speaking, they heard a deafening noise. Right before their eyes, Soviet tanks rumbled into the city like iron warhorses. Young boys who saw what was happening climbed up on roofs and waved red flags. Romanian soldiers were seen fleeing from the tanks on the city streets as they fired their weapons behind them without aim or direction.

Anton and Machiku ran to the doorway of a building to escape the chaos. After catching their breath, Machiku decided to return home instead of going to the office. As he neared his home at 17 General Mircescu Street, he saw that the Russian headquarters was located right in front of it. In the distance he watched Russian soldiers dragging the dead and wounded to the entrance to his building and others nearby.

Making his way through the commotion in the street, Machiku managed to get to his stairwell and run to their apartment. Donika opened the door slightly; seeing that it was he, she hugged him tightly. Litti clung to her, holding Baba Yetti's pillow.

"Machiku, what is going on outside? We heard gunshots and screaming all morning. Litti keeps peeking out the window. I try to keep her away so she won't see the blood and death."

"My dearest," he hugged her, trying to soothe her with the warmth of his body. He tried to stay strong. After all, he had been an officer in the Austrian army, fought in the last war and was wounded on the battlefield. But his wife was seeing war in its savagery for the first time in her life. "There are new masters in the city. The Russians have taken over."

"This is terrifying!" Donya trembled in his arms.

"Yes, I know," agreed Machiku.

"What are we going to do?"

"We stay low. We don't stand out."

"How? What if we run out of food?"

"We hope for the best."

"What if they drive us out? How can we protect our Litti?"

"We wait until the rage is gone." Machiku remained calm and resolute, at least in front of his wife.

"You were outside when it started. What was going on? Did you hear anything about my parents, or Regina?"

Machiku shook his head. "I don't know anything. I barely left home when suddenly everything started exploding." He tried to figure out how to calm Donya down. "Donika, everything will be fine," he said. "We'll be unassuming and quiet, and we'll not stand out until the wave passes."

He wanted to sound self-assured, but he, too, felt frightened by the uncertainty of their situation. He, too, had more questions than answers. "What will happen to us in this war?" he wondered. "This time I'm not alone. I have a responsibility to my wife and child."

Once again shots were heard in the street. Machiku and Donya hurried to the window. They peered through it and saw Russian soldiers beating people in handcuffs with their rifle butts.

"Come, my darlings," Leon embraced his wife and daughter and led them away from the window. "We'll go into the kitchen. We'll have some tea and tell Litti the stories she loves. We'll all stay calm and wait to see what the day brings."

In his heart, Machiku was uneasy. The Soviets were staunch communists. Anyone who was bourgeois or Zionist, like him, would be in mortal danger. After all, he was the right-hand man of the chairman of the Bukovina Zionist Organization. He was a major figure at Zionist congresses and was photographed standing behind Chaim Weizmann on his visit to Bukovina. Machiku had been invited to Palestine many times as a representative of the Zionist Organization, and he was there at the inauguration of the Hebrew University on Mount Scopus. This had all been to his credit before the Russians entered the city. Now the wheel had turned. They must eliminate any sign of his family's prosperity and conceal his Zionist connections.

"We need to get rid of any evidence of wealth, luxury, ties to

Palestine and institutions of the JNF," he muttered to Donya when they were in the kitchen.

"But how?" Donya was alarmed. "We live in a modern building that even has an elevator. Our furniture is fine looking and all our books are about Judaism and the Land of Israel."

"We'll light the fireplace and burn the books," Machiku murmured, scarcely believing his own words.

Donya knew what suffering this would be for her husband. "But he's right," she thought to herself.

"And we can scratch and damage our leather furniture, like a dog would," she said with a sigh. They would have to destroy all that was beautiful in the home they had lived in for barely two years.

Machiku went to light the fireplace.

"What if the neighbors wonder why we have the fireplace burning when it's warm outside?"

"We'll tell them we need to get rid of some things we have too many of."

"All the books and lovely things in our home? We said we would always cherish them," Donya sobbed.

Machiku stroked her hair. There were tears in his eyes. Donya took Litti on her lap and kept her away from the fire. Her eyes also filled with tears. For both of them, burning books was a terrible act.

The fireplace did its work, devouring Eliezer Steinberg's poems, newspaper articles Machiku had written, the *siddur*-the prayerbook, with the prayer for the health of the Kaiser. All these were reminders of the good times in the days of the Austro-Hungarian Empire. The bookshelves began to be empty.

Machiku and Donya stood sorrowfully before the fireplace. They knew they had no choice; still, they were shocked by the great loss. Little Litti, who didn't fully understand the significance this horrendous act had for her parents, was happy to join the effort. She tried to help by bringing books to burn. Leon and Donya took them from her little hands and threw the books into the fire. They decided that if any neighbors came to ask about the smell and smoke coming from the chimney, they would say they lit the fireplace to clean it afterwards with rags.

When the books were ashes, Donya went to get a pair scissors. Her heart aching, she tore and scratched the leather armchairs. This would convey to the Soviets that they were poor, with old furniture that people had given them.

***

A few days later, towards evening, Machiku walked to the town square. He tried not to be conspicuous and wanted to see what was going on. Soviet soldiers were dragging merchants from their stores, shooting them or chasing them off, and happily looting their stores.

Suddenly he saw Anton.

"How are you?" Machiku asked.

"All right. I was hired by the municipality," Anton replied, looking around to make sure no one was watching him speaking to his Jewish friend.

"I have to go to the office every morning and work. I'm not allowed to be out on the street. They spy on everyone. Even to go to the bathroom I have to sign my name on the attendance list before I leave and when I come back." The terror in his eyes was obvious.

The two friends bid each other farewell.

Chapter 13

Machiku realized that a rope was tightening around their necks. He began to look for a place to conceal the money they had left from better days. Every authorization and license he sought depleted the small treasure trove they had. Who knew what else they would need to survive?

"Donya, can you think of where we can hide the money?" He turned to his wife.

"Why hide it?" wondered Donya.

"We'll need it if trouble comes," Machiku replied.

"What about in Litti's little bear. We could open the stomach and put it in the lining," she suggested.

"Litti won't part with one of the few toys she has left," Machiku said, dismissing the idea.

"Under a floorboard?"

"We don't have carpets. It'll look suspicious."

"The kitchen? In a jar of cookies, a canister of flour?"

"That's the first place they'll look."

"I know!" Donya grabbed his hand in a flash, "A few days ago I saw Mrs. Antonescu coming downstairs with a sack of potatoes. There must be a basement in the building."

"Why didn't I think of that?" Machiku smiled. "I'll go down and see."

When it was dark, he took a flashlight and went down the stairs, not taking the elevator so that no one would see him.

It was pitch black and there was the smell of mildew. He was a rational man, but at that moment it seemed that dozens of eyes were on him in the dark. He pointed the flashlight's beam on the walls. The place was quite empty, except for bottles of wine skipped by the Russians and a sack of potatoes, the happy owners of which seek to keep for times of famine. He shined his light on the basement floor. To his good fortune, it was composed of dark soil from which weeds and moss sprouted.

At the entrance to the building on his way up from the basement he met a neighbor, Mr. Petrescu, who had gone out for a smoke.

"What happened, the elevator again?" Mr. Petrescu asked, lighting his cigarette.

"No, no, I wanted some fresh air. It's stuffy in the house," said Machiku, hurrying up the stairs.

When he got home he looked for a tool he could use to dig. He couldn't find one and settled for a large serving spoon from the kitchen. He went down to the basement again.

It took him hours to dig a large enough space in the black dirt. He stuffed banknotes in separate bags, covered the pit and then paced back and forth on it to wipe out traces of his digging.

Tomorrow he would bring Donya down here to show her where he had hidden the money. It might one day save their lives.

**

That evening, when he returned home, there was a sudden knock on the door. Machiku gestured for Donya to go into the kitchen with Litti. He put a finger on his lips signaling silence. Fear fell on him like a thick blanket.

"Who is it?"

"Open up!" came a shout from the other side.

He looked through the peephole and saw two men in uniform, Russian soldiers. With a trembling hand he unlatched the security chain.

They didn't wait until he opened the door of his house, but pushed it roughly and entered. The soldiers looked like Romanian peasants. Big, burly men in intimidating uniforms. One had dark hair, the other blond, wavy hair.

"Donya, take Litti and go to her room," he told his wife. He hoped with all his heart that they wouldn't be killed.

The soldiers went to the display cabinet in the living room. One by one, they pulled out crystal vessels and threw them to the ground in a bizarre competition as to who could break the most. Machiku tried to calm them, but they barked at him. Donya sat in Litti's room, hugging her little girl in fear. She could hear everything. Litti clung to the pillow Baba Yetti had made for her, afraid they would take it from her.

The soldiers finished demolishing the living room and moved from room to room around the spacious apartment. They opened closets, pulled out the drawers, yanking out objects and putting them in large baskets they had brought in with them.

"Look what I found!" The dark-haired soldier had one of Donya's satin night gowns pressed to his body as he measured it.

"My Anna can go to the opera in this," he boasted to his friend, throwing the dress into a sack he had with him.

Another soldier shoved Machiku against the wall and motioned for him to show his hands. He grabbed his right hand and forcibly removed the wedding ring.

"Any more jewelry here?"

Machiku swallowed hard and nodded.

They took everything they could, reveling in the treasures they found. They cared nothing about communist theory. They merely obeyed orders, and did so happily. Machiku saw, with a heavy heart, how they took the silver candlesticks Donya got from her parents for their wedding. He watched them put the candlesticks in the basket along with the wine cup of Elijah the Prophet that Regina had given him. He stood to the side, heard Litti crying in her room and Donya trying to calm her, waiting for the nightmare to end.

Finally, after what seemed like an eternity, the soldiers left with their stolen booty. Donya and Litti fearfully came out and joined Machiku. The three of them looked around, heartbroken. The house was upside down; the doors of the emptied closets were left hanging, and discarded clothes, pieces of broken utensils and clumps of dirt from the soldiers' boots were all over the floor.

"They took all the family silverware, the wedding gifts, even the Shabbat and holiday utensils." murmured Machiku.

"And everything you lovingly bought for me," Donya added.

"The important thing is to survive," Machiku said, hugging her. "Nothing else matters." They huddled together. For the first time in her life, Donya saw her husband cry. Machiku trembled, and tears welled up in his eyes, tears of frustration and humiliation. He didn't try to resist the soldiers as it was clear that it would have been futile. The soldiers had taken everything, but they were still alive. At least that. Thank you, dear God.

In the two days since the soldiers broke into their home, Machiku and Donya didn't dare leave the house. They only occasionally peeked out the window at the street. On the evening of the third day, just as they were getting ready for bed, there was loud banging on the door.

"Not again!" Donya was stunned.

"Stay here with Litti," Machiku replied, closing the door to the bedroom behind him. He hurried to the front door and opened it: two Soviet soldiers.

"Leon Schmelzer?" They asked in a threatening tone.

"Yes."

"Come with us. For interrogation."

"But why?" He tried to sound naïve.

"We are N.K.V.D. (secret police commissariat). We were told that you're a leader of many Jews here, and you write in your newspaper. We want details on everyone in your movement. If you don't come with us, we'll kill you right here."

In his mind's eye, Machiku could see himself being tortured for the information. He would go with them, he thought. He won't speak, but he'll do anything to keep them away from Donya and Litti. He knew the secret police arrested and sometimes murdered people without trial. Their method was to persuade people to inform on each other. In Chernowitz they translated the initials of N.K.V.D. into the Yiddish: Look, but don't speak.

Chapter 14

The veteran interrogator, Oleg, awoke in good spirits. He was very pleased with the role assigned to him at Chernowitz. Every day he would go to his office at the Secret Police Headquarters. He would instruct his soldiers to round up activists from the Jewish community, and they would obey and bring him the Jews from whom information needed to be extorted.

He preferred not to use force, but as a hardened interrogator he knew that after a punch here and there, and a few slaps, they would start talking. In his youth in Russia, he had worked harvesting potatoes on a farm. With no hopes of a future, he enlisted in the Russian army and met with success. As a junior NKVD interrogator, the more people he managed to get on the list of exiles, the more satisfied were his superiors. He was promoted several times, and now here he was, in charge of the Secret Police in the occupied city of Chernowitz. He needed to justify his advancement.

Machiku was locked up all night in the cellars of the NKVD. The short, stocky interrogator, his face flushed from drinking every day, was decisive and cruel, a veteran Russian commissar, loyal to the regime.

Oleg enhanced his uniform with a metal belt buckle. "I'll break this Jew," he thought. "Once he opens his mouth, I'll be able to get to all the Jews who run this city. They think they own this town, but now *we* rule. They're opponents of the regime. They talk about Palestine as if God gave it to them as a gift. Who is this God? No such thing. We are the conquerors. Communism will take over the world. Equality for all; no rich and no poor."

He glared at Machiku, who sat on the edge of a chair, his hands tied behind his back. He was pale, tired, and anxious, but tried to look calm.

"Do you know why you are here?" Oleg began, menacingly.

"No."

"We want to know about all the people who have money in the city. Who are your friends who are connected to Palestine in a movement called 'Zionism?'"

"How would I know such people?" Machiku replied, hoping no one had pointed to him as a key figure in the community and that the Russian was only fishing for information.

"Tell me about your family in town."

"My father died as a refugee in Vienna during the war. My mother is still alive, eighty years old. Here in the city, I don't have important friends or relatives," Leon replied in a calm voice, trying to show that he was at ease.

Oleg approached him, his little eyes darting. He looked straight at him. "Who are your friends?"

"I have no friends," Machiku murmured.

"Everyone has friends," the interrogator grinned. "And you have such good, devoted friends, that one of them gave us your name as a leader of the Jews in this city!"

"Me, a leader?" Leon asked, to gain time. "I'm too old for that. I don't think of others, just want peace and quiet at home."

The interrogator lifted his hand as if about to slap him.

"I ask you again, who are your friends? I want an accurate list of everyone you know in the Jewish leadership of the city."

Machiku was silent.

The interrogator glanced at him, and then left the room to freshen up. On the other side of the door he pulled out the flask in the inside pocket of his coat and took a swig. He won't let this Jew off so quickly. He held the power.

He took another sip from the flask, corked it and put it back in his pocket. He pushed open the door and went into the room, asking the same question.

"Who are your friends?"

"I told you, I'm not a sociable person. I'm busy with my work."

"What do you do?"

"I keep accounts. Collect debts for people," said Machiku, as an idea flashed through his mind. "This could benefit you."

Oleg's ears perked up, and he stood up straighter. Now the Jew begins to speak. He is glad. In this city there are many high-minded people who would rather die than inform on friends. He had already sent some of them to Siberia and murdered others. His previous work was excellent. The heads of the NKVD will reward him, make him commander of the whole province. However, for that he must succeed with this Jew, who is said to be a major activist in the city.

"And how can that benefit us?" Oleg asked disparagingly.

At that moment Machiku needed all the wisdom his mother had instilled in him. Here he could not merely lower his head to let the wave pass by. He had to cooperate in a way that would be useful to them. It might save his life.

"The Austrians left a lot of debts to the Romanian Government," he said, trying to control the tremor in his voice. "I'm an expert in this field and can recover all these debts for you," he continued softly. As a lawyer he had experience in breaking down witnesses in court. Now he had to capture this Russian in his net.

"My office is on the second floor of a central building in the city. It overlooks the main street. It can serve as your headquarters. I'll sit with you there and manage the debt collection all over Bukovina."

"What will you need to do that?" Oleg asked cautiously. He wanted to take advantage of this detainee who fell into his hands and have him work for the regime. "When the time comes, I'll kill him," he thought. "First he will give me his office. Then he will work under us, and we'll get everything we can out of him. Only then will he and his friends be eliminated."

Machiku outlined his plan to the interrogator, who agreed to the details of the devil's pact. Machiku gave him his office, and in return was appointed a payroll accountant traveling through Romania and collecting for the Russians the forgotten loans taken by the Austrians from state coffers. To succeed at that, Machiku set up a special collection department made up of bank executives who had been dismissed and former lawyers.

He wrote the account sheets in Russian so that the NKVD people could send them to Moscow, but he was careful not to sign them. It was impossible to know what the future would hold. Who knows which way the war will go? What if the city is taken by the Germans or the Austrians?

He considered his actions, and then called into his room Vladi, a young lawyer who held socialist views even before the city was captured by the Russians. He would be perfect.

"Vladi," he said to the young lawyer, "I was thinking of you. I'm getting older, and I don't think I would have a future in our profession in Russia. But you are young and starting out. Would you like the honor of signing the account sheets?"

"Thank you, Mr. Schmelzer," the excited young man replied, "Gladly." It was a great, unexpected opportunity that came his way.

Machiku thanked him, and turned to Boris, the mission manager for the Russians.

"Tovarishch (Comrade) Boris. I have given power of attorney to Vladi to sign the account sheets. He's a loyal socialist. He will sign. I'll just go over the details."

Boris nodded.

"Now I must apply for a travel permit. I have no choice. I need to go to other places around the country to collect the debts for you."

Boris hesitated.

"And if I have questions? How and where will I reach you?"

Machiku squeezed his hat.

"I don't know where or for how long I'll be gone," he admitted. "Debtors are scattered all over the country, and there's a lot of work."

Boris nodded.

"I'll tell you what to do. Every day when you finish work, don't go to the hotel, and don't make contact with local Jews, because the NKVD will know. Stay in the office where you are and sleep at your desk so we can reach you if we need to."

Machiku nodded.

"And what about the travel authorization?"

"Before you leave here, I want the key to the safe where you keep the financial reports," Boris replied. "There are a lot of people here. I need the report in my hands only.

Machiku handed him the key in silence. Boris signed the travel permit and handed it to him with a solemn expression.

Machiku said goodbye to his wife and daughter, took provisions, and set off. He obeyed instructions and slept on two desks pushed together in each office he came to. Every night he would call home, say "Hello," and hang up so that the Secret Police would not have time to check where he was calling from. That was how he kept in touch with Donya and Litti without revealing his location.

Chapter 15

The Russian army took over life in Chernowitz. Like locusts invading from an east wind, soldiers were everywhere. They could not be removed from the fields and houses. They sowed terror. They shot people in the streets without putting them on trial first, and made arrests in the middle of the night. People disappeared and no one knew where they were taken to and what had happened to them.

On the days when he wasn't traveling to collect debts, Machiku continued to go to the place that had been his office as a successful criminal lawyer. The Russian underling who ran the office followed his every movement, every phone call, and enjoyed the convenience the office offered. From the second floor, the panorama of the beautiful city revealed high-rise buildings and now deserted cafés. They were just shadows of the good days before the war.

On his way home from the office, Machiku walked with his head bowed, not wanting to see what was around him. He didn't want to see the red flags of the Soviets on every corner, the grayish-hued people with worried faces, and he didn't want to hear the soldiers shouting *"Edie syuda,"* come here! Machiku shuddered. He had finagled some borrowed time by transferring his office to the Soviets and hiring out his services to them to collect leftover debts from the Austrian Empire. His travels throughout Romania gave him some space and time to think, but he knew he was only delaying the end.

His anxiety increased when the Soviets began issuing new ID cards to residents. Because he worked with them, he knew that anyone whose last digit on his new ID was 3 or 9, was doomed. The Russians roamed the regions in and around Chernowitz and dealt with the holders of these ID numbers. Some were shot, and others sent to Siberia or to forced labor camps, but sooner or later they would all be dead as well.

He, too, was given a new identity card with the cursed number 9 at the end of it. The sword was hovering above him, and any day it could come down on his family. Well- intended contributions to the JNF and honorable trips to Palestine were behind him. Now only his life and his family were precious.

If only he had someone to consult with, to share his concerns.

Every evening as he walked home, he would hear his footsteps echoing in the empty streets and think that he might not walk them again tomorrow. He devoted his whole being to contemplating how to extricate himself from his situation. How could he fulfill his responsibility to himself and to the ones he cherished?

Machiku was an intelligent man, aware of the fate awaiting him: deportation to frozen Siberia, or else death in the torture chambers of the NKVD. This was what befell the Zionists he knew as well as others who were unlucky to have been born Jewish. Every night, friends and acquaintances would disappear without a trace. Uniformed Russian police arrested people and killed them in cold blood.

On the cobblestone streets, where glorious carriages once transported city dignitaries, now lay rotting, unburied corpses. In the meantime, as long as he was helping the authorities, he survived. But it was clear that his fate had only been postponed; the death decree had already been signed.

One evening, before the end of the workday, Boris, the Russian communist who had taken over his office, called him in. He was at least a head and a half taller than Machiku, balding, with blue eyes and sparse light brown hair. He wore military trousers and a sloppy, disheveled black shirt.

"Schmelzer," he said with a threatening tone, "give me your office keys. Tomorrow morning you may not need them."

When Machiku heard those words, he felt the earth open up, ready to swallow him. The last digit on his ID ended with the number 9. He was destined for Siberia, that frozen end of the world from which no Jew had ever returned. Every day in Chernowitz there were groups of people in heavy winter clothes, carrying suitcases that looked like brown cardboard boxes. No one knew when it would be his turn.

Machiku swallowed hard, pretending everything was fine. He handed the office keys to Boris. Then he turned around and left the room, its warm fire burning. What will he do now? How should he act? Doomsday was upon him.

Darkness was already falling. Light rain filled the street with the smell of soil and wet foliage. He strode home. As he passed the synagogue, he noticed a figure cloaked in black pointing towards him. At first he ignored it; maybe it had nothing to do with him, perhaps a gypsy refugee. But as he kept on, he felt eyes fixed on the back of his neck, and his hair bristled.

Machiku stopped at the entrance to a building and looked around to see if the figure was following him. He saw no one, but clearly felt that someone was there. He looked in all directions, saw he had nowhere to run and decided to confront the character. He moved forward, stopping at the door of one of the houses. The figure in black was standing next to him, motioning for him to keep silent. Machiku nodded at the signal that he understood, and the figure pulled the veil from her face. It was the secretary of the local Zionist administration.

Machiku heaved a sigh of relief.

"I came to warn you," she said. "Those who help everyone need to know. Last night they took Weisselberger, your close friend from the committee, and his whole family, to God knows where. The Russians broke into our office, which was operating under the guise of an ordinary office. They took the paperwork and now I'm almost certain they know about you, your membership on the committee, and your high position."

Machiku shook her hand gratefully. She said goodbye, signaled something to someone across the road and disappeared. He intended to hurry home, but before he could, two gendarmes emerged from the shadows. They stood blocking his way, their faces like black storm clouds.

"You!" one of them yelled "What are you doing out after curfew?"

"I'm coming back from the office, where I collect money for you that the Austrians owe to Romania. It's a lot of money," he replied, in a soft, yet confident voice. Perhaps they will let him pass when they see that he's not afraid. This was a technique he used more than once in court, and it had always proven itself.

"Papers!" shouted the other gendarme.

Machiku handed him his ID. He looked at the certificate and showed it to his comrade. They shook their heads. Did they see the number 9 on it, Machiku wondered? Do they know that it means that sooner or later we would be sent to an unknown destination?

"Move! Fast! Don't let us see you walking around again at night!" The gendarmes said as they sent him on his way.

He hurried home. What he had to do was now clear to him.

Chapter 16

It was already evening, and it was bitter cold. No one was permitted to be outside. Machiku walked as quickly as he could, not wanting to arouse suspicion. A freezing wind blew. It was about to rain again. The click of his heels echoed on the beautiful stones that led from Herrengasse past the Opera House to his home at 17 General Mircescu Street. He had to rescue his family from the death sentence that awaited them. He dreaded his gentle wife's reaction to the news. She was only thirty-one and a new mother when the war broke out and totally changed their world. The Russians looted their home, she and Machiku had burned their books and fired their daughter's nanny so that they would not be accused of being bourgeois, and so that she would not report them to the authorities. However, all this was nothing compared to what he was about to hit her with. Will she panic? Will she cooperate? It was a matter of life and death.

The house was dark and cold. When she heard his key in the door Donya came towards him, shivering.

"Donika, we must leave at once," he told her.

She looked at him, dumb-stricken. "Leave? Now, at night? Litti is asleep and it's freezing cold outside."

"We have to leave now," he repeated firmly.

"Where can we go now in the middle of the night and why?"

"We have to hurry!"

Donya knew her husband well. He was always well aware of what he was saying. At sixteen years older, she saw him as a husband, father, and family head, as well as a leader of Chernowitz Jewry. Yet she could not think of going out at night to an unknown place without speaking to their parents and family.

"If they catch us, they'll kill us. Who goes out in the middle of the night?"

"We'll take the risk. Put Litti in the basket and walk with her. If they see us, we'll say she has asthma, and the doctor told us that in case of an attack we must take her out for air."

"It sounds too dangerous. Besides, today I didn't feel well and wanted to go to bed early. I won't be able to go out now. I'm weak just thinking about it," Donya tried to reverse the harsh verdict.

Machiku knew his Donya well. When she was having a difficult time or was ill he treated her like a child. Now it was imperative. There was no other way. As hard as it was to let someone else make decisions for her, she had always trusted him.

"We have no choice."

"It seems so illogical," Donya said.

However, Machiku was a practical, judicious man. He had planned their escape route in advance. He hadn't wanted to frighten her and hoped that quick, decisive action would stop her from overthinking the matter. He quickly moved on to a necessary sequence of actions.

"There is the black bag in the closet of my study, the one I always travel with. It has things in it I prepared in case of need."

"What need?" she tried to interrogate him.

"I'll tell you later," he mumbled. "There's no time. We need to hurry. Please bring the bag to the kitchen. I want to put a few more things in it. Also, add a few sugar cubes, a warm coat for Litti and anything else you need. But as little as possible."

"You're scaring me."

"Donika, I'm with you. Come, my dear, do what I ask."

Her hands began to tremble. Something very threatening has happened, but Machiku wasn't sharing it with her.

"You know how important you are to me. I'll never leave you and will always protect you. Now go, bring the bag here."

Rumors of people disappearing in the middle of the night had reached her as well. There was nothing else to do. She will go with Machiku and pray that the worst will not happen. The backpack was brought into the kitchen and opened. It contained several tins of meat. She added a few more things; a sweater for her, a diaper for Litti, a comb.

"Won't we tell my parents? They'll think we were sent to Siberia," Donya murmured. Machiku didn't answer. He went to Litti's room, carefully lifted her out of bed, wrapped her in the blanket and laid her in the portable crib. In his heart he prayed that she would not wake up and cry. Then he remembered the pacifier and took that, too.

They left the apartment on tiptoes so as not to wake the neighbors. Locking the door behind them, and just before they went downstairs, they looked back. This could be the last time they would ever see that door.

It was very cold outside. Huge drops of rain fell on them and thunder rolled in the distance. The streets were dark and desolate. They clung to each other, the crib between them.

"Where are we going?" Donika whispered.

"You'll see. I know the way. We're going to hide."

"Can't we tell our parents? They'll think we were taken to Siberia!"

"No time for that," Machiku whispered, pulling her after him. She didn't know where they were headed, but after crossing several streets she realized they were on the edge of a forest on the outskirts of the city.

Machiku was leading them into the woods.

"No, Machiku," cried Donya. "I'm so tired, and cold. Litika could catch a cold. I want to sleep. I want to go home. I can't take another step."

Machiku didn't answer her, just supported her under the arm as they always liked to walk with each other. His comforting arm reminded her that he knows what he's doing and was the responsible adult between them. They continued walking into the increasing dark, as if a black cover spread over everything. Machiku feared using the flashlight, so they groped their way carefully, step by step, among the trees.

They made their way in the dark for a long time, until small lights shone in the distance. It was the village lights on the outskirts of Chernowitz. Machiku knew it well. The Russians sometimes sent him to remind the residents of their debts and taxes they had to pay. He led his wife and daughter towards a solitary old house.

"Who lives here? Why did we come?" Donya asked, shivering and frightened.

Machiku again refrained from answering her. He knocked on the door, and slow footsteps were heard inside. The door opened to a narrow crack. Behind it stood Irena holding a candle.

"Irina," Donya said, surprised.

Irina was the farmer who had brought eggs and milk every week. Even when stocks were depleted, she would secretly come and bring them groceries in exchange for cash, of course.

"*Domnule* Schmelzer!" She was astonished, "What are you doing here in the middle of the night?"

She was a thick-fleshed woman. An old blanket was wrapped around her body and she wore a woolen scarf. Her face was covered with wrinkles, and she looked at them suspiciously.

"We had to flee the house in Chernowitz," Machiku replied to her in a confident voice. "We came to hide with you so we wouldn't be sent to Siberia."

"If you're caught, they'll kill you on the spot and kill me too!" She moved back a bit, continuing to stare at them with fear and a puzzled look on her face. Her eyes fell on Litti, who lay quietly in the basket.

It was only at that moment that Donya understood why they had made this terrible nocturnal journey, and a shiver went through her. However, she refrained from making a sound, clinging to Machiku and drawing strength from his self-assurance. In fact, Machiku wasn't at all sure that his plan would succeed, but he had nothing to lose.

"I can in no way hide you!" said Irina, as she was about to close the door. Machiku stuck his foot between the door and its jamb.

"If you don't hide us, I'll tell the Soviets you invited us to your house, and they will kill you anyway," he threatened. He knew very well how to convince people. It wasn't for nothing that he was considered one of the best criminal lawyers in Bukovina.

The peasant woman was astonished at his boldness. She lingered on the doorstep, coughing and pondering what to do. If she didn't take them in, they would report her, and if she hid them, the Russians may find out. Either way it would be bad for her.

"We won't bother you." Machiku took advantage of the respite. "Some milk for the child and we thank you. That's all."

What could she do, she asked herself, call the neighbors? That would be even worse. She looked at the round, serene face of the little girl in the crib. She couldn't just leave them on her doorstep. She thought of something. Looking carefully outside to make sure no one had noticed them, she moved aside and let them in.

"Follow me," she said, leading them through the house into the backyard. They went down stone steps and came to a pig sty next to a chicken coop. When the war broke out, Irena was selling produce on the streets of Chernowitz. The Russians arrived and confiscated most of it. The stench of mildew and the feces of chickens and pigs penetrated their nostrils.

They descended to a dark surface, where she kept the animals that she raised in the pen and chicken coop. Irena removed the old blanket she was wrapped in and spread it on the filthy surface on top of the dung.

"You sleep here. Tomorrow we'll see," she muttered, walking off with the lit candle.

In the middle of the night, Litti woke up and searched with her hand for Baba Yetti's pillow, the one she could not fall asleep without. Only then did the parents realize that they had forgotten the pillow. Litti started wailing. Frightened, they didn't know what to do to calm her down. In a moment of deep distress Donya put her palm over Litti's mouth, almost suffocating her. However, thanks to that, their lives were saved. Had anyone heard Litti's crying and discovered them, they would have been betrayed immediately.

Chapter 17

"Cock-a-doodle-doo," crowed the rooster, and the chickens answered with their clucks. Machiku opened his eyes in panic, not realizing where he was. It was still dark. There was a terrible, overpowering stench and he suddenly remembered the events of the previous night. He sat up at once as anxiety enveloped him like the darkness all around.

"Irina's chicken coop," flashed in his head. "It's a good hiding place. Who would think that people are in here?" Even he would not have believed it. He calculated quickly: roosters usually crow at daybreak, so at sunrise he'll think about what to do next.

Donya stirred near him. He felt her moving lightly, trying not to wake their little girl.

"Where are we?" she whispered. He stroked her cheek. His Donika. He loved her so much. He must protect and take care of her. They'll escape, he thought. Even on the nights the Russians interrogated him in the cellars of the NKVD, the thought of Donya gave him both strength and hope.

"We're in hiding with Irina the peasant," he whispered. "If she agreed to hide us, we'll be saved. I'm sure," he said with confidence, although inwardly he had doubts. He was an optimist, but also a realist. For now, they had survived. Every moment that passes is a lifeline. They snuggled against each other, in the darkness of the chicken coop, trying to give one another warmth and confidence, being careful not to wake Litti. Sleep closed their eyes for another period of grace, until Litti woke up. Donya gave her the pacifier.

"Good morning Litika," she smiled. "Today you must be quiet; otherwise, bad people will catch us."

"Who are the bad people, Mama?" Litti asked.

"We're playing hide-and-seek like we play with Daddy at the park near City Hall," her mother replied.

"Are they like the policeman who comes if I don't eat my porridge?" Litti persisted.

"No, darling," her mother replied, "other bad people. They're not playing and they don't want us to hide here."

"Why not?"

"Enough questions. Take the pacifier and go back to sleep."

"I slept a lot. Dark all the time here, and the chickens' noises and smells wake me up."

"Come closer. Imagine we are in a great palace. You are the princess. You pricked your finger and you go to sleep for a hundred years, until the prince wakes you up with a kiss."

Litti was quiet. Tears fell upon her little cheeks. This time it wasn't a game. If you cry, the bad men will come. She touched a little finger to Donya's face. It was wet. "Mama is crying? Is Mama scared, too? Mothers don't cry. Maybe because of the sad story of the princess?"

Mama told many stories like that. There were evil queens and good queens, witches who eat little children, and princes who turn into frogs. This time Litti felt it was real, so she curled up with her fear and everything faded – the smell, the cold, the chickens, and the bad men who might come and take them.

At daylight they saw that they were in a small, underground room. Feathers, mixed with chicken feces, were scattered on the muddy floor. In the corner were sacks of chicken food, which smelled of garbage. There was no air in the room, and only a thin slit close to the ceiling let in the light of day.

"If we got through this night here, we'll continue to survive," Machiku assured himself and Donya. "We must believe. The rest we leave to God."

***

Heavy footsteps were heard from the stairs.

"Who is that?" Donya whispered as she shrank into herself.

Machiku knelt on the filthy floor, trying to shelter his family.

"The bad men?" asked the frightened Litika.

The door creaked open. The light that penetrated inside illuminated a figure in the doorway. It was Irina, with a headscarf, a wide dress, and a worn coat over her body. In her hands she held a jug of milk, a slice of bread and a small glass.

"She didn't betray us," thought Machiku. "She probably decided that if she betrayed us it would be death for her, too. Maybe there was humanity even among those who rise up to kill you. Who knows?" He stood up. Irina handed him the food.

"I brought you what I could. You have such a little girl," she said.

Machiku thanked her. Irina glanced at Donya and Litika. Poor people, she thought. They come from a large family, a fancy house in the big city. She knew the whole family because she would provide everyone with fresh eggs and milk from her farm.

"What can I do with you? How can I stop the authorities from finding you?"

"They have already searched this area. There is a chance they won't come back." said Machiku.

"I don't know. Maybe the neighbors will hear something. Then they'll suspect that I'm hiding you."

He knew she was devout, and spoke to her heart. "God will reward you for your kindness," he said to her in Romanian.

"You have to stay quiet all day. There are workers here on the farm. They milk the cows and clean the yard. If they hear you, they'll be happy to turn over the 'damn Jews,' as they call you."

"But how can we breathe in here? What do we do with the child all day? After all, she could get sick and die from the dirt and contact with the feces," Donya spoke up.

"If everything is quiet, maybe at night I can let you out for a few minutes," Irena replied, stepping out of the coop, closing the door, and bolting it from outside.

They were left in a silence that was broken only by the clucking of the waking chickens. The hours crept by slowly. When would they be able to come out of hiding? How would all this end?" Would they be caught? Saved? To keep her sanity and reassure Litti, Donya began to tell her Grimm Brothers' fairy tales. In her soft, soothing voice, Donya knew how to elaborate and stretch the story so that Litti didn't know until the very end if the hero would triumph. Donya knew dozens of stories.

There was the princess who pricked her finger and slept for a hundred years. She knew the one about a prince who was turned into a frog until a real princess kissed him and he became a prince again. And Hansel and Gretel – where the evil witch lured them into her house of chocolate and tried to eat them. The stories were of good and bad, black versus white, the charm of the impossible – and especially the happy endings. "And they all lived happily ever after."

Litti didn't accept the fact that evil prevails in the story. The evil queen must die and Snow White will rule the kingdom. She grew up believing the world is a good place. Despite all the hell that people go through, they survive, and rise from the flames like the phoenix.

After a few months that seemed like an eternity, Irena the farmer said they could come out of hiding. The Russians were fleeing and German tanks were on the outskirts of the city. Machiku was happy. Although he had heard of horrible deeds that the Nazis had perpetrated, he was an intelligent, reasonable man. He chose to believe that the Germans were a cultured people and that it wasn't possible that the rumors of what they did to the Jews were true. Moreover, he was sure that as a decorated Austrian officer wounded in the first World War, the Germans would treat him with respect.

Machiku, Donya, and Litti came out of the chicken coop into blinding sunlight. After thanking the farmer, they made their way back to the city. At its outskirts, people were waving and throwing candies at the columns of German armored vehicles rumbling into Chernowitz.

Chapter 18

The people of Chernowitz's joy at the German defeat of the Russians was short-lived.

The Holocaust for the Jews of Bukovina began on June 22, 1941.

The Germans and Romanians recaptured Northern Bukovina, including Chernowitz, from the Russians. Robberies, looting, massacres, sending Jews to concentration camps, especially to the terrible ones in Transnistria, devastated the community. The suffering was unimaginable. German and Romanian fascists carried out inhuman atrocities.

Immediately upon takeover, the Nazis made the Romanians their accomplices. As had happened in other countries before Romania, they were often worse than their masters. Romanians looted Jewish property, or forced them to sell their offices, apartments, or shops for pennies. A dreadful cloud hung over the Jews of Romania as a whole, and over the Jews of Chernowitz in particular. It was dangerous to walk outside; one could be arrested, shot dead, or seized and sent somewhere from which there was no coming back. The Prut River overflowed with blood, and the people lived in constant fear.

Still, the Schmelzer family lived relatively well in those early days. Bubbi, the older brother, had hidden a great deal of money for his family, and Machiku had many acquaintances from when he was a successful criminal lawyer. He would occasionally collect what was owed to him in barter – waiving the debt in exchange for food for his mother, wife, and little daughter.

The atmosphere was stifling, like before a rainstorm. It was hot and oppressive. Everyone expected the big drops to fall at any moment. No one knew what tomorrow would bring, only that the situation would get worse. Polish refugees passing through Chernowitz on their way to Russia told horrific tales of the Germans' actions against the Jews in the places they occupied – killing, exterminating, deporting people *en masse*. Entire families were torn from their homes. To some, the stories sounded impossible, inconceivable.

Then came the order to force all the Jews into a ghetto. Machiku gathered the members of his family together. "As you know," he began in a solemn voice, "the Germans have issued a decree that all Jews must move to an area on the outskirts of the city. Everyone will live there and won't be allowed to leave. Every Jew will have to put a yellow star on the front and back of his clothes."

"How can thousands of people live in such a restricted area?" asked Bubbi.

"I don't know," Machiku replied. "The order says that every family is allowed to take only what they can carry, and all the Jews must move to the ghetto. Whoever disobeys will be killed on the spot."

"And what will we live on? What will happen to the children?" Donya cried out. "Let's just go out on the balcony and jump!"

"There will be time for that," said Machiku, reassuringly, but firmly.

Regina sat, her hands folded, shaking her head. She had been through so much. Deported in the previous war, she had fled with her whole family to Vienna. Now there was nowhere to run to. Machiku saw her suffering, and approached. He placed one hand on her shoulder and stroked her cheek with the other.

She nestled her head on his side. When Machiku, Donya, and Litti had suddenly disappeared she didn't know where they were and what had happened to them. Many tumultuous days passed until they returned from the forest. Regina thanked God with all her heart that they were alive, but the turmoil she experienced at their disappearance had taken its toll.

"Mother's house is on the upper border of the ghetto," said Machiku. "We can live with her and not have to go to other houses. From what I have heard, everyone has to hand over the keys to their homes and property to the authorities."

His sister Lottie burst into convulsive weeping.

"Donika," said Regina, "go home, bring your parents, your sister and her family. They'll also live with us. I'll not let them be harmed."

Long convoys of Jews trudged into the ghetto. Each one carried a small package or suitcase. The smaller children were in the arms of their parents or on their backs. They walked quietly, silently. No complaining, no rebellion, no cursing; they didn't fight. The Jews who already lived in the ghetto area opened their hearts and doors so that no one was left outside.

In the days that followed, thirty people were gathered in Regina's house. Anyone who didn't enter the ghetto was deported or was shot by order of the Romanian dictator, Ion Antonescu. There was scarcely any food or water. They tended to the needs of the children first. Every day they were ordered to be near the ghetto gate where it would be decided who would be deported and who would remain.

The mayor of Chernowitz, Traian Popovich, fearing that the city's economy would collapse without the Jews, demanded that officers, doctors, engineers, and lawyers be allowed to reside in the city outside the ghetto. Thanks to this, Machiku was able to obtain a special permit for his family to return to their apartment.

When they came back, they were allowed to go outside only for one hour. Every day men were taken from their homes; some were shot, and the others were ordered to bury them. Machiku witnessed Rabbi Mark and Rabbi Feldman being taken out and murdered. He was among the men who dug their graves.

Returning home after the burial, he sat on the floor for three days, not eating, not drinking or uttering a word.

In June 1942, the deportations to the camps in Transnistria were renewed. Donya's sister Nussia, her husband and two sons, Ziggy and Norbert-Natan, were among the deportees. A German soldier on the way hit Norbert-Natan in the head. He was near death for two weeks and finally passed away.

Machiku, who had already seen it all, began to believe the rumors that prophesied what was to come. From that moment, he was concerned with only one thing: how to escape. How can he save his family from the clutches of war? Europe was burning, with the Nazis conquering one country after another. The only place of refuge, he thought, was Palestine. But passage to Palestine now was not possible, like it was before the war. How can they get out of Romania and reach Palestine? He must get there with his wife and daughter, no matter what. They may die in the attempt, but anything is better than what could be expected here.

What of his extended family, especially Mammu Regina?

She could no longer stand on her own feet and function as before. If he leaves his beloved mother behind, who will take care of her? Who will protect her? She loved him so much, and now she depends on him. Tears welled up in his eyes. He realized that to ensure the survival of his wife and daughter, he would have to leave only with them, Donya and Litti. Alone they might be able to escape. However, how can he leave behind his whole family, including his mother? Although he had a strong character, at that moment he was overwhelmed by sorrow.

The only possible way out was by sea. Slowly he began to formulate a plan. At that time, there were ship dealers around the city who offered to sell vessels to sail beyond the country's borders.

The Romanians supported this because they wanted to get rid of the Jews in any way possible. In those days in Romania, money solved all problems. But how could he sail out to sea with his family? Would the authorities approve the trip? The voyage itself would be dangerous. The sea was infested with German submarines and underwater mines. He had heard about the "Struma," with 768 Jewish refugees on board, that was sunk in the Black Sea. How could he be sure that he wouldn't suffer a similar fate? He had to try; the decrees and the worsening of the situation demanded it. Better to drown than be shot in the street or sent to Transnistria. What about the ban on landing on the shores of Turkey? How will they equip and refuel on the way? He didn't know the answers and understood that anything could happen. One thing, however, was certain: If they stayed in Chernowitz, they were doomed.

Machiku made a decision, not sharing it with anyone, not even Donya, to purchase a ship to sail to Palestine. A small vessel might more easily elude the Soviets and the Germans. He would raise the funds needed by selling places on the boat to a few people whose discretion he could count on.

He contacted a ship dealer and made an agreement to buy a small craft, a simple boat the size of a bus. Machiku still had connections with high-ranking people in Chernowitz. He consulted with them and formulated an exit plan from Romania. Since he was on the deportation list anyway, he would use it to get out of the country.

The authorities were happy about every Jew who managed to get out. In this way, their country would be *Judenrein* – free of Jews – a term they copied from the Germans.

He began selling seats on the ship. Each passenger paid approximately $1,500 for the voyage, whose final destination was Palestine. Fifteen people bought seats. There were five children, five men, and five women. He swore everyone to secrecy and asked them to pack one small suitcase for each family with some canned food, warm clothing, shoes, and scarves.

At the same time, Machiku was involved in organizing another, larger ship, called "Europa." His protégé, Harry Zucker, was on this ship. Harry's father had died, and his mother was alone like many other adults, unable to leave the city due to their age and health.

Chapter 19

Donya knew nothing of Machiku's preparations until he shared them with her. Except for a visit to Regina's home in the ghetto, where her parents were also housed, she avoided leaving the house. She locked herself in with her daughter. Litti was a young child, but aware of what was going on. For hours she would stand at the window and observe what was happening in the streets.

"Look, Mama," she would say as she pointed her little hand to the street. "People fall down and don't get up."

"Move away from the window, Litika. That's not a good thing for you to see," her mother pleaded.

"Why don't they get up? It probably hurts to fall like that."

"Litika, come away from the window. Come to your room and I'll tell you a story."

For Litti, a story from Mama was a temptation that even looking out the window couldn't compete with.

***

Machiku shared his escape plan with Donya only after he had purchased the ship. He cautioned her not to tell any of the relatives about it, because it would upset everything.

Donya listened in astonishment. They were about to leave Chernowitz, most likely forever. To Palestine, out of the ghetto, away from the terror, shootings, murders, and the missing.

They were leaving their families behind, not even bidding them farewell. Donya was thirty-two years old, but had never really been away from her mother, Yetti, and her father, Hersch. They had always lived in the same city, and even when she married and moved in with Machiku, their apartment was very near their parents. She thought of Mammu Regina, her beloved mother-in-law, her sister Nussia and the children. Would she ever see them again? Would it possible for her to come back, even for a visit?

She wiped away the hot tears sliding down her cheek with the back of her hand. "What is it, Donya?" asked Machiku.

"It cannot be that I won't be able to say goodbye to my dearest ones," she murmured.

"That's what the authorities ordered, so as not to jeopardize the escape."

"Escape?"

"Yes, Donika," he replied as gently as he could. "There is no other way to look at it."

She shuddered.

"Please, Donya, enough. There's no time," he finally blurted out. "I beg you. Pack one valise for all of us. We must hurry. We have to leave."

Donya could never have imagined packing her whole life into a single suitcase. How do you pack your life into one suitcase? What is needed for the sea? What would be needed in Palestine? She heard that it was hot there and life was hard. What do you take to cope with a hard life?

Machiku had been to Palestine eight times. He knew some of the answers but didn't want to frighten her. Donya was young, tender, and gentle, and had barely begun her life as a wife and mother.

"My Donya," he said, "we'll be together, safe from the threat of death. That's more important than taking one item or another."

Donya went through the rooms, gathering what she could. After the looting, the house was practically empty, with not much left of their comfortable past. Suddenly she saw the fox fur scarf that Machiku had bought for her as an engagement gift. It had been in a suitcase in the attic and the looters missed it. The fox eye shone brightly at her, as if to say, "I'm staying here! What will you do with me, a fox fur scarf, in Palestine?"

"I don't know how to do this," she sighed. "I'll take care of Litti's things first. Her clothes won't take up much space. Here is the dress with the white collar that Regina bought for her third birthday. She can wear it in the evening, on the ship."

"Donika, it's not a ship, just a boat with a motor." Machiku couldn't restrain himself. "There won't be any evenings of entertainment. Just take something warm for you both." He knew the journey would be hard and wanted to shield her from worry of what was to come.

"There's no room for the story books I read her at bedtime," she said to herself as if she had not heard him, "I'll only take her favorite – the funny 'Strubel Peter' (Wild Joshua)."

"You're so creative," he reassured her. "She'll love your stories, even without books."

Yet the more she tried to decide what to leave behind and what to put in the suitcase, the greater the fear of the unknown.

"I've never been to sea," she blurted out. "I was never even on a boat."

"I'll be with you and take care of you," Machiku replied.

She had always trusted him, and was accustomed to his authority, determination, and ability to take action in difficult situations. Even after a night in the Russian interrogation cellars, he returned home tired and pale, but upright. He hadn't betrayed his comrades. This, however, was different. She had to pack their whole lives into one small suitcase. He cannot help her with that.

There was Baba Yetti's pillow, the one Litti would not go to sleep without. She'll put it in the suitcase only when the packing is done so the pillow will be there for her as soon as they open the suitcase.

No room for toys in the little suitcase, not a single doll, puzzle, or toy animal. She'll improvise, tell the child stories and create things from whatever is at hand. Maybe in Palestine they'll buy new toys. There must be toys there and it will only be a few days' voyage.

The thought raised Donya's spirits in those difficult moments. She looked around at everything in the house that she couldn't take. She put in a photograph from their wedding, and one of their parents. The rest of the things were left behind; they wouldn't keep well in the humidity on the seas.

A carton of cigarettes for Machiku, but no room for shoes. They'll have to make do with the shoes on their feet. Out of the corner of her eye she noticed her doll shoes with the heels, but decided not to take them. The suit that Machiku wore at the wedding remained on the hanger in the closet – the Russian looters had decided it was too small for them. Together with the suit was the memory of the wonderful day that united them forever. She remembered feeling like Cinderella. Machiku was the prince she always told Litti about.

She hadn't yet gotten used to life as a young wife, and already had to leave everything behind. The coffee cups at the shared breakfasts, the dairy and meat dishes they still had left. Everything would have to be replaced.

"Take Litti's little sunglasses," Machiku said. "She'll need them on the boat."

Donya put the glasses in the little brown suitcase, which was already beginning to fill up. She put things in and then took them out, hesitating, not comprehending how she could make do with one suitcase for the whole family. They were going to a country she knew little about. It never would have occurred to her that even the few belongings she packed would not always be hers.

Suddenly she remembered a dream from the night before.

"Last night I dreamt I was falling into a deep, dark abyss," she told Machiku. "In the dream, you're holding my hand. I struggle not to let go, but my hand slips from your grip. I become weaker. I have no more strength, and I fall." Machiku went to her, took her hand, pressed it to his heart and didn't say a word. Dreams are not false imaginings; in their metaphorical way, they reflect reality.

Litti observed her parents. She realized with a child's wisdom that they were facing a colossal change. She watched in dismay as her mother took things out of her room and put them in the suitcase. She wanted to tell her to take Sophie the Doll and Max the Bear, but in the face of the silence between her parents she dared not speak.

Machiku gazed at his wife and looked around his home. He felt the weight of responsibility on his shoulders. He must bring his small family to safe harbor. He tried not to think about his beloved Mammu Regina, his brother, Donya's parents, her sister and family, and everyone else left behind. In light of the killings, deportations, and disappearances, he didn't know if he would ever see any of them again. Machiku shrugged off these thoughts; there was no point to them. The only thing he could do in the little time he had left was to leave a letter for his mother. While Donya was preoccupied with what to take and what to leave, he sat down and wrote to his dear mother – a letter he knew he could never send.

***

August 13, 1942

My good and dearest Mammu,

I say goodbye to you. I know I shall never see you again. Your wrinkled visage is before me: the neatly pulled-back white hair, your wise eyes full of warmth and love. You loved me so very much, and I cannot return the favor and leave you – old, alone, and sick.

I cannot take you with me. You no longer have the strength to leave the house and stand on your own feet. You came to father Yossel's home as a young girl after he had two wives before you and thirteen children. Some of them were close to you in age. They saw in you the one who had stolen their mother's place and tried to spoil your marriage. You knew how to bring peace and warmth to the house you came to and you succeeded, Mammu. You kept a strict religious home as Father wanted. You gave birth to Bubbi, Lottie, and me. Father died when I was young, and you raised us alone. I could always talk to you. It was enough for me to look into your eyes, for you to hug me, to feel the comfort of your support.

You always told everyone what a smart child I was. I remember the story of how I once was crying for almost half a day, and when I was quiet for a moment, you said, "Good for you, Machiku, you're finally calm." Impish me said to you, "No, I'm just resting for a minute."

When Litti was born, you adored her immediately. You would ride in a high carriage with the baby by your side so that everyone would see 'the Schmelzer granddaughter.'

Now we're leaving and leaving you behind. You won't ride in the carriage with her anymore and let everyone know she's your granddaughter. Litti will grow up without a loving grandmother, without cuddling in your welcoming lap. How much I would give for things to be different. I hope and believe God will keep you safe and that no harm will come to you.

My dear Mammu, I miss you already. I write these words because our decision is secret, and I cannot part with *you face to face. I cannot even send you this letter. But perhaps the words from my heart will miraculously find their way to your heart.*

I leave you in your big house almost alone. I can see you wandering around in the empty rooms, sad and heartbroken.

I don't believe you can forgive me, yet I beg your forgiveness. You know how much I love you and so do Donya and Litti. Perhaps you can find solace in the thought that we can raise the child in a place without fear of persecution, in a Jewish country. You always thought Palestine was a desert and life there was hard. Every time I came back from a trip there, you breathed a sigh of relief. There is no choice now; I must escape to freedom and save Donya and Litti from what awaits us if we stay.

People like me, who led the Zionist movement and the Jewish community, will be the first victims of the Romanians, and an example of German cruelty. Since I'm a decorated officer from the first World War, I had hoped to be spared. Today, it is clear that will not be the case. The die is cast. I leave everything behind, including you, dearest Mammu, and escape to freedom.

I love you more than words can say,

Machiku, your little son

Chapter 20

On Thursday evening, August 13, 1942, fifteen men, women, and children left Chernowitz. They traveled in a specially designated train carriage heading to the coastal city of Brăila. Litti didn't understand what was happening. She had never been in a train before. However, she quickly connected with the other children. They had no toys, so they improvised. They took a string and made different shapes with it using their fingers. The children laughed among themselves until Litti stuck her tongue out at one of them.

"Phooey! Don't do that!" Donya scolded her. "A girl from a good home never sticks out her tongue!"

Scolded, Litti lowered her head, looked at the other child and was silent. From her mother's tone she felt that something unusual, different from what she had known, was happening. She sensed her parents trying to hide it from her and pretend everything was normal.

"Why aren't Baba Yetti and Baba Regina and Grandpa Hersch going with us?" she pleaded. "I want to see them."

"We'll see them another time," Donya replied, turning away so Litti wouldn't see her tears.

"Mama, can we play 'Hoppe Hoppe Reiter?'" asked Litti. It was her favorite game with her parents. They would sit her on their knees facing them – either Mom or Dad, depending on who was giving the ride – and bounce her to the song "Hoppe Hoppe Reiter." When they reached the line "the rider falls," they would tilt backwards and shout, "Then the rider falls, ker-plunk!" Her mother relented and played the game with her until Litti got tired. She rested her head on Donya, closed her eyes and stuck her thumb in her mouth. Litti groped for the precious object, Baba Yetti's special pillow, her sleeping potion since she was a baby. It was enough for Litti to stroke it with her little hand and she would soon be asleep.

To her dismay, Donya saw that she had forgotten the pillow at the very last minute. Because of the stress in deciding what to take, she neglected to put in the suitcase Baba Yetti's pillow, the one most important thing for Litti.

The little girl burst into tears – at first quietly and then loudly. "I want Baba Yetti's pillow!"

Her parents tried to calm her. They were afraid they would be caught or killed. And because of a pillow? The fear was with them all the time. They had already been in this situation, and they couldn't quiet the child. The enormous pressure they were under made them less able to function effectively. Donya reached out, covered Litti's mouth, and forcibly silenced her. This was the second time; the first was in Irina's pigsty. Sometimes you have to shut someone up, she reasoned, in an attempt to justify her behavior.

Litti was shocked. She stopped crying. The pillow wasn't forgotten, but slowly the little girl fell asleep.

***

The train finally arrived in Brăila. Machiku guided the other passengers to a hotel where the authorities had organized rooms for them. They would not be permitted outside until they were told that the ship was ready to sail.

General Antunescu was a friend of Machiku's from his days in the Austrian army. He was the one who had helped Machiku buy the ship and had come to the hotel upon their arrival.

"How are you, Dr. Schmelzer? And your family and the passengers with you?"

"We're all well. Excited and weary from the preparations and the train journey."

"I understand. It's not easy to leave everything behind for an unknown place."

"It's particularly hard to leave our families behind without saying goodbye and just leave the country."

"That is what I want to tell you. You cannot just depart from Romania."

"What do you mean?"

"I initiated a plan that would enable you to do that."

"I see. I wondered if there were some details missing."

"All the heads of the families must appear in court tomorrow morning for a hearing."

"What? Why in court?"

"It is a necessary act, to arrange for a passport."

Machiku didn't close his eyes that night. Thoughts of the unknown – and now this matter with the court. "All the heads of the families must appear. What could it be?" he wondered. "Will they send us to Transnistria, to a labor camp? All our efforts and it will end badly, without anyone knowing about it? Without even saying goodbye to our families?"

Several policemen entered the hotel the next morning,

"Machiku, why are the police here?" Donya asked anxiously. She was exhausted. "Where are they going to take us? Will they arrest us?"

"Everything will be fine," he answered, trying to sound self-assured.

"Every head of a family will go to arrange departure," Machiku said as he turned to the other men still at the table finishing their meager breakfasts – tasteless coffee, a slice of stale bread, and a dab of jam.

"I thought it was all sorted out," said Dr. Mann.

"You deceived us!" Alfred Wacher cried out threateningly.

"What now? Are we going to jail? After all the money we gave you! We thought everything was set!"

A chorus of angry voices arose. It appeared they were about to assault Machiku.

The police stared them down with menacing looks and said nothing.

They lined up the men and stood at attention, their guns drawn. Images of the massacre in Chernowitz passed through Machiku's mind. Are our lives in peril again? He had been sure that that was behind them.

The men marched with the police escort, not knowing where they were going or why. Each one was filled with the fear of impending doom. No one knew what to expect. Would they be arrested? Sent to a labor camp? And after all the planning, what fate awaited them?

After a short distance they reached a gray building, very different from the magnificent courthouse in Chernowitz. The Habsburg influence on the architecture was absent in this place.

"A death sentence," thought Machiku. "But the general assured me that everything was arranged. I trust him. A comrade in arms is forever."

Tired and bent over, the men were seated on the simple wooden bench for defendants. General Antunescu sat near Machiku.

"Is this the municipal court?" Machiku asked the general.

"No, a military tribunal," Antunescu replied.

Machiku broke out in a cold sweat. He wiped the wetness off his forehead with the palm of his hand.

"All rise!" roared the bailiff.

Everyone stood. As a lawyer, Machiku was well acquainted with the procedure.

"What will they charge us with?" he whispered to the general.

"Shhh. Wait and see."

The judge entered in an army uniform along with two high-ranking Romanian Army officers. He perused the documents before him. "Who is the leader of this group?"

Machiku spoke up. "I am, your honor. Dr. Leon Schmelzer."

"You are charged with treason, along with the other men here."

The Jews were stunned. Some of them went ashen, others beet red. A few coughed nervously. Wacher felt tears streaming down his face.

The charge hit Machiku like a hammer. "Treason? I fought for this country all my life."

"Does the chief defendant have anything to say before I pronounce the sentence?"

"Your honor, we are loyal to Romania. We desire the welfare of the state as law-abiding citizens."

An agonizing silence followed. Each man was suspended in terror, awaiting the ruling. The judge whispered to the army officers, turned to the accused and declared: "I sentence you to deportation from Romania. Let that be a lesson for all traitors such as you."

A huge sigh of relief erupted from Machiku's throat, but he stifled it. Unobtrusively, he shook the hand of his friend, the general.

"Deposit your passports with the court clerk to be stamped for deportation."

It was a meticulously planned show trial. The Romanians were interested in expelling as many Jews as possible, and this was an opportunity for just that. What's more, each member of the court, and particularly the judge, was well compensated for taking part in the mock tribunal.

The men were marched back to the hotel, again under guard. The women and children were waiting there, frightened. When they heard what had happened, the relief was intense.

However, sorrow soon overtook the joy. They were leaving their native land and, saddest of all, their families.

They had been under house arrest at the hotel for the entire weekend. The siege was difficult for Machiku and Donya. He thought of Mammu Regina and was wracked with guilt for disappearing without a word. Donya was overwhelmed with anxiety about the journey and their unknown future in Palestine. As for Litti, she played with an imaginary doll, restlessly throwing it back and forth inside their small room. It was only on Sunday evening that the captain of the ship Machiku had purchased sent word that the ship was ready to sail. They were to embark the following day.

Monday morning. Everyone got ready and after a quick meal, left for the port. They carried the small suitcases, their hearts in their throats, anxious and afraid. What was to come?

The port was much bigger than they imagined. Scores of ships and smaller vessels were moored in the waters. How would they know which ship was theirs?

To their great relief, a red-faced, burly man approached. He recognized them by the little brown suitcases. "Is there a Dr. Schmelzer here?" He asked.

Machiku stepped forward. "I am Dr. Schmelzer."

"Gregory, your captain. Follow me."

Leon looked at the man and felt his stomach turn. A face flushed from the sun, and from what looked like heavy drinking. Was this the stalwart captain who would bring them to safe harbor in Palestine? And where was the ship?

This was no time for hesitation. Captain Gregory led them almost to the end of the harbor, where a motorboat the size of a bus swayed in the water.

Leon looked at the vessel, horrified. "This is what the dealer sold me," he thought. "How do we make it to Palestine in this thing? The sea is filled with danger. There is war, explosive mines, and menacing ships." He straightened up, regaining his composure. He was the leader of the group, and he would see them through.

The captain stood beside the ship in an official posture, welcoming the men, women, and children. He wore a threadbare blue uniform. It was important to gain the trust of his passengers – like a spider weaving its web.

He directed them to the narrow, swaying ramp leading to the ship's deck. The first to board was the beautiful Susie Mann. He flashed a sideways leer at her, revealing yellow, tobacco-stained teeth. Holding out his hand to help her in a chivalrous gesture, Susie boarded. Next in line was her husband, Dr. Mann. He shook his hand warmly, as though they had been friends since time immemorial.

Machiku again took a hard look at this man in charge of their escape. He had a strong feeling that Captain Gregory wasn't up to the task but didn't know at that moment just what his feeling foretold. He prayed that the captain knew how to navigate the shipping lanes and could bring them safely to Palestine.

The dealer who sold him the ship said he deliberately chose a small vessel to escape the notice of enemies and obstacles along the way. But *this* small? And with *this* captain?

"No time, no time, load everything fast, store the suitcases. Hup-hup!" the captain hurried them and looked at the "goods" he was transporting. His gaze fell on the Wacher family, who carried a small, sleek black suitcase with a gilded lock. "Valuable customers," he thought to himself, reaching out to help them on board.

His gaze fell on Donya. "What a rare, young, lovely woman the old Doc has," he thought. "Maybe I'll throw him in the briny and sail off with her." But then he saw that she was holding a little girl's hand. "No, I won't mess with a married woman who has a child," he virtuously declared to himself.

The captain was busy imagining what he would do with the money his passengers paid him. He saw himself in a new suit, going to the tavern, celebrating his good fortune. He was putting himself in mortal danger, but the sum he received was worth it. All he had to do was get the job done. These men and women were paying him for taking them to a remote hole called Palestine, which he had never been to. He figured that because of the mines the British and Krauts had thrown into the sea, the storms, and the October rains, he would look for a shortcut.

Chapter 21

Machiku had previously arranged with Moshe Shertok (later Sharett) from the Jewish Agency that when they arrived in Turkey, he would provide certificates enabling them to continue to Palestine. It was agreed with the captain that on entering Turkish territorial waters, he would pretend that something was wrong with the ship. They would have to dock and be able to access the visas.

The captain, however, had other plans. He had no intention of sailing to Palestine.

The ship sailed through the Bosporus to the Dardanelles. Apart from the passengers vomiting up their insides from the ship rocking back and forth on the sea, the story of the voyage passed in peace.

On the sixth night of the voyage, a strong wind came up. In an instant a storm was upon them. The sea was pitch black, and huge waves pounded the sides of the vessel. The small boat shook like a leaf on a branch at the edge of a tree, battered by the storm.

"Captain! Where is the captain?" shouted Machiku. No answer.

Suddenly there was a jarring, creaking sound. Machiku ran on deck, held on to the rail, leaned over and looked down. In horror he saw that the ship was about to split in two. One section hung up on a rock and the other half was flooding with seawater.

Everything on deck slid downwards. Some of the other men joined him, their faces lashed with spray, their eyes assaulted by water and wind. What was happening?

"The ship has run aground! It's going to sink!"

"Where's the captain?" they shouted. "Where is he?"

Machiku realized that if he didn't take command, everyone would drown. He was the one who had taken them on this journey. He alone had the responsibility to save them. Five women, five children, and four men besides himself were in mortal danger.

The ship, which seemed the size of a walnut shell in the vast sea, was stuck on a sandbar, split in two. In a matter of minutes, parts of it would break off, fall into the water, and sink into the deep.

Again the ship rolled sideways with a terrible creak and a breaking sound. The children were shrieking, the women ran back and forth, terrified. Some vomited up whatever remained in their stomachs.

Machiku was a man of faith. He had grown up in an observant home; his parents kept all the mitzvot, no matter how "light" or "serious" they seemed. He himself didn't keep them all and would secretly leave synagogue on Saturday and light a cigarette without his father knowing. Still, the most important thing he had learned in life was that one must not despair. True, there was destiny, but two great forces are always with you: Almighty God – and you yourself. Providence had been on his side at important crossroads in his life. He accepted its help and it had gotten him through many of the crises that he faced.

"Oh God," Machiku prayed. "If you give me the strength to save these people, I won't ask for anything more in this world, not for any other purpose. I brought these people to this moment. I must work to save them."

He was used to taking initiative and making difficult decisions. He concentrated solely on helping everyone survive – his family, and all the others. The night was cold and black; the sea was stormy, with waves as high as walls. He didn't know how far they were from shore. However, he estimated that if they had run aground, land could not be far.

"Tie together anything you can find – sheets, towels, clothing. Make a rope," he shouted at the men.

They looked puzzled. Strong, salty wind whipped their faces. In the dark, the ship's rocking intensified, rising and falling. Things began to slide off the deck into the water.

"Doctor Mann!" shouted Machiku, over the roar of the wind. "Take the men and find anything we can use to make a rope. We'll tie us up together!"

"In the meantime, the waves will sweep us away," Dressler responded, whining.

"Do it! It's the only way we can save ourselves!" he yelled as he tried to embolden Dressler. He knew that if he failed to lead and they would not work together, all of them would sink into the water like sacks of potatoes.

The scene that ensued on deck was men quickly searching for clothing and bedding to tie together and make a rope.

"Machiku, I can't take it!" implored Donya, shivering and scared.

The children kept crying, even the oldest, a seven-year-old. Little Litti, his three-year-old daughter, was frantic. He wanted to go hug Donya, but just then saw a huge tower of water coming at them, angry foam bristling from its crest. He hurried to safeguard the children, afraid that they'd be swept off the deck.

Dr. Mann came back with two sheets. Two other men, Dressler and Leon Wacher, began fastening the ends together. Then they added Max's sweaters, tying them by the sleeves.

Again, the frightful creaking rose from the ship's hull. Black waves crashed onto the deck. Darkness obscured their vision, and the salty water burned their eyes.

"I'm finished!" cried Lottie, an old friend. She was so sturdy and had always joined the rugged mountain treks he organized.

"No time for that!" he cried, tossing the end of the makeshift rope towards her, "Help me secure the children!"

The rope they made wound around the deck like a snake. They gathered child after child, lined them up along the length of the rope, and wrapped it around their waists. Nelo, Wacher's son, didn't know why his father was tying him up and struggled, trying to escape.

"Nelo! Be quiet!" his father shouted. "This will save you from being swept into the water!" He quickly tied the rope around his son.

Litti cried out, "Tata, give me your hand!" She raised her arms pleadingly, but had slipped away, sliding down the deck.

"Look out! She's falling!" Donya screamed between spurts of vomit issuing from her mouth.

A huge wave roared over the boat, almost taking them down into the abyss.

They tied each other quickly and carefully in a long line: a man, followed by a child, then a woman. One by one they cautiously descended from the tilting deck into the black, frozen water. The men swam in front, dragging the women and children after them.

"I'm exhausted. Can't go on," groaned Leon Turkfeld, swallowing and spewing seawater.

"Just a little more, another meter," Machiku called out to him.

They swam in what seemed like an endless sea. Machiku ducked his head and swam, inhaled, and again went below the surface, inching forward. Slowly the night began to clear. Dawn rose on the horizon. They could see shadows of huge rocks and prayed that they were approaching dry land.

Chapter 22

Machiku could barely open his eyes. His face was covered with sand and coagulated salt. In his mouth was the taste of brackish seawater. The morning was cold and grim.

He heard waves breaking on the shore close by. Birds circling above were making odd squawking sounds. Crows or herons? Machiku was lying on the beach, half-naked. At first, he didn't understand where he was. He lifted himself up on one elbow and looked around. The beach seemed deserted, desolate. Not a tree, not a bush – as far as the eye could see, there was nothing growing.

Next to him lay three-year-old Litti, sound asleep, a thumb firmly in her mouth. Donya was close to her, hugging the child to shield her from the morning cold and wind. Machiku sighed. Thank God his wife and daughter were alive and well.

Not far from them, scattered on the sand was a man's shoe, a soaked notepad, a book that had lost its shape, individual planks torn from the side of the ship, a carton of canned tuna, the key to a house they would never return to, a child's sunglasses, and a lump of waterlogged cardboard that was once a suitcase.

In the distance he saw other members of the group and counted them. Thank God, everyone was there. They were in shock after the harrowing night, but no one was missing.

"Mama! Mama!" cried five-year-old Nelo, a child with blond curly hair. "I'm cold!"

His crying, mixed with the squawking of seagulls and the waves of the sea, woke up the rest of the people. Alfred Wacher rubbed his burning eyes; Dr. Mann tried to shake off the sand that clung to him as if he were wearing a cloak. None of them had yet spoken. They looked around with bleary eyes, each of them recalling the night's events to himself. The storm that tore their ship in two. The sandbar. Swimming for their lives through the icy water.

They didn't know where they were, but at least they understood that they had avoided drowning in the sea. Everyone lay on the sand wet, tired, and hungry.

Machiku was the first to recover. He approached the others. "Friends, friends, let's see where we are and what can be done to make things better," he said in a self-assured tone that in no way reflected his true feelings.

Donya stroked Litti. She was stricken with the terror that engulfed her when the ship began to sink and they were hurled into the icy water. She said nothing; only her eyes spoke, seeking deliverance. The women clung to their children. The men stood and gathered around Machiku. "First, let's see what's left of the ship," he said. "Maybe we can find some clothing to keep us warm, or some food."

They nodded and trailed behind him, closer to the shoreline.

"Here's the rope we made." Alfred pointed at what looked like a wet trail of rags. "If we leave it in the sun to dry, we can use the cloth and sweaters to protect ourselves from the sun, the sand, and the salt."

Meanwhile the clouds began to disperse and the sun rose high in the sky, shining brightly. The sky was clear, unlike last night's darkness. Even the waters were calm and non-threatening.

The women and children joined in searching for articles that had been swept ashore.

"Look, Papa!" cried Nelo, pointing to a shoe that was half-buried in the sand.

"I found a hairbrush!" shouted Mrs. Wacher.

"Here's a book! 'Strubel Peter' (Wild Joshua)," added Susie Mann.

Donya hurried to her. "Wonderful! I read it to Litti at bedtime."

She walked to Susie but stopped when she saw what she was waving in her hand. The book was soggy and shapeless

"Here," Susie gave Donya the book, "it's still wet, but it'll dry."

Donya examined it. All the pages were intact, including the familiar illustrations of the evil twins who tied people to their chairs. It smelled of salt water, but Susie was right – if she puts it out in the sun, it'll dry. Maybe she could once again be able to read her daughter the stories in the best German tradition.

"There are some cans that floated in and landed on the beach!" Turkfeld shouted. Everyone rejoiced and ran towards the precious cans gleaming in the sun. They picked up cans of fish and vegetables that would ease their hunger. They had eaten nothing since last night's horrific events.

"We don't have an opener!" Mrs. Wacher complained.

Machiku put his hand in his pocket and took out the pocketknife he always carried, jubilantly waving it in the air.

"It didn't fall into the water?" They were amazed.

"I fastened it to my belt loop." Leon replied. He took a can of sardines, struck it hard with the knife handle, pushed the tip of the knife under the lid and removed it, using the length of the blade.

Everyone sat down in a circle on the sand. Each in turn, with their fingers, pulled out a sardine dripping with oil and devoured it. None of them would ever have imagined that they would eat like that in the company of others, but this was no time for niceties.

"Look!" exclaimed Dr. Mann, his mouth full of sardine. He pointed to the south as everyone turned and saw what he saw in the distance: riders on horseback were approaching them.

"Do you think they're coming to rescue us?" asked his wife Susie.

"Hell, no one even knows we're here," Fritzie Turkfeld replied morosely. He hadn't wanted to come on this journey and had done so only because of the incessant nagging of his mother-in-law, Bertha. In addition, Dr. Schmelzer had aggravated him by taking over complete leadership of the group. Even though thanks to him their lives were saved, Fritzie was envious. Such a short man, and yet women fall at his feet. "What's he got that I don't?" he thought. "The first chance I get, we'll go our own way without him. It's hard for a person who considers himself to be superior to depend on someone else."

"Who can they be?" Mr. Wacher wondered. "You would think there wouldn't be anyone else around in this isolated spot."

The riders drew near, ten in all. They wore Turkish khaki-colored army uniforms with gold buttons, and riding breeches. Some had medals on their lapels. On their heads were high hats and on their feet were boots with spurs. They were soldiers of the Turkish Coast Guard on their morning patrol.

When they reached the group of refugees, the caravan leader dismounted and approached, checking that they weren't enemy invaders.

Machiku stepped forward. The Turkish officer stared at him suspiciously. He spoke, and from the tone of his voice it was clear that he was asking who they were. Machiku didn't know any Turkish, but realized he had to make it clear they were not a threat to Turkey in any way.

"Sir, our ship sank last night." Machiku pointed to the wreckage of the vessel, and then gestured towards the other members of the group.

"Wasser, wasser!" cried Nelo.

Machiku could not translate from German to Turkish but pointed to the canteens on the soldiers' belts.

"We need to convince them we are not enemies," he hissed at his comrades. "Get down on your knees!"

Body language is international, especially when in distress. One by one the men got down and raised their hands in supplication. They hugged the children to them, hoping the soldiers would not harm them, and each one whispered a prayer.

At this sight, the commander turned to his men. It was obvious from his tone of voice that he had decided they were not enemies or spies. He pointed to the children and gestured to his men to give them water.

He took the canteen from his belt, walked to Nelo, and let the boy drink. Nelo gulped with great thirst. The other soldiers did the same. The refugees sighed, relieved. The tension was somewhat dispelled.

Meanwhile, the sun rose in full force. The heat of the day beat down mercilessly. The refugees could barely stand, wondering what would happen next.

"What are we going to do with these people?" One of the soldiers gestured to his commander.

"For now, we hold them captive on the beach," the commander answered.

The group tried in vain to understand. They saw one of the soldiers carrying a large cloth sheet, and another bringing pegs and ropes. They put up a large tent and with hand signals urged the refugees inside.

The refugees thanked them for the shelter with gestures. The sun was scorching hot. No one knew how long they would be there and what would become of them.

"Machiku," Donya sobbed softly, "I'm so tired, thirst, and hungry. Litti is exhausted too, and clings to me all the time. She won't take the thumb out of her mouth, makes whimpering sounds, and then cries loudly."

The other women saw Litti crying pitifully and began to weep. Soon it was hard to tell who was crying and who was trying to calm their children. From the behavior of the parents, the children understood that they weren't in a normal situation, but a frightening one. The soldiers watched them all day from a distance. It was a day of intense pressure. The sun roasted them, hunger had weakened them, and no one knew what was going to happen.

"What have I done?" Machiku asked himself. "Where have I taken all these people who trusted me, believing they could escape the inferno and reach Palestine? Donika is frail and delicate; she won't last long in these conditions." He, too, was overwhelmed by the sadness that affected everyone in the group. Worse, for once he didn't know what to do.

Somehow the day went by. There were those who lay exhausted on the sand, and others who went into the water to cool their feet. The children saw this and started running on the beach, playing tag and throwing fistful of sand at each other.

When evening came it was cooler as the wind coming off the sea ventilated the stifling tent. It was a welcome change in the weather for everyone. They began to search for more provisions and belongings that had been swept to shore. They were able to improvise a light meal from some canned meat that Machiku had managed to obtain with great effort in starving Chernowitz. To this they added green beans from another can, along with some sun-dried sardines.

Each family gathered in a corner of the tent for the night. It was chilly in the desert-like climate. The children curled up in their parents' arms for warmth. Litti also lay between her parents, stroking Donya's hair with one hand and sucking a thumb with the other, as she was taught to do when hungry.

***

Hearing a sudden noise, Litti woke up in the middle of the night. They were lying at the edge of the tent, close to its opening. The child thought she could see two pairs of eyes gleaming at her in the dark. She turned to her father.

"Tata! Tata! Animals," she whispered in his ear, waking him.

Machiku stood, carefully approached the entrance to the tent. Two hungry jackals. They were sniffing around, watching them.

"Shoo! Shoo! Get away!" he shouted, waving his arms frenetically to drive the animals away.

The group woke up from the shouting and the howling of the jackals protesting their rude dismissal. They had just found food and had to abandon it. The refugees tried without success to get back to sleep.

At sunrise, everyone was shivering with cold, frightened and hungry.

Chapter 23

The days passed with no relief in sight. It was depressing and frightening. Searing heat during the day, bone-chilling cold at night. Stomachs rumbling with hunger, and worst of all, the uncertainty of what would become of them.

> "It has been a week," Machiku wrote in German, in pencil. He had found a notebook in the ship's wreckage, and dried its pages in the sun,

> "Nothing has changed. Our hardships and suffering have only increased. Jackals continue to howl at night. A few days ago, a huge sandstorm rolled in, destroying our tent. The cover ripped off and pounded our bodies all over. Torrential rain followed, drenching us. We had no cover, helpless in the storm's fury. What did we do to deserve this death sentence, defenseless before God? Innocent people perishing in the desert. Have we forfeited our right to live? Are we to die in the desert like lowly dogs?"

Life, as it always does, settled into a routine. But what kind of routine could a group of people with little in common have? Bound together by a shipwreck, destiny having put them on a vessel that was intended to carry them to their destination and instead spewed them out onto a desolate shore. In the mornings they rose after fitful sleep, shivering from the cold night and the rain. Every day they searched the sands for remnants of food or objects swept off the ship.

Late in the day, the Turkish Coast Guard patrol would pass through, its soldiers bringing a small quantity of fresh water and one slice of bread per person. They, too, didn't have a morsel of excess food.

The children played tag around the tent, and rolled in the sand, laughing. When they were tired of the games, they joined the parents in collecting seashells or merely stretching their legs. Litti had amassed a large collection of pretty shells in various shapes and colors. On one of the days, waves washed over the tent, sweeping her entire collection back into the sea.

Lonio's father led gymnastic exercises for everyone. They stood and stretched their arms up in the air, and then down, bending their legs, going as low as they could. Children and adults alike took part.

The favorite diversion was building sandcastles. Even the adults competed to see who could build the biggest one, complete with towers and turrets fashioned from drizzled lumps of muddy sand.

When Litti was afraid, she would cling tightly to her Mama and Papa. She was fearful of almost everything, especially colonies of marching ants on the sand, and huge sea turtles that looked like walking houses coming out of the water to bask in the midday sun. She was afraid of the tiny fish that wiggled and darted about in the water. Even the flickering rays of the sun seemed like giant threatening animals ready to pounce on her and set her on fire. The rain that sometimes fell in torrents terrified her. Her teeth chattered from the cold. The sandstorms that whirled like giant revolving pillars and knocked down the tent looked to her like the evil witch from Hansel and Gretel.

She especially dreaded the jackals that came almost every night and howled at the entrance to the tent. She would wake up, see their eyes blazing in the darkness and tremble all over. "What will they do to us?" she thought. With her three-year-old's imagination, she pictured them leaping inside and attacking her.

"Tata, Tata! *Ayn Shakal*, a jackal!" she would cry out to her father and wake him up.

She didn't make friends with the natural world, living or inanimate, and felt that everything was a threat. At the same time, her rich imagination diverted her attention from constant fear. She could sit for hours on the sand, watching the waves crashing onto the shore, imagining Cinderella's chariot and horses falling into the sea, as had happened to their ship that night.

For Litti, nothing felt safe anymore. The adults, too, were afraid. They tried to hide it from the children, but they sensed their parents' fear. No one knew what the sand, the sea, and the sky would bring forth.

When she was very scared, Litti would whimper quietly, as she had been taught, soundlessly, hoping to ward off evil. Her father would take her in his arms to calm the fears, and her mother would caress her.

"Litika, my little one," Donika would whisper, "we're with you and will always keep you safe."

Litti would calm down from her parents' touch, and Donya would say quietly to Machiku, "Our little girl – what'll become of her? How'll we get out of here? We'll all die here."

***

The sky was dark gray. The sea looked grim, blaring like an off-key orchestra of strange, jarring instruments.

Donya felt unwell. Ever since they arrived on shore, her body temperature had risen and remained high. Her joints ached and she often vomited. Her head hurt and she felt weak. The depression she fell into since the shipwreck was getting worse. Three-year-old Litti looked as fragile as a skeleton. The others seemed like walking dead.

"There's no hope," she thought. "We'll die here of hunger, cold, and solitude." The thought of Litti's fate broke her heart. Why did I bring this little girl into such a terrible world? Instead of playing with dolls, she sits and builds castles in the sand that the waves wash away. We have no future, only this onerous present."

She sighed out loud from the painful despair. Machiku hurried to her and she rested her head in his arms. How good he is to her. He sees the changes in her delicate face, where lines of worry and anxiety are now firmly etched.

The wind picked up and began to blow with a force that whirled clouds of sand around them.

"A Sandstorm!" shouted Dr. Mann. He had been a physicist at the University of Chernowitz. "Get into the tent and cover yourselves with whatever you can!"

The wind howled like a wounded beast. Sand swirled, creating funnels in the air, getting into their mouths, noses, and ears. Machiku feared that they would suffocate. The rickety tent was swaying, its sheets threatening to break off. Parents shielded their children with their bodies. Terror seized them. They were sure that they would be covered over by sand and even their burial site will never be found.

"Why has no one come to rescue us?" Susie Mann whimpered.

Leon Wacher, nicknamed "Big Leon" to distinguish him from Machiku, "Little Leon," grew pale, his teeth chattering. The hot wind didn't let up on its fury and went on relentlessly.

All that day they cowered in the tent, trembling. The storm was relentless. When it got dark, it started to rain, first in small droplets, then in huge globules that washed away the sand. The sea's waves rose two meters high.

"What else is going to happen to us?" Donya groaned. "If only we had some water to drink."

The men heard her cry and an idea came to mind. They seized every empty container at hand to catch the rainwater. They quickly set the containers outside the tent, and ran back inside, away from the fierce storm.

Everyone was thirsty. Litti occasionally peeked out, trying to catch raindrops with her dry, cracked lips.

The sea rose higher until a huge wave came rolling towards the tent. Everyone jumped up in panic, trying to protect themselves and their children. Wave after wave followed. They weren't the nice little waves from their games on the beach, but giant, angry waves that threatened to drown everyone and everything in their paths. The smell of wet, salt, and a horrible clamor filled their senses. Then a massive wave roared in, collapsing the tent on top of them.

Bedlam ensued. They pushed their way out of the entangling tent sheets and found themselves outside in the strong wind, facing a black night, with no moon or stars to be seen.

"This is the end," thought Machiku. "This time there is no escape. We got away from the Germans and we survived the shipwreck, but now there is nowhere to go."

He could no longer fight; nature was stronger. It was the first time on this journey that he, too, had lost hope. "The hunger, distress, hot sun, wind, and rain have led us to our end. Help has not arrived. We are forgotten. No one is even looking for us. Sentenced to death without a trial. God will open the Book of Life on Rosh Hashanah and write, and on the Yom Kippur fast he will seal our fates. "Who by water and who by fire, who by hunger and who by thirst," he recalled from the Rosh Hashanah and Yom Kippur prayers.

"We have lived a life and sinned," he thought, "but what sin did little Litti commit? Is this how fifteen human beings are going to vanish from the world? I have devoted my life to Eretz Israel, and now, mere hours from its shores, my family will die like dogs."

Machiku felt that life had betrayed him. He, who had always looked to God, felt that even He had forsaken them. Day after day he prayed, "Please God, save us. Please God, spare us." Tears rolled down his face, now creased by the sun, and there was no sound, no answer.

"He who made the covenant with Abraham," he stood and prayed, yet only the waves crashing to shore answered him. He watched as every day a little more life left the bodies of his loved ones. Donika vomited up her soul, until she stopped, simply because there was nothing more to vomit. Litti sat quietly on the wet sand, tiny as the ripples of the waves, all skin and bones. She no longer sang and stopped jumping into the puddles left by the sea foam on the beach.

He looked around – as far as the eye could see, there was only desert sand. "How much longer until we die?" he thought. "What would this death be like? Who will go first and who will stay yet another hour?"

In those moments he felt everything about to collapse and fade. But he kept his despair inside so those around him would not see it.

The storm intensified. Mountains of water poured down from the sky. The tent had collapsed and no longer provided shelter from the raging nature. The Turkish soldiers had disappeared. There was no one to help them.

For two whole days the refugees lay on the cold, wet, deserted beach. They were half conscious, weak from hunger, terrified, waiting for the grace of Heaven, which wasn't forthcoming.

How much of this can a person bear?"

Chapter 24

Two days later the storm subsided. The Turkish Coast Guard came and gave them some food and water and went on its way. After eating and drinking, they all looked at each other and broke out in ironic laughter. Dressed in rags covered with dust they looked like mummies from the age of the Pharaohs.

Machiku, always a leader and planner, took advantage of the respite. They could not continue to wallow in this morass. He took the notebook, whose pages had dried, and the pencil salvaged from the wreck, and wrote letters of entreaty to all the organizations he had served in his many years of Zionist activity, addressing their leadership.

To Dr. Nahum Goldmann

Dear Dr. Goldmann,

For years you and I have worked together for a common goal – Palestine. I am now in dire straits. Thirty days ago, we washed up on a desolate shore – fifteen men, women, and young children. We are on a barren beach, at the mercy of the elements. And there is no mercy from the rain, searing sun, windstorms, and sand. We are all sick and hungry. My wife is all skin and bones, vomiting up her soul every day, losing all hope of salvation. My three-year-old daughter no longer laughs or plays. Her small body is almost transparent.

Why do you not save us? Why have we been sentenced to die like dogs?

All my life I have worked for others and now I have been forsaken by God and Man.

Please! Please hear my plea!

The address:

Dr. Leon Schmelzer
Karataş Beach, Turkey

"Machiku, what are you writing?" Donya asked him, her voice weak.

"A letter to Dr. Nahum Goldman of the Zionist Organization."

"How will you send a letter? There is no post office here," she said with a bitter smile.

"I'll ask the Turkish guard to take it. Perhaps God will be with us and send the letter to its destination," he replied mournfully.

"You and your fantasies!" Leon Wacher burst into their conversation, waving his fist at Machiku.

"A man of no substance. All wind and hot air," Melina Wacher added, mockingly. "It's your fault we're stuck here, sentenced to death without a trial."

Machiku recoiled. This was no time for squabbles. The situation was bad enough without fighting among themselves.

"You know very well I did everything I could to save us from the Germans and Romanians," he defended himself.

"Would you rather have stayed and been murdered in Chernowitz?" Dr. Mann suddenly spoke up in support.

"We all agreed and even competed for a place on that boat," Susie Mann reminded the Wachers. Do you think he would have taken his wife and daughter with him if he had known this would happen?"

There was silence in the tent.

"But how could you trust that lowlife captain and give him all our money?" Leon Wacher persisted.

It was the first time the captain's disappearance had come up in conversation. Everyone had their own idea about it, but so far no one had raised the issue.

"He must have fallen overboard. In the storm we couldn't hear him calling out, and he drowned," offered Dr. Mann.

"Oh, really? You're so naïve. A sailor doesn't just drown like that," Bertha Turkfeld countered, angrily.

"Maybe he lost consciousness and fell into the water," Susie Mann wondered.

"I think he just lowered a lifeboat and fled in the storm," Bertha Turkfeld argued.

"But why would he abandon the ship?" asked Machiku.

"For God's sake, you're such a fool," came the angry retort. "He got all his money! You gave it to him, so why should he continue on this endless journey!"

"I think maybe from the beginning that was his plan. He brought the ship near the shore to escape, and we ran aground," Machiku admitted in a sober, painful voice, "I take full responsibility for that."

"Don't be so hard on yourself. You could not have imagined that he would do such a reprehensible thing," Dr. Mann responded.

Machiku's confession of guilt took the wind out of everyone's sails. Once more there was silence. Why should they continue hammering at Machiku when he took the blame for what he had done? Meanwhile they were on a desolate beach, hunger gnawing at them, with no rescue in sight.

Every day Machiku wrote to those who would never receive his letters. He spoke from his heart, entreating God to save them. He would entrust the Turkish guards with the letters, hoping they would forward them to their destination.

There were no responses; apparently not one of his missives had been received.

The situation worsened. Hunger, sandstorms, cold, and rain greatly weakened the refugees. In difficult situations such as this, they looked for someone on whom to vent their anger.

"You're to blame for all this!" Wacher shrieked at Machiku on a particularly gloomy morning. The others gathered at the sound of the screaming, which sounded like a wounded bird on the empty beach. "How could you put all our money into the hands of a deceitful degenerate who left us to die?"

Machiku paled. He thought the issue was already settled, but apparently it continued to fester. He tried to behave in a restrained fashion. "It was impossible to foresee that things would turn out this way," he said quietly. "If I had known, would I have taken my only daughter and my wife on the ship?"

"Maybe you didn't know, but you were tempted by the money. How much did you get from this deal?" Wacher's tone intensified. He moved towards Machiku threateningly, as if about to hit him.

"Do you think that I would have been tempted by money? I lacked for nothing in Chernowitz! We were going to be exterminated. We had to escape; it was the only thing to do. At least we got out. With God's help we'll get out of here as well," Machiku replied. He barely kept himself from attacking Wacher. Donya took his arm and tried to calm him.

"Just how do we do that, eh?" Wacher asked scornfully, "Walk to Palestine?" He was flushed with anger.

"Stop! Please. This won't solve anything," Susie Mann interjected quietly.

Her voice was like ice on a scald. They were all quiet. Each went to their corner of the tent to calm themselves.

Machiku understood that the agitation was still there, but he had no way to quell it. He looked at Donya. She was frighteningly thin. Her lovely face was burnt by the sun. Her eyes closed, she held Litika tightly. He loved the child so much, the daughter born to him after long years of bachelorhood. Litika was skinny and so tiny she looked like she could soon fade away. What can he do? He wondered. His anguish was unbearable. He recalled the revolt of the Israelites against Moses when he led them into the wilderness.

"Were there no graves in Egypt that you have taken us to die in the wilderness?"

He prayed: "Dear God, save these people. If I must die, so be it. But how have these innocent children sinned? Or my Donika?"

★

As if the heavens had heard his prayer, loud shouting was suddenly heard. Everyone turned in the direction of the noise.

"Doctor! Doctor!" A soldier from the Coast Guard ran up to Leon and fell at his feet, holding his finger and writhing in pain. The other soldiers followed.

"Scorpion, scorpion," whimpered the soldier. A large spot appeared on his fingertip, clearly a sting, most probably from a venomous species. They were a terror to everyone, roaming freely on the beach, concealed in the burning sands.

The soldier came to Machiku as the soldiers had heard the refugees call him "Doctor Leon," and assumed that he was a physician.

Machiku's devoutly religious father had not allowed him to study medicine, so he chose law. However, he secretly also studied medicine. He did his doctoral dissertation in law and not in medicine so as not to anger his father. Now, if this Turkish soldier has come to him, he must at least try to help him.

He sent everyone out of the tent, leaving only the two gendarmes who laid the injured soldier on one of the sheets spread out in the tent. From the mountain treks and trips he had made in his bachelor days, he knew what to do. He gestured to the gendarmes to bring him the bottle of liquor they had with them. He had seen them get drunk in the evenings when they thought the refugees weren't looking.

He asked the soldiers to grab hold of the wounded man and demonstrated with his hands how they should do so. He then poured the alcohol on the wound to disinfect it. This would reduce and perhaps prevent infection.

The wounded man screamed holy hell. The refugees kept the children far enough away that they would not hear his cries. The soldiers stood in the entrance to the tent as a guard of honor, and to be sure that Machiku wouldn't harm their comrade. He disinfected the blade of his knife and dug into the wound to remove the scorpion sting. The soldier fainted from the pain. Machiku signaled to the soldiers to bring him a bandage and he dressed the wound. The soldier lay on the stretcher, murmuring in pain.

The guard commander approached Machiku and patted him on the shoulder.

"Thanks," he said in Turkish.

Machiku, who had never been in such a situation, had almost fainted himself while treating the sting, but outwardly he kept his composure. He had acted to save the soldier's life. How ironic. On the battlefield a doctor had saved Machiku's leg, and now he functioned as if he were a medical doctor, to save the life of a soldier who holds him captive.

After that day, the wounded soldier came to Machiku daily to change the bandage. He would enter the tent and hand him a fresh bandage. Machiku would open it with his usual care and patience, check that the wound wasn't infected, and bandage the soldier's finger. When the treatment ended, the soldier would put his good hand in his pocket and take out a cube of sugar or a dried apricot.

Litti already knew that when the gendarme arrived, she would get something sweet to eat. Machiku made sure that when they changed the bandage they would be alone, so Litti would not arouse the envy of the other children. She herself knew not to talk about it. The child would bite off a piece of the apricot and slip it to her mother, so that she, too, would have something sweet.

Machiku healed the gendarme without thought of compensation. It was how he had behaved his whole life. But now that he felt responsible for the troubles that had befallen him and the others, he wondered how he could induce the soldier to help them.

The opportunity came without his expecting it, as they say, from an act of God.

That night Machiku had a dream:

> He is again a young officer in the Austrian army
> during the First World War. He's on the battlefield
> somewhere in Italy. The soldiers kneel in rows
> and aim their rifles at enemy positions. When
> the first row finishes firing, the second row takes
> its place and so on. The officers pass between the

lines on horseback, encouraging their men. He hears gunfire, smells charred corpses. The cries of the wounded. "It hurts, I'm dying, Mommy! Mommy!" A sharp pain pierces his body. A bullet has penetrated his leg. The blood pours out and he groans in agony. His horse has run away and he cannot move. He lies wounded on the battlefield. Around him are the cries of the wounded again: "Medic! Medic! Save me!" The stench of blood, death, and burning dust are in the air. Figures dash back and forth with stretchers, trying in vain to take control of the killing field.

Machiku feels his leg. It is drenched with blood. Probably a torn artery. The pain is unbearable. He almost loses consciousness. He is bathed in cold sweat, nauseated. He wants to vomit. He shouts like the others: "Medic! Medic!" Suddenly he sees a figure leaning over him, a man with blue eyes and a gentle face wearing a white robe. Next to him stands a medical assistant, a boy.

"Evacuate the wounded man to the tent to amputate the leg. There is nothing more to be done," the doctor ordered.

"No, no! I need my leg. Please! I have to climb the mountains, keep hiking and boating. I just started living my life. Please don't take the leg! Please!"

He's an officer, but he cries. He has cried all his life when in terrible distress.

Something in the young officer's plea touches the doctor. "All right, son, we'll take care of you and your leg," the doctor says, turning to his assistant. "Take him to the train for the wounded going to Vienna."

Machiku woke from the dream, the image of the leg still with him; only a big scar remained from the injury. It seemed to him for a moment that he still saw before him the blue-eyed doctor, but then realized that he was in a tent by the sea with the families who had sailed with him.

Chapter 25

The following day was cloudy and the sea was calm. Squawking birds flapped their wings over the rippling waves. The refugees kept to themselves. At the water's edge, the children built castles in the sand, and when the tide came in and destroyed them, they built new ones. Donika lay in the tent thinking about her past and the future she would not have. She had lost hope that they would come out of this alive.

***

The Turkish soldier Machiku had saved came and signaled for him to follow. They moved a little away from the group. While pretending to be talking about the injury, they walked along the shoreline so as not to arouse suspicion. They had had several such encounters since Machiku saved the soldier. He taught Machiku some Turkish and Machiku made a list of useful words and phrases in his notebook.

"Doctor," said the soldier, "the guard is changing and we're leaving," he explained with hand gestures, "but I'll do for you whatever you ask."

Machiku's body tensed, his senses alert. How could he make use of this unexpected opportunity to save the refugees from their miserable existence? He will ask the soldier to forward a letter to the governor of Adana, perhaps to the rabbi there or to the Jewish Agency. The main thing is that someone knows where they are. Until now he was sure that everyone believed they had dropped off the face of the earth. "How could he write a letter so that the reader could not hide or ignore it?" he thought. If he wrote in German, they would need a translator. So there would be someone else to know about them. In addition, he would encode the letter, but not too much.

He hurried to the tent, took his notebook and pencil, and wrote down a poem of absurdities by Heinrich Heine in German, from memory. It was a poem he used to recite to Litti. It would serve as a code to indicate that the writer stems from German culture:

> Dark it was the moon shone bright
> Green the grass the snow so white
> When a carriage fast in speed
> Slowly drove across the street
> Inside people sitting stood
> Talking loud in silent mood
> As a dead shot rabbit
> Slid on ice skates just to grab it.
> (Translated from German by the author)

And he added:
Fifteen people are we
Discarded on the shores of a sea
Men, women and children are we
No one to save us, to set us free
Come quickly or we perish
And lose the dear ones whom we cherish.

Dr. Leon Schmelzer, one of the directors of the JNF in Bukovina
Address: Karataş Beach, Turkey

He ripped the page out of the notebook and hid it in the skin of a potato that had been emptied of its contents. He handed it to the soldier, explaining in hand gestures and the fragmented Turkish they had taught him that he had hidden the letter inside a potato peel, in case the commanders of the guard would search the vehicles of the soldiers leaving the area. The soldier looked at him approvingly, buried the stuffed potato in his pocket, and to show Machiku that he would do all he could to bring the letter to its destination he crossed his arms over his chest

Machiku mimicked his sign and added a bow. Now there was no choice but to pray that God would see their misery and save them.

Friday morning he woke up sweating and wet from a night of incessant rain. He looked around. The others were still asleep in restless slumber. Donya to his right, Litti between them. That was how she felt protected, the sweet, beloved child. Who would have thought she'd have a sunburned, hungry, thirsty childhood with no childish pleasures?

"What have I done?" he again thought with bitterness. "I took my dearest ones, left a warm home, and brought them to this wilderness, to this hostile environment. I ran like a thief in the night without saying goodbye. Who knows if my family is still alive?"

Every day he thought about what would have happened to him, his wife, and child if they had stayed. This particular morning he was exceedingly troubled, despairing over everything he had done. He began to speak in his heart with God, pleading and justifying himself as King Saul did when the Prophet Samuel rebuked him for not waiting for his arrival before going to war.

"What have you done?" asked Samuel. Saul replied in deep despair "I saw that the men were scattering, you had not come, and the Philistines were gathering to attack…"

The other people with him were hungry, thirsty, and sick, lost on an unknown beach, helpless against the forces of wind and rain, the cold and sandstorms.

Every day they became more despairing of rescue. And he, Dr. Leon Schmelzer, for the first time in his life, was powerless. He could see no salvation. Maybe God had turned His countenance from him.

Each day someone else in the group attacked him because there was no one else to blame for their misery. The cries of desperation of these people whom he had persuaded to come with him were present wherever he went. He had nowhere to run. There was nothing to do but wait, he told himself. Wait for what? For whom? However, a man like him will not give up, will not despair. Yet he, too, had reached the bottomless pit, and there was no one to pull him out of it.

These thoughts tormented Machiku all day long.

In the evening there was a commotion among the refugees. Machiku saw Donya holding Litti's hand, Malvina Wacher took her Nelo, each mother with her child, all the women walking into the sea with their children.

"Hey!" shouted Machiku. "What are you doing?"

Dr. Mann was also stunned and began running after them.

The line of women and children began marching into the water. The men rushed after them. In an instant Machiku understood: They had decided to descend to the depths of the sea with the children and disappear. They could no longer stand the suffering and chose to end their lives along with their children.

"This must not happen! We must stop them! Even in our situation there is still hope. As long as we're alive we must not cease hoping. After me!" Machiku shouted, recovering from the shock. "Everyone go to your wife and child and bring them back to shore!" he urged the men.

"We almost drowned before," muttered Wacher. "Now again?" But he had no other choice and ran with the others toward the women. They were already up to their knees. The children thought it was a game. After all, mother was with them and mother always protects them.

"Susie, my darling, please come back!" begged Dr. Mann. "We're together for better or worse!"

Machiku struggled with Donya. "Leave me alone," she said as she tried to free herself. "We'll die here like animals anyway. There is no point in going on!"

The sound of the waves silenced the men's shouts. They were in terrible anguish. The water again met their deep despair. In a short time, all evidence that humans were once here would disappear. Even their burial place will not be known.

Each man struggled to save his little family. They had no hope, it was true, but letting the women commit suicide with their children was unthinkable. This would be the second time the sea was trying to take them down to its depths.

"How did I bring this misfortune upon us?" moaned Machiku, lying on the beach exhausted after dragging Donya and Litika out of the water. Even he, the eternal optimist, the believer, had reached his breaking point as a result of what had just happened.

Chapter 26

On Monday morning the sun rose and lit up the sky. Machiku awoke and went for a short walk on the sand to stretch his legs. The shoes he wore on the ship had dried but they had shrunk and hurt his feet, so he walked barefoot. The warmth of the sand on his bare feet felt good.

Most of the time they walked barefoot, dressed in the bits of clothing they had on at the time of the shipwreck, or things gathered from what had swept ashore. Since the ship was small, they had been told not to take many belongings, only a single small suitcase with clothing and food for a few days. After all, when they arrived in Palestine, they would start all over. Surely, Machiku had thought, he would be received in Israel with honor. He was the JNF representative in Chernowitz. He personally knew Ussishkin and Weizmann, and had sat on the podium at the opening ceremony of the Hebrew University of Jerusalem.

The memories flooded over him.

Machiku had no way of knowing what was going on at that moment in Chernowitz. He knew that Jews were being deported to labor camps in Transnistria and that there were killings for no reason on the city streets. He was tormented by worry about what was happening to his mother, who was no longer able to go outside, and whether his brother Bubbi's family were protecting her.

Until he left, he had been the one who took care of her. He loved his mother with all his heart and made sure she lacked for nothing. It was a good thing Bubbi had been able to move in to Mammu's spacious house in the ghetto. But if they had one slice of bread left, he would surely divide it first among his own family, and only then consider someone else.

Machiku loved Mammu so much. She had raised him, showered him with warmth and love, shared her wisdom with him, and always gave him good advice.

"How could I have left her in such a situation? An elderly woman, sickly, alone?" were among the thoughts that tormented him. "You had no choice," whispered a voice from within. "Did you want Donya and Litti to die or be sent to a labor camp? Why did I have to make such a cruel choice? She's my mother. It was my moral and humane obligation to take care of her. Nevertheless, she's my dear Mammu and she's in my heart wherever I go," he reasoned, trying to console himself.

These thoughts assailed him whenever he was alone. He shared with no one what was going on in his mind regarding this matter as well. When he finished his morning walk, he turned back to their temporary quarters and the harsh reality.

This time on his way back to camp, he shielded his eyes and looked away from the blinding sun out to sea and could not believe what he saw. He blinked, looked again, and saw the same thing. A sailboat on the horizon seemed to be coming closer to shore.

Mad with excitement, he ran back towards the others and couldn't utter a sound, just pointed towards the sea.

"A boat! A boat!" cried Dr. Mann.

"They're coming!" Wacher joined in the chorus of shouts.

"Thank God," thought Machiku. Donya came and laid her head on him. He placed his hand on her emaciated shoulder. "Donika, they have come to save us," his voice trembled with emotion. "They're coming, they're coming!"

"Oh, Machiku!" Donya's whole body was shaking. Tears of pain and relief filled her eyes. She couldn't believe it. "But who are they? Have they really come to our rescue? How will we all fit into the little boat?"

Litti alternated between laughing and crying at the sight of her excited parents. She didn't understand what was happening but saw what everyone was looking at and realized that whatever was coming made everyone happy.

As the boat approached, they all shouted. "Hello! Hello! We're here! Save us!"

The children clung to their parents. Lonio cried, as usual.

The Turkish Coast Guard soldiers saw the boat and prepared their weapons, ready for anything. "Maybe they're enemies," the commander wondered.

"Or maybe refugees like us?" asked Donya.

"Just don't shoot at them. I'm sure they came for us," cried Susie Mann.

"Please don't shoot!" Machiku beseeched the guards' commander, signaling for their rifles to be lowered.

"*Ekmek* (bread in Turkish), Machiku added, from the essential words he had learned in Turkish.

The commander and the soldiers looked at each other and then at the small group of prisoners. They didn't put their rifles aside, but neither did they raise them to fire.

The boat approached the shore and the engine cut off.

A tall, bearded man in a black coat and hat alighted from the boat. He was accompanied by a younger man, also with a beard, wearing black trousers and a leather jacket.

"He looks like the rabbi of the Chernowitz Synagogue," said Donya.

Machiku went up to the man and looked straight into his brown eyes. He surveyed his dress and friendly facial expression and decided that they were there to help them.

"With whom do we have the honor?" Machiku asked in German.

"I am Rabbi Rosen of Adana, and this is the governor's aide."

The guard commander heard the word Adana and immediately ordered his soldiers to put down their rifles. The rabbi stood still and everyone gathered around him. He looked at them and saw only misery dressed in rags, shielding the children with their bodies, bloodshot eyes, and sunburned faces.

"Who are you? Where are you from?" asked the rabbi, puzzled.

Machiku immediately stepped forward. "We are refugees from Chernowitz. Our ship sank off the coast more than a month ago and we have been here ever since. Prisoners without food and water, hungry and abandoned."

"The governor of Adana called me and forwarded a letter from a Dr. Schmelzer on behalf of your group. He ordered me to come and check what was happening," said the rabbi. "I have brought food and clothing sent by the Jewish community in Adana."

"I'm hungry!" Nelo cried, on hearing the word food.

The rabbi spoke to the soldiers in Turkish. They went with him to the boat and unloaded packages of food, cakes, fresh *challah*, dried fruit, sugar, and tea.

Everyone's eyes widened. They hadn't seen such delicacies for so long, they had almost forgotten what they tasted like. When you're starving, you can only dream about food – or else try to forget about it so as not to increase your hunger.

Immediately after the introductory meeting, the rabbi and his assistant gave out candied dried fruit to the children. As after the Yom Kippur fast, they explained to the refugees, it is best to start with a little something sweet and only then break the fast.

The children held up small, dirty hands to the miraculous rabbi, who handed out the delicacies, while the assistant distributed them among the adults.

The Turkish Guard soldiers stood around, incredulous.

The refugee group sat down on the sand.

"Now tell me everything that happened," said the rabbi.

Chapter 27

Three weeks had passed since the rabbi of Adana and the governor's aide visited them. During that time the refugees set up the tent, which collapsed in every storm. The food supplies the benefactors brought with them ran out, as did the rainwater they had accumulated. No word from the rabbi and the aide.

The sea was calm. The sun warmed the refugees, but their worries grew. The remains of their ship were wedged on rocks opposite the shore. The Turkish soldiers renewed their patrols. They gave them only a bit of bread and a little water. Rescue was nowhere in sight.

Desperate, Machiku wrote heart-wrenching letters to the governor of Adana, to the Jewish community in the city. He even drafted a telegram and asked the Turkish soldiers to send it.

"We are a group of refugee men, women, and children stranded on Karataş Beach, plagued by hunger, abandoned. Nature strikes us mercilessly with cold and heat. We have no defense against jackals and scorpions. There are women sick with high fever, children who are all skin and bones. Winter approaches and we'll die if help does not come soon. Please save us. We are human beings, not animals."

Machiku entrusted the telegram to the soldiers, but in the days that followed there was nothing. He realized that the message had not reached its destination. No one was interested in their plight.

"What happened to the rabbi and the governor's aide? They were here three weeks ago and promised to get us out. Why is it taking so long?" Machiku wondered.

The refugees didn't know that a struggle was being waged in Turkey over their case at that very moment. The Turks didn't want them to remain on their land. Where could they send them? It was prohibited to enter Palestine. What was their crime, these walking skeletons marooned on Karataş Beach?

On the forty-ninth day of their stay, the sun rose on a pleasant morning. The children went running on the beach, building sandcastles. The adults withdrew into themselves, some in pain, and others in despair. Desperation gripped even the strongest among them and wouldn't let go, like jackals holding prey in their mouths, leaving only the scraps of their victims near the tent each night.

Leon Turkfeld was the first to see it. He couldn't believe his eyes. "It's a mirage!" he murmured.

Leon Wacher saw Turkfeld and joined him. The sun's rays beat down on them. Nelo saw the two men shading their eyes with their hands and hurried to them. Slowly the whole group gathered, at least those who were able to stand.

A boat coming in the direction of the shore was clearly visible on the horizon.

They didn't dare hope. Maybe the boat was coming to bring more gendarmes to guard them. No one could speak from excitement. Nelo jumped up and down, even forgetting his usual "I'm hungry" refrain.

Machiku's optimism began to perk up.

"We'll see what this boat is soon enough. Perhaps God has finally sent someone to save us."

The boat moored cautiously near the shore. Three men disembarked. To the refugees they seemed like the angels at the tent of Abraham.

"We have come on behalf of the Turkish Government," the tallest of the three men addressed them.

"The Jewish community in Adana fought for you. We came to take you out of here," added a man wearing a black hat.

They brought with them some food, dried figs, and apricots. The children stood around them, their eyes bulging.

"Tata! Papa!" Litti clung to Machiku. "What are they saying?"

"They're here to save us," Machiku smiled and patted her head.

Litti took a dried apricot from the strangers. In the excitement, she didn't chew on it; instead, she sucked it and rolled it around in her mouth, refusing to relinquish the marvelous flavor. How long had it been since she had tasted something so sweet?

The foreigners explained that the ship on which they were sailing was anchored some distance from the shore. Because of the rocks they had to come in on a small boat. The refugees would be taken to the ship three at a time.

Machiku resumed his leadership role, determining the order of transfer to the ship. They were all so weak that no one argued about who would go first. It was clear to Machiku that he, Donya, and Litti would be last.

The boat went off with the first group of refugees. When it disappeared over the horizon, they feared it would not return.

"What if they don't come back like before? Maybe we'll stay here and die?" lamented Donya.

It was finally their turn. Machiku took Litti in his arms, supporting the sick but joyfully weeping Donya. They approached the boat. The sailor who worked it helped them on board. They sat down on the wooden seat built across the width of the boat and took one last look at the dreadful beach where they had been trapped. It now seemed so peaceful. Machiku's gaze also turned to what was left of their ship, the "Dora."

The sailor took hold of the oars and started rowing. In silence, Donya and Machiku looked at the beach, at the sea and then at each other. Litti didn't fully grasp what was going on but saw that the adults were sad or depressed. As usual in such situations, she curled up in her mother's lap, reached out her little hand and stroked Donya's face. It was wet with tears. Litti wiped them away with her little hand.

When the boat reached the large new ship, Litti didn't want to get on. Machiku took her in his arms. Her entire tiny body was trembling in fear.

"Again a ship?" she pleaded.

"Papa will hold you tight and you'll see that we'll reach a good place. There we'll have food and drink and the sweets you like."

"And the big waves of the sea won't eat us up?"

"This time the good people who came to pick us up will take good care of us."

"Can Mama sing the song she likes to sing to me before bed?"

"Yes, my sweet girl, she will sing to you."

They boarded the ship. Litti crouched between Machiku and Donya, listening to her mother's quiet singing.

It was her favorite song. She didn't understand all the words, but she was spellbound by its sad, quiet melody:

There where tall cedars kiss the clouds and sky
There where the Jordan River flows in waves so high
There where the ashes of my forefathers lie
This beauty of a land
Stretches along a blue sea strand
This is my dear homeland.
Words: Yizhak Feld, Folk tune, Translated by the author

Litti knew that far, far away is a beautiful country where everything is good. Her parents had told her this land was called Palestine and they would travel there together. Sometimes Papa called the land "Zion."

Her mother sang her many songs about this faraway land. They were in German and also in a language called Hebrew, spoken by the people in that distant land. Papa told her that she would be called Margalit there, her Hebrew name. The songs were sometimes sad and at other times like a march for soldiers. Papa and Mama would sing together, he in a thick bass voice and she in a gentle, delicate tone:

To Zion carry a banner and flag
The flag of Judea
Some ride some stride
All come together and unite.
Words: Noah Rosenblum, Tune: Noah Zlodkovski, Translated by the author

When they sang the song, they would stand with their hands at their sides like singing an anthem. Litika didn't understand all the words, but the melody was lovely and calmed her spirit.

She fell asleep in the arms of her Papa and Mama and woke up when big waves began pounding.

Tired, hungry, and almost apathetic with the despair that had been their lot for so long, they all sat on board the ship. None of them knew where she was sailing to, and no one had the strength to ask. Machiku, too, was shattered. He felt that now, with the rescue, he could relinquish the yoke of leadership and determination to remain optimistic. A great burden was lifted from his shoulders.

The ship went out to the high seas and began rocking on the waves. Most of the people vomited. The joy at the ship's arrival was replaced in a haze of sorrow and sickness. After enduring so much together, their spirits fell as one. No one spoke, no one asked for anything, no one questioned anything.

Machiku was the first to recover and began to speak to the ship's captain. He knew how to count in Turkish and also knew words like bread, water, and a few others. With hand gestures and his meager vocabulary, he asked the captain how long it would take to reach Palestine.

"No, not Palestine," said the captain.

Machiku paled – as if the earth had opened up under his feet.

"What? Then where are we being taken to? Adna?"

"No, no."

"Istanbul? Izmir?"

"No."

"Then where?" cried Machiku.

"Cyprus," said the captain.

The mere mention of the word "Cyprus" filled Machiku with rage, and he turned crimson in anger. The disappointment was enormous. Why Cyprus? He didn't understand. The Land of Israel was where they were supposed to sail. He was almost tempted to strangle the captain and end this journey.

"What does the captain think? That after all they have been through, and not be taken to Palestine?"

Machiku felt that his legs couldn't support him any longer. The hardships they had suffered, his responsibility for the people he put on the ship, leading the rescue from the shipwreck, safeguarding everyone from despair and the forces of nature that threatened their extinction, and trying to get the soldiers and others to save them. All these things had finally taken their toll on him.

The constant anxiety of how to get them off the desolate beach, and the endless worry about starvation and disease had weakened his mental capabilities. It was particularly hard seeing Donya physically and mentally drained, and little Litti shriveled up from hunger. It was precisely when he saw her playing on the sand with the other children that the tears welled up in his eyes. This was not how he imagined raising their firstborn daughter: without food, clothing, or toys. No childhood joys. For several minutes he wallowed in self-pity along with his pity for the others. But, as always, he came to his senses and thought about how to turn the situation around so that it would end well.

He was stunned by the captain's words and where they were sailing to. "What can I do?" His feverish mind and his anger triggered all the warning bells in him. He must change the course of the ship. But how? They were miserable refugees and this was an experienced captain who knows how to sail a vessel and navigate a stormy sea. He had to try. Maybe he could have a heart-to-heart with the captain and get him to change their destination? No. That wouldn't work. The man obeys orders. His hardened, sunburned expression negated all possibility that he would succumb to supplication, weeping, or begging for mercy.

Then the solution came to him. Machiku knew in his heart what to do.

"Leon Wacher, Leon Turkfeld, and Dr. Mann," Machiku called out and took them to the stern. He told them to pretend they were vomiting. He ordered them to hold the railing tightly so as not to fall off the slippery deck. The water continued to wash over the ship, wave after wave.

"What did he say to you?" they asked in panic. They saw Machiku in a state they had never seen. He didn't know whether to tell them or not, and decided there was no choice. They had to know, whatever happens.

"You have to know," he said in a quiet but determined voice, "this ship is taking us to Cyprus and not to the Land of Israel."

None of the other men could believe it. They didn't even know where Cyprus was!

Many questions flooded Machiku's mind, but this time he was helpless. He, too, didn't have the answers. They had been cut off from the world for so long. The war continued to rage all over Europe. How was it that Jewish refugees could be so abandoned and unable to reach the one place that is their natural home? How is it that after surviving so many hardships, they won't be able to enter their homeland?

"How long until we reach Cyprus?" asked Dr. Mann.

"What will happen to us? Who will take care of us there? We'll starve again!" Susie Mann intervened in the conversation.

"How can he dare take us there?" Wacher complained.

"Who gave him permission to sail to Cyprus?" wondered Leon Turkfeld.

"We will not agree to this under any circumstances!" declared Susie Mann.

"The question is, how do we change the route?" Machiku asked. "He is young and strong and we are weak and worn out."

"One of us will call him over here, and then we'll push him overboard!" suggested Leon Wacher.

"Can't you think of something more stupid and impossible?" Dr. Mann was angry. "Who'll sail the ship? You?"

"Then we'll all shout, create a commotion. The women will fall at his feet, begging," Leon Wacher said.

None of them came up with a practical idea of how they could rebel against the captain. For now, all they could do was accept the decree in silence and survive the trip at sea.

Throughout the voyage, Donya shivered and complained of excruciating abdominal pain. In normal times she would hurry to a specialist for an examination. But who will check her now, on the deck of a ship heading towards the unknown?

"Machiku, I feel like I'm going to die," Donya whispered. "I was terrified when we almost drowned. I was sure I would never survive," she said in a frail, feeble voice. "I know you did everything for me and Litti, but the pain is awful."

"My poor thing," thought Machiku. "She's so young. Donya hadn't had time to enjoy marriage, motherhood, and the good life I wanted to give her. It's well known that the mind and body are closely intertwined. The more her heart aches and her spirit fades, her body reacts with pain and illness.

"My darling, you know that you are my life," he tried to encourage her. "I won't let you part from me and Litti. I'll protect you until the day I die."

"She's very pale," he thought.

"I don't have the strength to stand on my feet, Machiku. Look at how high the waves are. The sea is endless. Nature is constantly against us. Maybe it is time for me to give up."

"You are strong and beautiful. You're sick now because of everything we've been through," Machiku cheered her. "I promise you that when we reach safe harbor, you'll get your health back."

He felt deeply sorry for her. "And what about our tender little child who needs her? How can I help her?" he thought to himself. "I would give anything to make her well."

From his medical experience he knew that she probably had an inflammation in one of her internal organs – perhaps the gallbladder, pancreas or, God forbid, the liver.

"How did I bring her such trouble?" he thought, remorsefully. "What could I have done differently?" said another voice within him. "If we had stayed in Chernowitz, we would have been slaughtered. "Who knows? Maybe we'll be saved after all."

Outwardly Machiku showed nothing of his emotional turmoil. Nevertheless, he felt the weight of responsibility he had taken on himself, and as the waves rose and the storm intensified, thoughts of death crept into his head as well. The self-confidence he showed Donya and the other passengers was his armor in times of crisis. Within, he felt like they did, utterly helpless.

"We are now at the mercy of heaven," he thought. "Maybe this storm will subside and we won't capsize again. Perhaps God will spare us, as has happened before."

Faith is a powerful thing. More than once, it had stood by him in times of crisis. He has no control over the sea or the ship. "Is it too much to ask, Oh God, for You to save us?" he silently prayed.

The other passengers were also in a dreadful state. Stress and fear came over them and they started squabbling with each other.

"You're the one who decided to run away," Bertha screamed at her son-in-law.

"And you certainly didn't object to joining us," Dr. Mann replied firmly.

Leon Wacher, who was a large man, leaned against the railing, struggling in the wind and spray, vomiting up his soul. In these moments he didn't feel like a hero, rather like a motherless little boy in kindergarten.

For hours the ship tossed between sky and water, tumbling in the waves like a nutshell, small and helpless against the forces of nature.

Suddenly the ship's horn sounded. The fog began to lift. In the distance were mountains that bordered a strip of coastline.

The captain emerged from his cabin and summoned them to the bow of the ship. The group members approached and huddled around him, clinging to the deck railing so as not to fall into the water.

"As I promised," said the captain. "Cyprus," he said, pointing to the panorama before them.

Chapter 28

One by one, pale, thin, and destitute, they descended the ship's gangway. They were aided by men from the shore. They couldn't believe it. Finally: land! At last, solid ground.

Donya got off the ship, her legs wobbling. Two men held her, Machiku on the right and Dr. Mann on the left. Litti ran behind like a flower girl holding the hem of a wedding dress, trying to support Donya so she wouldn't fall. The little one realized that her mother was ill and needed assistance. She liked to help but worried about what she would do if something terrible happened to her mother.

"Are we hallucinating?" Machiku asked Donya, trudging beside her in an unsteady gait. He could barely walk after such a long period at sea and the upheavals of the weather. The only thing he had tucked under his arm were pages from the notebook in which he had penned letters of supplication to the wide world, beseeching help and rescue.

"Machiku, there are real people here. There is land here. We're on land!" Donya cried, her voice trembling.

British officials came to greet them because Cyprus was a British colony in those days. They controlled Cyprus and Palestine and took responsibility for the fate of the refugees. They adhered to the "White Paper" policy, which strictly limited refugee entry visas to Palestine. They endeavored to give out as few entry permits as possible and didn't even meet the quotas they set, which was how the British closed the gates of Palestine to the Jews. Those who tried to enter were either forced to retrace their steps or be sent to Cyprus. For these fifteen people who had gone through such hell, had fled Europe at war, and had nowhere to go back to, Cyprus seemed like heaven.

As refugees, they were quarantined in barracks to determine the status of their health. The British wanted to be certain they weren't carrying, God forbid, any terrible diseases. To the refugees this was not a sign of disrespect; on the contrary, they considered their housing in barracks a blessing.

"Look, real beds with blankets and sheets," an ecstatic Susie Mann pointed out.

"And a real roof. Finally, it won't rain on us," added Mrs. Wacher.

They were soon taken to what seemed to them like a feast fit for a king: an elongated wooden dining table on two wooden stands, laden with cauldrons of hot stew. At last they could eat and satisfy their hunger to their hearts' content.

The relief they felt was so great that even being in quarantine didn't bother them. This safe haven had brought hope back into their lives, and the phenomenon was evident on their faces.

For the first two days, Donya scarcely put anything in her mouth other than dry crackers dipped in tea. At night she tossed from side to side, finding no relief from the nightmares haunting her. Litti would curl up beside her, sucking her thumb so as not to make a sound. She still missed Grandma Yetti's pillow that was left behind. Machiku stayed awake, guarding the two souls dearest to him and outlining the letters he would write to gain entry to "The Promised Land."

No one could tell them how long they would remain in Cyprus. After a few days of quarantine, Machiku noticed that Donya was very pale and as yellow as a mezuzah scroll. There were red spots on her cheeks, her auburn hair was shaggy, and she was skin and bones. She also complained of chills most of the time, although he had found a warm blanket to wrap around her shivering body.

"What's wrong with me, Machiku?" Donya implored. "I can't stand up. It's as if I'm still at sea. All the time huge waves wash over me and I disappear into the waters. There is no sunrise, no sunset. Dark waters as high as a wall open wide and envelop me as if I don't even exist."

Machiku comforted her with a warm, caressing hand. He held her close, as if trying to transfer strength to her with his love.

"I'll take care of you, and God, who has safeguarded us this far, will also not forsake you," he promised her, although in his heart he wept.

He had to be strong. He was responsible for her and their child. He had brought them here. True, this wasn't Palestine, but they will get there. Right now, the main thing is to safeguard Donya. First of all, he has to get a medical diagnosis and decide on a treatment for her.

Machiku was very worried by the vomiting and the color of her face. He feared it could mean inflammation of the gallbladder or liver. "What if she had to be operated on here in Cyprus?" This, after all, wasn't Europe.

The next day the quarantine doctor determined that they should take Donya to the hospital in Nicosia. Machiku left Litti with Susie Mann, whom he trusted, and rode with Donya to the hospital. When they arrived she was examined.

"She has a severe case of jaundice. Her liver is badly damaged. Leave her here. You should say goodbye."

"I'll stay with her. She will recover, and if not, you can say goodbye to your hospital!" In his agony he threatened them. He sat on a chair and didn't move from her side.

Two doctors entered the room. "This woman is a lost case. We need the bed," one physician said to the other.

"We'll inject her with something that might at least lower the fever," his colleague suggested.

They talked about her as if she weren't there, as if she didn't understand. Donya was very ill, but she was educated. She knew many languages and had studied French, Romanian, German, and Yiddish. For a girl from a religious background, she was exceptional. When she was younger, a broad education was not for girls, yet she had developed and progressed. During all the years she ran Machiku's office, she also learned accounting and customer relations. Nevertheless, now she was in a Cypriot hospital, an old stone building whose yellow color was peeling off its walls, closely resembling the yellow tint of her skin.

She was burning up with fever and imagined she saw her dead sister Ruzika. Donya had been very attached to her. She was a beautiful girl who died of diphtheria when she was only sixteen. In her nightmares, Donya saw Ruzika standing in the doorway, pointing at her and saying, "Come with me."

"She has come to accompany me on high. Anyway, my life no longer has any meaning. The dream of Eretz Israel has faded. We survived the sea but now it is too hard. I cannot go on. No more, no more," she murmured.

Because of the high fever, for a moment she didn't know who or where she was.

The words, "This is the end," slipped from her lips.

Then clarity returned and she asked, "Where is Litika?"

"Susie Mann is taking care of her," said her husband. "Moisten your lips. Just a tiny sip of water, please."

Machiku applied a wet cloth to her lips and wet them. She's his Donika again, his darling girl. He won't leave her lying feverish and sick.

Donya sank back into hallucinations. She didn't know whether she was dreaming or if this was reality. In her dream, or hallucination, she goes deeper and deeper into the sea. The waves wash over her. She cannot breathe and tries to shout, but no sound comes out of her mouth. "Mama!" she shouts, and there is no answer. She's wet all over, sweating from fever. Machiku tries in vain to lower her temperature. He puts cold cloths on her forehead and face, squeezes them dry and dips them again in the water. The night passes without any relief.

She dreams:

> She is a young bride in a blue dress, carrying a bouquet of gorgeous flowers. She and Machiku hold hands. The dream is in beautiful, soft colors. A lovely day in Bucharest. They march towards the clerk who marries them, only she and he. His arm is warm, he holds her by the elbow, arm in arm, as they liked to walk. Again she sees herself as the young bride Donya. She will have a beautiful life. In the dream there is a little girl who follows them, holding flowers for the bride. Whose child is this? Maybe it is hers? Why is she so wet? Is it raining? Someone has poured cold water over her. She sees the clerk baring his teeth, laughing wildly, his mouth open, snarling like a demon. "Ha, ha, ha." Are they married

or not? They must marry. Only then they won't be in the ghetto. She sees the whole family – Regina, Bubbi, his wife Clara, Ruthie, and Yoji, their children. There is Nussia her sister with her son Ziggy. They wait for a knock on the door. They have come for them. To take them where? To the open pits they dug. She hears sounds of the machine guns. Soon she, too, will fall into the pit with the others. It is cold and dark in the pit.

She's trembling. Machiku is beside her. The night is not yet over. Around them is the smell of Lysol and strong disinfectants so people don't get infected with disease. Through the small, barred windows, dawn begins to seep in and finds Machiku on the chair by the hospital bed.

"Who shall live and who shall die, who in good time, and who by an untimely death, who by water and who by fire..."

Machiku recites prayers from a small book of Psalms he has with him. Prayer had always helped him in times of need. Now he needs that help. He begins to read:

"Yea, though I walk through the valley of the shadow of death, I will fear no evil: For Thou art with me."

He closed the prayer book and fell asleep on the chair.

Chapter 29

Within a few days, Donya's condition improved. Her body temperature dropped and she felt better. She was discharged from the hospital and they both went back to the camp. After ten days of quarantine, the British decided the refugees were free of germs, lice, and other diseases. It was time to move them to a more permanent residence. Where? Of course not to Palestine. The country was closed to Jews by virtue of the "White Paper," and even Dr. Leon Schmelzer, the respected Zionist activist, failed to find a way around the rigid immigration policy of the British. They were condemned to stay in Cyprus for an indefinite period.

Since at that time the British had no organized places or camps to send them to, the British authorities decided to transfer the "Dora" refugees to the village of Pedoulas, nestled in the mountains of Cyprus.

One morning, two cars arrived at the Displaced Persons camp and the group was told to get into them.

"Papa, Mama! Where are we going?" Litti asked.

"For a ride in a car," Machiku replied.

"I can't," murmured Donya. "I'm not yet fully recovered. I won't be able to stand it."

"You have no choice," Machiku told her firmly, helping her into one of the cars.

It was cold out, but the skies were clear. The cars meandered along a narrow, winding, unpaved path leading up to the Troodos Mountains.

"Where are they taking us? We'll soon be as high as heaven," muttered Donya. She hurriedly opened the car window and stuck her head out to vomit.

Machiku took a handkerchief out of his pocket and handed it to her so she could wipe her mouth. She thanked him with a nod, but in another moment the car took a sharp, crooked turn around the mountain. The vomiting reflex rose again, although she hadn't eaten or drunk anything that morning.

Litti looked out the car window at the landscape. In the distance, she saw a thin mist covering the mountaintops. As they ascended, she sensed the air becoming cleaner and colder.

Olive trees grew on the mountain slopes, and a carpet of green grass covered the ground. Here and there she saw goats grazing on the grass; suddenly her eyes caught sight of a huge animal standing on a stretch of grass, staring at her with huge eyes.

"Papa, Mama! Look at the big animal!" Litti pointed to the cow. She had never seen such an animal. Suddenly the beast made a funny noise.

"Moo, moo!" the children answered.

While the adults found the journey uncomfortable, the children felt good. As long as they didn't get nauseated from the twists and turns of the road, they looked around them with pleasure. Nature was smiling at them. The trees, the grass, the farm animals, and the clear air rekindled their joy of childhood.

After two hours of driving, the cars stopped at the edge of the dirt path, a high spot overlooking the mountain slopes. Here and there they could see small houses with fences.

"This is the village of Pedoulas," said the British driver. "You'll live here from now on."

They drove slowly towards the village until they came to a two-story house made of stone, with bars on the windows.

"That's it, we've arrived! This is the "Marangos Boarding House," the driver exclaimed.

The car with the rest of the group pulled up, stopping behind them, and everyone got out. The clear, cold air that hit them was comfortable and embracing.

When Machiku heard the words "boarding house," he was relieved. The staff would no doubt come out to greet them, serve them home-cooked food, and offer them comfortable beds. To feel at home was all they needed now.

He glanced at the "Marangos" sign, which swayed in the wind on a half-cut wire on the building front. "Strange that no one fixes it," he thought. He helped Donya and Litti, and together they climbed a stone staircase into the building.

To their astonishment, they were greeted by an abandoned building. It had once been a boarding house, but from the dirt and cobwebs in every corner, it was clear that it had long been out of service.

They went through the rooms. Each had several iron beds and a mattress without bedding except for a gray blanket folded on top.

"These are your rooms," said the driver. "Take any one you want. Shared toilets are down the hall."

"You'll live here for now," he explained. "Every morning the head of each family is to report to the local police station and sign an attendance sheet to show that no one has left."

"How will we survive like this?" Machiku asked.

"Don't worry, sir. You'll receive a daily allowance of food, clothing, and essentials," the British driver assured him.

Donya looked around the desolate, dingy structure, and her spirits plummeted. The dream of a pleasant stay was replaced by the despair so familiar to her in those days.

"It won't take long and I'll die here," she whispered to her husband.

"Donya, this is after all a place where people live. We'll find a way to improve the conditions," Machiku said, trying to cheer her up. "I know what to do. I'll write to the Zionist leadership. They'll help us and eventually we'll be able to enter Palestine. We haven't come all this way to go back to Chernowitz or die in Cyprus."

"Again the fantasies about the Zionist leaders?" Donya was angry. "They haven't responded until now. Why should their attitude change?"

"They probably didn't even receive the letters I sent with the Turkish soldiers. But here there is mail, and even if it takes time, they'll get my letters asking for help," Machiku answered. He was optimistic by nature and had to keep his hopes up so as not to sink into despair.

Donya shrugged, stoically. Her pale, beautiful face looked at him in sorrow. "What a pity she had to go through all this." Machiku thought as his heart pounded. "I'll never forgive myself if I lose her now, after the worst is already behind us.

British drivers unloaded crates of provisions from the trunks of the cars and placed a crate in each room. The refugees opened them and found bread, tins of soup, oranges, tea, and sugar. Litti stroked the orange with her little hand, but Machiku took it from her.

"It's not for now, Litika. That is an orange for dessert," he told her. "First we'll have some soup and drink tea together."

"But it's cold," Donya protested. "We can't eat cold soup."

"Haven't you learned to trust your husband yet?" He smiled at her.

Machiku called one of the other men and together they went to look for branches and twigs to light a fire. One of the British drivers had given them matches. They arranged a circle of stones in front of the building, threw twigs and small branches in the middle of the stones, set the tins of soup on top, and lit the fire.

After the soup boiled, they each took off their shirts, grabbed the hot tins with the shirts and brought the soup to their families.

Machiku poured it into the glasses they had received in the crate. Donya sipped the soup slowly, blowing on it to cool the hot liquid.

"Oy! What a *mechaiya*! What a joy! Hot soup. So good," she exclaimed. "We can even warm our hands with it."

Machiku looked at her and gratitude filled his heart, thankfulness to God, Who had answered his prayers once again and saved them.

"Papa, now can I eat the orange?" Litika reminded him, after finishing her soup.

"Of course," Machiku said as he smiled at her.

He took the orange and cupped it in his hands reverently. The bright orange fruit was beautiful and smelled like the oranges grown in Palestine. Their fame had spread far and wide thanks to their sweet taste. The orange had a wonderful citrus scent, and Machiku remembered the orange orchards he had encountered in Eretz Israel on his visits.

"What a wonderful fragrance," he said. "Hold it to your nose, Litika. Smell it." He dug his nails into the orange and peeled it; then he carefully sliced it into segments and distributed them to his wife and daughter. They bit into them with zest, sucking on the marvelous sweetness.

"So sweet! So delicious!" rejoiced Litika.

Machiku wiped the juice off his hands. "Wonderful, Litika, I'm happy," he said. "Now that we're full, we'll go to bed, and tomorrow with God's help we'll clean the room and find a way to get more groceries."

"I don't know how we can fall asleep here with the musty odor," Donya mumbled, her eyes already half closed.

"It'll be all right, Donya. The important thing is that we're off that terrible beach. Here there are other people. It seems like a quiet place, so let's hope for the best," Machiku said before he also fell asleep from fatigue.

The next day, Donya woke up shaking all over and feverish. Machiku glanced at her and immediately realized that she had again been stricken by the sickness she had contracted on the beach where they were prisoners. He hurried downstairs, boiled water in a tin, made her sweetened tea, and fed it to her sip by sip.

Towards noon the British driver arrived with daily provisions. Machiku told him about his wife's condition and begged him to arrange for them to see a doctor. The British driver left immediately, and a few hours later Machiku heard the rumble of the car and hurried out. Indeed, a British military doctor got out of the car with a small bag of equipment and medicines. Machiku hurried the doctor to his wife's bedside. The doctor looked around the damp, musty room, clicked his tongue, took a thermometer and a stethoscope out of his bag, and examined Donya.

"I'm not sure whether it's just fever or some internal ailment," he told Machiku, "so it would be best to get her to a hospital."

"No, not another hospital!" Donya murmured weakly. "I'm not moving from here."

The doctor took Machiku into the hallway.

"Your wife is in serious condition," he whispered. "She ought to have the kinds of thorough examinations that are possible only in a hospital."

"My wife is sick, but very stubborn," Machiku replied. "She has endured great hardships so far, and with God's help she will get through this one as well."

The British doctor shrugged and left. Machiku returned to Donya. She was still shaking, and her face was the color of parchment. He gave her a little water, set the blanket under her head like a pillow, sat down next to her and prayed. "God Almighty," he silently invoked, "You have kept us and safeguarded us this far. Don't abandon us now."

In the evening, as if someone from above had heard his silent plea, a couple – a man and a woman who were refugees from another ship sent to Cyprus – arrived. They were housed in another "boarding house" in the village. Hearing that other refugees from their country were there, at "Marangos," they received permission from the British authorities to visit them. The couple was from Bucharest, the capital of Romania. The husband was Dr. Arnold Kutten, a lawyer, a tall, burly man with glasses on his nose, a gleaming bald head, and a constant smile on his lips. His wife, Dr. Susie Kutten, was a gynecologist, tall and also full-bodied. Her black hair was cropped, except for an artificial curl she had managed to stabilize in front of her head even under refugee conditions.

When Machiku learned his female guest was a doctor, he told her of his wife's condition. Dr. Susie asked him to take her to Donya's room and leave them. She examined Donya, and from the symptoms determined that Donya apparently suffered from acute gallbladder inflammation and mental trauma etched into her psyche from the shipwreck and prolonged stay, not to mention captivity, on the beach.

"The lady needs an injection of penicillin every day," Dr. Kutten said, turning to the British soldier-driver who came every evening to check if the refugees needed anything. "Can you obtain antibiotics? Do you know how to give an injection?"

"I can get the medicine, but I have no medical training," the British soldier informed her.

"If so, I'll ask for permission to come every day to take care of my compatriot," Dr. Kutten said.

The soldier nodded in assent. From that day on, the Kuttens came every morning in the daily delivery car, carrying liquid antibiotics and syringes. The doctor injected the medicine into Donya and sat down to talk to her. She well understood that if she wanted to help Donya heal, the injections weren't enough. She needed to calm her spirits from the terrors she had experienced. Her husband, nicknamed "Puyoo," who was a kind, warm-hearted man, entertained Litti while his wife dealt with the trauma.

"Here, Litti, look. I can make all sorts of shapes with my hands. See the shadows on the wall?" He cupped his hands and moved his fingers this way and that. "What do you see on the wall?"

"Butterfly! He spreads his wings and flies!"

"Right," Dr. Kutten smiled. "And now?" He changed the position of his fingers.

"Is it a parrot?"

Dr. Kutten laughed.

"No, it's a lady with a bent back. You see, she's going to the doctor. He knocks on her back. Tuk, tuk. And then she gets better."

Litti sat on Dr. Arnold Kutten's lap, watched the silhouettes shown on the wall, and listened to his stories.

"A dog!" Litti rejoiced at the silhouette of a dog with upright ears.

"Woof, woof!" The doctor made a barking sound, and Litti joined him, laughing.

After enough of the silhouettes, Doctor Kutten played another game. He took one of the pillows that the soldiers had brought to the boarding house, put it on top of his head, shaped it until it looked like a high hat, and began to walk back and forth, as if he were an officer in a military parade.

Donya recovered, but her gallbladder and liver remained damaged forever.

Chapter 30

Life in Pedoulas settled into a routine. The refugees survived from day to day without knowing what tomorrow would bring. Machiku kept busy; every morning he and the other men had to report to British headquarters to make sure no one had escaped during the night. Donya, meanwhile, lay in bed most of the day, tormented by pain and trying her best to hold on to her life. After all, she had a lovely little girl, already three years old. She had a husband, a friend for life who protects her; only the wild storm waters threatened to drown her in her dreams and hallucinations, undermining her sanity.

Machiku didn't give in to despair. He fought to keep his wife lucid until salvation came, and he also wanted to make a living. Practical as usual, he looked for a solution. In the streets, he found it in a big, empty, water barrel. He turned it over here and there and came up with an idea.

He rolled the barrel up the street all the way to the house and brought it into the yard.

"What's that noise?" Donya awoke from her nap. "What is that thing? Why did you bring it in here? Isn't there enough dirt already?"

"Patience, Donika. Wait and see," Machiku said as he smiled at her.

He found four bricks on the village streets and lugged them inside. He then made a mixture of mud pulp, placed the bricks around in a circle as a kind of base, and poured a bucket of mud on them. On top of the base, he put the water barrel with its opening facing sideways. He looked at what he had fashioned and rubbed his hands with pleasure. Now all he had to do was build a middle shelf.

He hurried out again and returned with a tin plate that had previously been a temporary roof for one of the village houses. He creased and bent the board until he could break off a piece of tin the size he wanted and pushed the piece firmly into the inverted barrel.

"Here, Donya! I've made you a baking oven!" he exclaimed joyfully.

"That's an oven?" Donya looked at the inverted barrel. "It's a water barrel!"

"It's a wood-burning oven, not an electric one," laughed Machiku, "that has no thermometer and rapid heating capability, but it is an oven for all intents and purposes!"

"And what are you going to do with it?"

"First of all, we'll use it to warm us in the winter," said Machiku, "and if you have the willpower and the desire, you can also bake us a loaf of bread or a nice cake."

For the first time in a long time, he managed to put a smile on his wife's face.

"What about flour? And eggs?"

"If I've already built you an oven, how hard will it be to get the eggs and flour?" he laughed.

The next day, the British driver brought more supplies to their room, including a crate containing eggs, flour, and oil – all the things on the list Donya had written for her husband.

She knew many recipes from her parents' house by heart, and the activity relieved her depression. She sat with her husband and wrote down the recipes. He brought the ingredients she asked for and they got busy. Machiku mixed, stirred, and whisked the eggs, and Donya rolled up her sleeves to knead the dough. The feel of the dough and the need for strength to do the kneading, breathed life into her. But all this was nothing compared to the joy that surged in her after Machiku lit the wood under the stove, heated it, and put inside the loaves of bread and the cakes the two of them had prepared together.

The wonderful aroma of freshly baked goods was in the air, chasing away the smell of burnt wood. The scent began to spread to the corridor, and from there to the stairwell and the other rooms.

The other men and women of the group gasped in disbelief and followed the scent of the baking dough.

"What is this? What's going on here?" Susie Mann asked, breathing in the delightful aroma.

"Did you really manage to bake something in that tin contraption?" Leon Wacher asked, with hope in his heart.

"Come, sit down." Machiku and Donya invited the others in and began taking a variety of baked delicacies out of the tin barrel oven.

"Here's bread," Donya declared proudly, "and here's a braided challah like the ones in my mother-in-law's house, and also a cake, only without the hole in the middle."

The group sat on the beds with them for a long time, eating the pastries, praising the taste that evoked thoughts of the good old days in Chernowitz. Those days were gone, but at least some of the fond memories were baked into these pastries.

From that day on, Machiku gave the lists of the ingredients that Donya wanted to the British driver. When he went to sign the form at the local police station, he spread the word about the opening of the new confectionery at Marangos.

The villagers couldn't believe it. However, after Machiku brought with him some of the pastries he had baked with his wife, and gave them a taste, they decided to go up to the boarding house. They wanted to see if it was indeed possible to find such delicious foreign pastries there.

The villagers began to come to Marangos regularly; they bought from Machiku and Donya an assortment of baked goods, even a Viennese strudel made from Cypriot flour that was stuffed with apples from the village and baked in the miraculous tin oven.

The business flourished, providing Machiku and Donya with money to buy all the necessary supplies and improve their living conditions. They weren't hungry anymore. At noon they would make meatballs, soup, and delicious stews, and invite the young people without families from the other refugees housed in the village to eat with them in exchange for a few pennies. Among them was young Harry Zucker. Every day the youth would climb the mountain to the boarding house and satisfy his appetite at lunch with the Schmelzers.

One day, while eating to his heart's content at her parents' table, Litti spoke to him.

"What's your name?" she asked him in English.

"I'm Harry. And yours?"

"Litti, because I'm little."

"And what do you do all day?"

"I'm already big, and I go to Susie's kindergarten."

"Who is Susie?"

"She's a nice lady who was with us on the ship and she likes children. She opened a kindergarten for us so we could be happy."

"And what do you do there?"

"We play in the sand and make up stories to act. There is even a doll there that opens and closes its eyes. Puyoo, Mama and Papa's friend, brought it for us."

"Would you like to go to an older children's school?"

"Sure. I'm already three," Litti said proudly, standing tall.

"If I open a school, will you be my pupil?"

Litti nodded enthusiastically.

"Then," Harry declared, "I'll open a Hebrew school for the children of Pedoulas, and you will be my first student!"

Litti began to jump up and down. The idea fascinated her. She would be the first student to go to a school for older children. She thought, "I wonder what Nelo, who always laughs at me for being as small as a match, will think about that."

***

The next morning Litti woke up and heard someone singing under the window. She didn't understand the words but recognized that it was Hebrew. She peered out through the bars and saw a young man with curly black hair standing there singing. It was Harry, whom she had met the day before.

"Cock-a-doodle-doo, the rooster crows to you. Get up, lazy bones. Come and study too."

The heads of adults and children started slowly peeking out of the building's windows.

Harry Zucker was eighteen years old. Machiku and Donya had known his parents in Chernowitz. He had tried to reach Eretz Israel on the "Europe," but the ship was seized at sea.

Harry knew Hebrew from Chernowitz and suggested that the refugees in the village have their children learn Hebrew so that they would understand the language spoken in Palestine and would be able to study at the local schools when they arrived.

It was the first morning that he stood under the windows and sang like the Pied Piper of Hamelin. The children followed him and thus he gathered more and more children and began to teach them Hebrew.

From that day on, Harry came to the boarding house daily, had lunch at Donya's, and after the meal would stand outside and sing his song. That is how the children knew it was time for their Hebrew lesson.

They would gather in an empty room in the boarding house yard. The children sat on a wool rug that Machiku purchased on the outskirts of the village. They didn't have a chalk board, but Harry improvised on a small board with a wooden frame that the children played with in kindergarten. Harry taught them songs, recitations, and stories of historical heroes like Judah the Maccabee and the mighty Biblical hero Samson. He had a wonderful memory, and he taught them everything he remembered from his own studies at the gymnasium.

He loved little Litti very much. Although she was small, she was sharp, full of humor and had an excellent aptitude for languages. She was also the actress of the class; after every recitation he taught them, she would stand proud before the rest of the children, stretch her tiny body, and repeat the words verbatim, without a mistake.

It was great to go to Harry's classes. He got the children's interest, and they learned from him the new language that they would need in Palestine.

Chapter 31

Six months later, while still in Pedoulas, Machiku and Donya woke to loud, hoarse coughing. They jumped out of bed and hurried to their daughter. Litti had a coughing fit, non-stop, and was having trouble breathing. They waved their arms wildly in despair and didn't know how to help her. She was very thin and had no appetite.

Machiku summoned the British military doctor, who examined the girl and diagnosed whooping cough.

"The best thing for her is mountain air," he said. "You must take her out daily for fresh, clean air to cure her."

Machiku nodded. That same day he lifted Litti onto his shoulders, carefully descended the stairs so he wouldn't drop her, and left the building for the main road.

He started walking. His three-year-old daughter was getting heavy for him, but his athletic past helped. He continued on the road until he saw the village stretched out before him. There were small, old houses, some with red-tiled roofs. To the right, the path leading to the top of the mountain branched off, and the Troodos Mountains were visible all around it. He began to climb the mountain. Sparse vegetation grew on the sides of the path and a small spring trickled between the rocks. The sky was cloudy and it was cold. As he continued climbing on his way to the summit, he was met by cool mountain air. Every breath brought Litti closer to recovery.

He recalled his wonderful climbing treks in the Carpathian Mountains. He had led a group of young men and women from Chernowitz. Together they would gasp for breath in the thin mountain air and laugh. They enjoyed the climbing trips so much that young people competed for a spot on Schmelzer's trips. But those images quickly disappeared. Now there were no young people around him. He carried Litty on his shoulders, and he was responsible for her recovery.

Each morning he got up, lifted Litti on his shoulders and set off. She loved these hikes with her Papa, just the two of them, with the cold air hitting their faces. Occasionally they would see a goat that had strayed from its flock, and Litti would bleat at her playfully. A thick olive tree with olives scattered at its foot was the harbinger for harvest when the villagers would come for the olives to make oil, soaps, and hand creams from them. The Schmelzers had already witnessed one harvest since their arrival, and to Litti it was a wonderful happening. The villagers would spread blankets on the ground around a tree, beat on the tree with sticks, and the olives poured down on the people and on the ground.

Machiku continued climbing until they reached the top of the mountain and he lowered Litti to the ground. She jumped and hopped from place to place.

"Look, Tata, there's a yellow flower – and another one!" she exclaimed as she picked the wildflowers and made a bouquet, bringing it to her nose and breathing in deeply.

"They don't have any smell," she pouted, disappointed.

"That's all right, Litika," her father consoled her. "The important thing is that we're here together and that you're happy."

He was glad to be with her, and especially content with the peaceful moments and joys they shared.

Upon their return home, Litika found that a surprise from her mother was awaiting her. Donya had gathered pieces of cloth and goose feathers in the village and sewed them into a pillow for Litti, like the one grandmother Yetti had made, only without the embroidery.

"Baba Yetti's pillow!" Litti exclaimed. That same night she got to fall asleep with her head on the pillow, with a warm, comforting sensation enveloping her. To sleep with the pillow her mother made for her was almost like being back home in Chernowitz.

In his spare time away from the baking and cooking, the lawyer Dr. Leon Schmelzer wrote letters to Zionist leaders in Europe and Palestine, entreating them to make it possible for them to reach "Eretz Israel," the homeland.

***

Months passed and everything was seemingly fine. They were able to adapt to a steady routine. The children went to school and the bakery business supported them. But deep in his heart, stark loneliness engulfed Machiku, in physical pain. Sometimes he would go off on his own, away from Donya, from their friends, and from the house. He felt alone in a battle, the end of which he could not foresee. In his troubled state, he sat and wrote letters to anyone he knew from the JNF in Israel. The following day, on his way to report to the local police station, he would go by the post office and send the letters.

However, Palestine was closed off to immigration. Without certificates, no one could go there – and no one answered his letters.

Machiku felt isolated. It was good for him to take Litika to the mountains every morning. Walking up there with her distracted him from the pain of solitude, he thought, increasing his pace to the summit. He could not share his distress with a friend, and not even with Donya. She had more than enough of her own. He was no longer the boss, and she no longer his loyal secretary. He gasped for breath when they reached the mountaintop, and thought, "She's my wife, the mother of our child. We have a daughter, a common past, and an unknown future." He had to accept that and hope for salvation.

"Tata, I'm cold," Litti said, pulling on his sleeve and waking him from his reverie.

"Yes, Papa will make a bundle out of you to get you warm," Machiku replied. He wrapped her up in his coat like a small package and together they slowly climbed back down to the village.

He comforted himself with thoughts: "Tomorrow at the same time we'll return and look for a new path to the top of the mountain." Or "Tomorrow maybe the sun will shine down more clearly, and we'll be able to see farther in the distance," or "Tomorrow maybe the cough will stop, and maybe Donya will be able to get up and come hiking with us."

However, long months passed without any change in their situation.

***

One morning Donya awoke, sweating in her sleep. She rolled over in the narrow, uncomfortable bed feeling sick and wanting to vomit. Everything hurt. She was dizzy and couldn't eat anything.

She hadn't yet fully awoken from her dream.

In the dream, she was in a room full of sunlight, lying on a white bed. Machiku is standing at her bedside, stroking her forehead.

"A son, Donika, we have a son!"

"Is he alive, Machiku?"

"Alive, Donika, alive!"

A flash of heat came over her. They had survived. They had a son. She wasn't sure where she was in the dream – in the hospital in Nicosia after jaundice, or in a maternity ward, but the light around her was gentle and caressing. Was it a dream or did she really give birth to a son, to a brother to Litti? She wanted them to be a family. She so wanted another child. This longing filled her thoughts day and night. She didn't want Litti to grow up an only child. But the war was stronger than this longing. They had barely managed to save Litti's life.

Yes, she wanted another baby. She was still young. She will knit him little socks and a hat. She was skilled at these crafts. She'll tell him all the stories she knows and she'll make up others.

When she came completely out of the dream, the thought of another pregnancy and birth filled her with terror. In her state of health, could she give birth and function as a mother? There was no way of knowing.

She awoke fully, and to her great surprise, the room was dark. It was still the middle of the night. But the great, soft light that surrounded her in the dream was with her, as if to say, "Do not despair. You still have hope. Soon there will be light."

Will there be another child?

Chapter 32

They remained in Cyprus for two years, trying to keep their heads above water and fighting for health, hope, and their human spirit.

In 1944, rumors began spreading that the Germans would reach Cyprus. The British decided to rid themselves of the refugees so they would not reveal any "secrets." They gave everyone certificates and sent them to Palestine. A registration sheet at the Immigration Bureau of the Jewish Agency in Haifa, read:

"In March 1944, Leon (50), Ida (34), and Margarita (5) Schmelzer arrived in Haifa by ship."

When the ship docked and they landed on the coast of Palestine, they knelt and kissed the ground. They couldn't believe they were finally treading on the soil of "Eretz Israel."

There were many people at the port. The three of them stood stunned on the beach that was bustling with people in costume. Parents held their children's hands and showed off to each other a little "policeman" and a "Queen Esther" in a white dress with a crown on her head.

Litti looked at them, confused. She didn't understand what new place they had come to and the meaning of the odd clothes the children were wearing.

"What a strange place. Look at what people are wearing here. It's so funny," she told her parents.

Papa and Mama explained to her that today was a holiday called Purim, and one of the customs is to dress up in costumes. For one day, Purim, you can be whoever you want to be and wear the clothing that suits what you choose to be.

"I want to be Cinderella, like in Mama's stories!" Litti jumped up and down excitedly, "But how can I find the right clothes?"

"Next year you'll be whatever you want," her mother assured her. "I'll make you a beautiful dress and you'll be a real princess."

Margalit smiled, took her Mama's hand and stroked it.

A tall, fat man holding a megaphone blared out, "Dr. Schmelzer, come to me."

Machiku approached him with Donya and Litti following.

"Welcome to Palestine. We'll take care of you from now on. From here you will be transferred to a detention camp at Atlit, where you will stay in quarantine for two weeks to make sure that you're healthy."

"Machiku," Donya whispered, "I'm not well. Will they expel me from here? Another quarantine!?"

He wrapped his arm around her slender, drooping shoulders, looked into her eyes and whispered back, "We're home. We won't move from here."

They were asked to get on a small, light brown bus that would take them to their new abode: Atlit.

The camp they came to was quite large and surrounded by a barbed wire fence. There were long barracks scattered throughout that housed the people in the camp. As soon as they entered, everyone was disinfected with DDT, a spray with a terrible smell of oil that was also used at that time to repel mosquitoes. They underwent medical examinations and waited impatiently for the day they would be released. Everyone assembled in a large hall and each was given a bed.

A senior British officer who came to inspect the camp saw Litti, a cute little girl, and asked her, "How do you like Palestine?"

She answered him in plain English. "This is not Palestine. This is a barbed wire fence."

On one occasion, Moshe Shertok – later a minister in the first Israeli Government – came to visit. Litti met him. She had collected ladybug beetles, put them in a matchbox, and handed them to him as a gift.

Time passed very slowly. They had nothing to do and were merely waiting to leave the camp.

After two weeks, each of the refugees was asked to provide the address of someone in the country willing to accept them into their home. They gave the address of distant relatives living in Jerusalem who had agreed to house them for two months.

In the evening of March 28, 1944, an "Egged Company" bus arrived at the Central Bus Station on Jaffa Street in central Jerusalem. It was cold and rainy. When the bus stopped, three people got off with a carton suitcase, a rag doll, and a tattered sweater.

Machiku held the brown suitcase with the few pieces of clothing they had received at the Atlit Detention Camp. Margalit was holding the doll that Susie Mann had made for her from rags. Donya tried to shield herself from the rain, tightly wrapping around her the sweater she received at the camp.

The three new immigrants waiting on the street corner were lost, not knowing where to turn or what to do next. They were Leon Schmelzer, now called Arieh; Ida, now called Yehudit; and five-year-old Litti, now officially called Margalit.

They stood on the street corner, waiting.

This was not how Machiku pictured the fulfillment of his dream of Palestine. In the eight times he had come to "Eretz" before, he was greeted on a red carpet. Ussishkin made sure that his protégé, head of the JNF in Romania, would receive a proper escort and welcome. Machiku had raised a great amount of money for them and had earned special treatment. This time the drainpipes of heaven opened up and poured down on them, as if to say, "Well, you've arrived in Palestine. Now let's see what you can do."

Machiku, who had always known what to do, this time stood helpless and wet in the rain. His face betrayed nothing. He looked as determined as ever, but inside he felt very tired, tired of making decisions, tired of having to know everything. All he wanted was to lay his head on a pillow, close his eyes, and have someone else take care of everything.

From the corner of Rabbi Kook Street, which descends and intersects with Jaffa Road, both in the very center of Jerusalem, a couple emerged. The woman was hefty, with blond hair and a beautifully white complexion; the man was average-size and bald, with brown eyes. He had on a shiny plastic raincoat and wore a hat.

The couple spotted the three refugees standing on the street corner in the rain, approached them and reached out to shake their hands. At once they began to speak.

"We're Raya and Max Gottlieb. The JNF informed us you were coming. We're your distant relatives on Grandma Yetti's side of the family," they said, surprising them. "We'll take you to our home until they find a place for you to live."

A sigh of relief issued from Donya's mouth. Machiku looked at them and smiled.

"And what is your name?" Raya Gottlieb leaned over to Litti.

"Litti."

"From now on your name is Margalit," her father corrected her.

"You'll be glad to know that we have an eleven-year-old son. His name is Hagai, and he'll be happy that you have come."

Margalit jumped up and down in a puddle and splashed water on everyone.

They walked on a few steps until they came to what the Gottliebs called a "bus station." They waited there for a while, until what looked like a ship on wheels arrived at the bay of the station. It was similar to the one that had brought them from the Haifa Aliya Gate to Atlit. It was a kind of vessel on wheels that moves on land. In front sits a man who turns a round wheel called a steering wheel, and when he presses the handle, the ship's door opens with a spring.

This time they boarded the ship traveling to their home in Talpiot, a south-east Jerusalem neighborhood.

A few days after arriving in Jerusalem, Litti started kindergarten. It was a real kindergarten with a teacher, toys, plays, and stories. It was so good for her there. Before then she could only dream about having a doll or having some of the things that children grow up with. Nevertheless, she didn't forget the desert and the jackals and the high sea waters that covered them. Sometimes at night she would still wake up fearfully and whisper, "Tata, Tata, *Ayn Shakal*, a jackal," and her father or mother would take her into their narrow bed and lovingly comfort her until she fell asleep again.

Margalit went to the kindergarten almost by herself. Donya would accompany her to the huge Shell gas station across the busy road and let her walk the rest of the way alone to the nearby kindergarten gate.

Donya had gotten some work washing dishes.

One day she was late picking up Litti from kindergarten. Litti went out of the gate, walked the road familiar to her across from the Shell station, and turned to the man working there.

"Mr. Shell, could you please cross me over the street?"

The gas station worker burst out laughing.

"My name is not Mr. Shell, my name is Mr. Weisberg," he told Litti. "Shell is the name of the petrol company. Come, give me your hand and I'll gladly walk you across the street."

As they crossed, Donya came running, panting from the effort. She hurried towards them. "Oh, thank you Mr..."

"Weisberg," the man completed her sentence. "Your little girl thought my name was Mr. Shell," he laughed.

"Ah, well, she speaks Hebrew, English, and German," Donya apologized, "a completely mixed-up five-year-old."

"Like the rest of us," sighed Mr. Weisberg. "It'll take time for us to be absorbed here properly."

Donya thanked the stranger again and went home with her daughter. Even now, when they had reached the "land of ancestral covetousness," that they had sung about, they still didn't have their own house and lived with their relatives. No wonder Litika was confused.

Hagai, the eleven-year-old son of the Gottliebs, hurried towards them.

"Margalit, do you want to jump rope?"

"Yes!" Margalit exclaimed happily. "Mama, may I?"

"Just for a little while, until I warm up your lunch," answered her mother.

Donya went inside and stood at the burner to heat up Litti's meal. How good to have Hagai here, she thought. Without knowing it, he serves as a cultural and emotional guide for Litti. He teaches her all the children's games they play here – jump rope, tag, and hopscotch. They throw a stone on the squares, and then jump into them or between them.

One day at kindergarten the children had to get a typhoid vaccination. Everyone stood in a long line waiting their turn. A powerful fear gripped Litti. What are the children doing? She got out of the queue and ran home. Hagai went out to meet her. He had already returned from school and heard about the shots.

"Well, how were the shots? You're a real hero!"

"They were okay," she replied in a soft voice.

It was the first lie she told, for fear that her parents would find out she had avoided the shot and be angry with her. Her parents were very strict. They taught her to behave properly and what to do in any situation she encounters. If in their opinion she behaved improperly, she would be punished, and they would not speak to her. The silence lasted a short time, but to her, as a child, it seemed very long, maybe two weeks. Then, at the end of the grim silence, her mother would say, "Now go and apologize to Papa."

Litti didn't always understand what she did wrong and why they were angry with her, but she apologized so they would not be angry anymore. Papa would pretend to look angry, flushed red. But then he would break down and hug her, and they would laugh together. Sometimes she still thinks about the injustice in apologizing for not doing anything wrong, out of fear that they would be angry with her.

That morning, of course, she was caught lying, and finally had to get the shot.

Chapter 33

Thanks to his work for the JNF in Romania, Machiku was hired as a clerk in the JNF legal department in Jerusalem. The person who arranged the position was none other than Ussishkin's son. Machiku didn't have a fancy office on the main street like he had in Chernowitz; instead, he sat with a secretary in a small room in "Beit Yahalom," a small building in Jerusalem. He didn't practice his profession as a respected lawyer sought by upper class clients either, but as a simple clerk registering the ownership of JNF lands and properties. He didn't even have a license to practice law in the country. The people he worked with were secretaries and clerks like him.

The department conducted inspections regarding the status of lands, their registration, and the issuance of ownership certificates. Dr. Leon Schmelzer became a minor subject of Her Majesty's Government in his new country, dealing with daily life in Palestine. He understood the deep divide between his dream of immigrating to Eretz Israel and the reality.

The public figures who had received him with great respect during his visits to the country either disavowed him or were busy with other matters. Ussishkin and Weizmann were occupied with national affairs and negotiating with the

British Mandate authorities concerning the establishment of an independent state. Even so, Machiku was grateful for the wages he could bring home and the miraculous rescue of his family. For a new immigrant getting a job, and moreover in the JNF legal department, it was like winning the lottery. This job was the closest thing to his past as a famous criminal lawyer who many people turned to and would pay handsomely for his services.

For that reason, he never complained, and was happy that he had enough money to pay rent and provide food for his loved ones, Donya and Litti. Although this position wasn't the job he dreamed of in return for his services in Romania, he secretly believed that one day he would study for the certification exams to become a lawyer in Palestine. Then he would be able to return to the profession he had studied and practiced in Romania, but that day still seemed far off. Before that, he had to deal with other challenges, such as making sure that Donya recovered and overcame the mental and physical trauma that plagued her for so long. Her hair had turned white, and she was still too thin and had a hard time eating.

Every day, Machiku would walk from Talpiot to his place of work at Beit Yahalom in the city center to save on bus fare. Besides, he needed exercise and found that walking was a good way to get it.

He was small and energetic, and he wore a light-colored ironed shirt and khaki pants down to the knees with a brown belt to match the brown shoes he bought. He wore heavy black plastic-rimmed glasses and looked almost like a person born in Eretz Israel when he walked down the street; maybe they, too, were just new immigrants.

No more jackets and ties. His pince-nez glasses without the earpieces had also gone out of fashion, which wasn't so terrible. "This is how to build a country," he thought to himself.

One day Machiku received a letter.

"You won't believe it. Look what they wrote to me from the JNF main office. They should be ashamed to write such a thing to someone who was chairman of the JNF of all Bukovina and made so many contributions to the redemption of Eretz Israel."

"What did they say that you're so upset about?"

"Here, look at this:

> 'We must point out that since you arrived here you have not acquired sufficient knowledge of the Hebrew language. This of course greatly interferes with your present work and any position offered to you in the future. It is therefore recommended that you learn the Hebrew language in the coming months to the extent that you can dictate letters when needed.'"

"And who exactly will pay for these studies?"

"They're happy to give me a 5 lira increase in my salary, which will now be 15 lira."

Although he was angry, Machiku saw that the letter also contained good news. He had been made a tenured employee of the JNF. He knew that tenure was one of the most important things for a worker. He would not be fired and could be assured of an income for his family. Then he also saw the addendum later in the letter. As if it weren't enough for him to go into first grade to learn Hebrew, they appointed Mr. Wexler and Mr. Weiss to be what they called his "advisers."

"You understand that these men are my supervisors? I'm not trustworthy enough for them? I have to meet with one of them at least twice a week, and with the other one once a week."

"Machiku, I know how committed you are to what you take on. What can you do? This is a different country and we have to start all over again."

"Yes, you're right. The main thing is that we're alive and Litti is with us," he said with a sigh and stroked her hair.

She already had so much white hair. Where did the mahogany glow of her hair go, and what happened to the smooth skin that was now replaced by wrinkles all over her beautiful face?

Mr. Wexler was Machiku's boss in the legal department. Gradually, Machiku began to sense that Mr. Wexler was harassing him. He was constantly spying on him, checking the bills, going through the records. To Machiku it felt as if he were once again a little boy with the melamed in heder.

"Maybe that's how it is at the JNF in Palestine," he thought to himself. He was so meticulous in each and every number he wrote in the books.

One day he and Wexler bumped into each other just as Machiku was about to open the door of his room. Wexler – short, and lame in one leg – swayed back and forth.

"Yesterday I saw that you didn't include in the book of records the new land we purchased in Hadera," he noted in a heavy Polish accent.

"I didn't? That's not possible."

"No, you did not. I checked."

Machiku's face immediately turned crimson. He was steaming with anger. All the rage that had been building up in him was about to overflow. He wanted to shout, to hit. He had never physically beaten anyone before, but he had fits of anger on occasion.

"That cannot be," he replied with restraint.

"Are you calling me a liar?"

"I didn't say that." Machiku was boiling, like a steam kettle about to blow.

"I'll see that you're fired!" bellowed Wexler.

"Dwarf," Machiku muttered quietly in German. In times of stress people sometimes revert to their mother tongue.

"What did you call me?" Wexler puffed up and raised his hand to hit Machiku.

People came out of the rooms to separate the two sparring males.

"You're grown men. Please calm down!" pleaded Machiku's secretary.

Slowly things subsided and the fierceness between them faded. Each licked his wounds, but neither apologized. "How did I let myself get so enraged," Machiku thought as he went into his room. The humiliation he suffered gnawed at him. Mammu had always told him, "If a big wave comes, lower your head and it will pass." He remembered her and felt like he was her child again. He bowed his head in silence.

That same afternoon, at home, he told Donya about what had happened at the office. They both sat down on the bed in the little bedroom at the Gottlieb's. Margalit was playing outside with Hagai.

"You know, Donika," he said to his wife, "it's incredible how very different the land we envisioned and called the 'Zionist dream' is and what I meet with every day."

"What do you mean?" Donya asked him, startled.

"People here are engaged in a war of survival: vis-à-vis the Arabs, the British, and the shortages. They're not at all aware that it is they who are the Zionist dream. They don't conceive of themselves as being the realization of the dream. Perhaps only history will perceive it in that way over the years. People here are too busy with their everyday problems."

"I also feel that what we encountered here is very different from what I imagined," Donya admitted. "It's difficult here with so many flies and mosquitoes, and we have nothing. We live in someone else's house. What is 'Zionist' about it? Even the land is not ours but controlled by others who don't allow Jews to enter."

Since recovering from her illness she had tried not to complain. She told herself that she had to survive, recover, and bear the burden along with Machiku. She's by his side and not his child. Machiku, who was ashamed of complaining of the difficulties, changed his tone.

"But the main thing is how Litika is blossoming, like a little flower. Dreams are wonderful, but the everyday is completely different."

"Yes, there's no doubt the child is happy here, practicing her Hebrew, and will soon start going to a real school."

"The truth is that I'm worried about the situation in the country. It's like standing on the edge of a volcano. In Europe there is still a war and here the gates have been closed to Jews. Where can they go?"

"Once a leader, always a leader," smiled Donika. "You can't just relax at home without involving yourself with public and national affairs."

"True," Machiku admitted. "Anyone who has entered the country must be involved in everything that happens here. When I visited before the war, I didn't see the hardships of life here. My experience was influenced by the honor I was given."

"Oh, I still remember when you told all of Chernowitz how you were a guest of honor at the inauguration ceremony of the Hebrew University on Mount Scopus."

"That was then," sighed Machiku. "Another world, another time. I don't even have a single photograph from those days."

"Do you know anything about our families in Chernowitz?" Donya asked.

"Not a thing. There is no communication yet. Maybe they're alive or maybe not. They're at war there and we are here."

Chapter 34

Each of the Schmelzer family members, being new immigrants, tried to become absorbed in the new country at their own pace and in their own fashion.

Four months after immigrating to Israel, in June 1944, Machiku, Donya, and Litika left the Gottlieb family's home and moved into a rented detached house in the Romema neighborhood of Jerusalem. The owner of the property was an Arab named Hassan Hula. There were three rooms with decorated floor tiles, arched windows, and high ceilings. The house was surrounded by a fenced-in yard with blue and yellow flowers called "the stork's bill." Other flowers had tails that wove around like clocks.

Hassan Hula would often check on the house, but only from the outside, without speaking to the tenants. To help meet the cost of rent and also to aid in their *aliyah* absorption, the Schmelzers rented a room to Gertrude Noymann, a single immigrant from Germany. The Arab property owner really liked Gertrude and enjoyed watching her through the bathroom window when she forgot to close it while showering and singing Zionist songs. But if she noticed his figure lurking outside the window, she would scream in terror and he would run away as fast as his legs could carry him.

Donya began volunteering, doing social work through WIZO, thanks to their recognition of her activities in Bukovina. The Jewish Agency sent her to take care of children whose parents had been killed in concentration camps. There was one girl in her care who had seen her mother's corpse eaten by a dog, as well as many others with equally horrifying histories. Donya cared for them with all her heart.

Each neighborhood had its own characteristics. In Romema there were Arab stone houses, and next to them were long rows of attached apartments with green railings and stairs that led to a long, narrow, common balcony for all the tenants. The streets were unpaved, and only a dirt path led to the main street that was a continuation of Jaffa Road, which crossed the city from east to west. On one side was a bus stop that went to the "city center," and on the opposite side a bus stop for Beit Hakerem, a beautiful, green and distinguished neighborhood. On the corner, not far from their house, were little shops that had all the necessary everyday products: milk, bread, eggs, fruit, and vegetables. The store used brass, double-pan balance scales; the goods were placed on one pan and on the other pan were different sized weights. Sometimes, when the buyer wasn't looking, the vendor would tilt the scales slightly in his favor.

Margalit was so proud when her mother sent her to buy eggs. All the way home she jumped up and down, finding, to her great sorrow, that the eggs turned into an omelet.

At the corner was Ali's small grocery store, which resembled a treasure cave with the kinds of sweets that Litika loved: licorice, fruit leather bought by the piece, and a glass jar with a black lid filled with colorful chewing gum that you could blow big bubbles with. The owner kept apricot kernels for the children to play with while sitting on the sidewalk; they would throw five of them in the air, and the winner would be the one who caught more kernels. In front of the shops, it was also possible to draw on the sidewalk with chalk and play hopscotch.

Margalit grew taller, her face took on a healthier color, and her hair grew longer. Her mother arranged it in two braids and wound white ribbons around them, tied like butterflies. Margalit already spoke Hebrew; she had an almost complete grasp of the vocabulary. Only at home, with her parents, did she speak German, which was their mother tongue.

"Machiku," said Donya one evening as they sat by themselves in the tiny kitchen, "I would like Margalit to grow up surrounded by culture, as we did."

"What do you mean?"

"For example, to learn to dance, and play an instrument."

"Where can we find such things here?"

"I keep hearing someone playing the piano from the house next door. Let's go see what's going on there."

The next day they both went to the neighbors' house. In the yard adjacent to them was a house like theirs, built from Jerusalem stone with arched windows and a courtyard with decorated tiles. Outside were olive trees and a blackberry bush. They knocked on the door without knowing who would open it, because they didn't yet know the neighbors.

A tall man opened the door.

"Shalom," they said together.

"Shalom to you, too," answered the man, greeting them warmly.

"We're Arieh and Yehudit, the neighbors from next door."

Only at that moment did they notice that the man's eyes were blank. He was blind.

"I'm Avraham Greenberg. Come in. Would you like something to drink? My wife and I have long wanted to come visit you."

"Thank you. Very nice to meet you."

"Where are you from?"

"Romania. We fled from there and were in Cyprus for two years until we received a visa from the British to enter the country. We have an almost six-year-old daughter named Margalit."

"We have two boys, in the third and fifth grades, at the Beit Hakerem School. Oh, this is my wife, Mira."

Mira entered the room and greeted them. To their amazement they saw that she, too, was blind. "We're glad to meet you at last," Mira said. "Where we are from, it wasn't customary to just go to the neighbors uninvited. But here in Eretz Israel it is very common. All the people of Israel are friends with each other."

"We heard piano playing and wanted to ask if you know where our daughter could take lessons."

"Here, of course," Mira immediately replied. "I'm a piano teacher for children, and my husband Avraham is a sought-after piano tuner. He has a perfect ear for music and achieves wonderful results.

"What luck we have," said Donya. "We so want Margalit to have as broad a cultural education as she would have received if we had stayed in Europe."

They drank tea, ate cookies baked by Mira, shook hands with the pleasant neighbors, and went back home.

"Where will we find the money to pay for piano lessons?" Donya pondered.

"We'll think of something," Machiku replied.

When Margalit was told she would be starting to study piano, she jumped for joy. She, too, had heard the music from the neighbors' house, but didn't dare ask for lessons. After all, they didn't even have a piano.

Machiku was a heavy smoker. He decided to quit, and from the money saved by not buying cigarettes, Margalit would be able to take piano lessons. It was hard quitting like that, all of a sudden. Even on the beach he would get a cigarette from the soldiers now and then. But for his little girl he was willing to do anything.

Twice a week Margalit went to Mira. She was also given permission to practice there. She wanted to play songs she heard on the radio, but Mira supervised her practice and said she was to play only classical music. This didn't satisfy Margalit's longing to play popular songs as well, but she was disciplined and dreamed of the day when she would have her own piano at home. Then she could play whatever she wanted. Margalit continued learning the piano with her blind neighbor, Mira Greenberg. Over time she realized she would not be a great soloist, but found that she loved music and the way it calmed her spirits.

Shlomko Weissbrot, one of the owners of the British Institute for learning English, would come to their home frequently. He was a distant relative, a tall, broad-shouldered man with a mane of white hair and bright blue eyes. He helped them greatly in their absorption into the country. He brought blankets, toys, and even books. When he saw how much Margalit loved music, he started coming up with musical surprises for her. He wore a long leather coat with inside pockets, and always had something for her in them. It was usually a book about a composer, such as "Haydn the Village Boy," or "Schubert and His Merry Friends."

The books were illustrated and printed in big letters. Margalit enjoyed learning about these people, who already at a young age had composed music.

Whenever Shlomko came to them, Margalit would jump up impatiently. "What did you bring this time?"

He reached in his coat pocket with deliberate slowness and whup! A book, a rectangular hardcover book with the title, "Mozart, the Musical Magician."

"Thank you!" exclaimed Margalit, a polite young girl with good manners and a "*yekke*" education, as those of German origin were called in Eretz Israel.

Since she had already learned to play piano, she loved reading about famous composers and their lives. It was magic for her to learn about how they composed their pieces, and about the lives they had in the courts of the emperors who commissioned music from them. Haydn even composed a piece that had a "boom" in the middle because the emperor always fell asleep at a concert and the noise would jolt him awake!

Shlomko once brought her an encyclopedia of music. Margalit's parents read it to her because the Hebrew writing had no vowels. Shlomko also taught her to read musical scores, in which the notes of all the instruments together were inscribed.

That is how Margalit received a wonderful musical education from various sources. At that time there were no phonographs in the country, but sometimes entire works were played on the radio at the request of listeners. She would sit, close her eyes, and listen, a smile spreading across her lips.

***

Margalit also had a talent for languages and fairly quickly began chatting in Hebrew with her piano teacher's children. She was a quiet girl from the Diaspora, from the exile, with two braids tied with ribbons and pierced ears. She wanted so much to be like the *sabras*, those born in the country, but didn't know how. She was embarrassed by her mother, who wore odd dresses with buttons and flowers, and her hair had remnants of a reddish color woven into the white. She wasn't proud of her father, either, although he had actually become popular among the locals. At least his style of dress was suitable, going to work in khaki pants down to his knees, long khaki socks on his feet, and rubber insoles beneath them due to his problem with varicose veins. Her mother no longer sang her lullabies in German, but occasionally she would tell her stories from the Brothers Grimm – like how the witch seized Hansel and Gretel, or how the prince kissed Snow White, and she woke up. The fairy tales always had happy endings: "And they lived happily ever after, and if they didn't die, they live until today." She memorized the endings, and it became part of her character – in the end, all will be well.

In the meantime, they had not received any word about the family left behind in Chernowitz. Like the rest of the Jewish community, Donya and Machiku heard on the radio about the European countries occupied by the Germans and the fate of the Jews there. They worried terribly about the family and would often be stricken with great sorrow – Donya with a yearning for her parents, Machiku longing for Mammu Regina and the rest of the family.

One day, in midsummer, the entire country was covered with strange insects that crawled, flew, jumped, and got into everything. Margalit was outside wearing white doll shoes, and one of the insects got into her shoe. She started screaming in fear. Locusts had descended upon the land, covering everything in a huge cloud. There were rumors that some people even ate them.

"Ugh, how can they?" Margalit asked.

"Don't say 'ugh' about food!" her mother retorted and burst out laughing, but Margalit didn't laugh. She trembled with fear and refused to go outside until the plague was over.

"You know, when the children of Israel were in Egypt, the Almighty struck the Egyptians with a plague of locusts that devoured all the grain," her father explained.

"But we're not in Egypt and don't have to eat those disgusting things," Margalit protested.

"Of course not."

"Yes, but we don't have good food to eat."

"You know your mother does the best she can. The day will come when we'll have better food," her father tried to comfort her. But in his heart, he had to admit that they weren't getting the right nourishment. Their daily diet was quite lacking in both quality and quantity.

Chapter 35

Margalit was almost six years old, and it was time to enroll her in school. Her parents wanted her to go to the old Beit Hakerem School, named for the neighborhood where it was located. She would have to take a bus back and forth every day on her own.

Donya and Margalit arrived at the school. It had a big schoolyard. At the end was a long, narrow balcony with green doors that opened onto classrooms. The second floor had a similar balcony, also with a row of classrooms.

When they arrived, David Benvenisti, the principal, was waiting for them by the railing on the ground floor. He had a mane of white hair, glasses, and a pleasant smile.

He invited them into one of the classrooms and they followed him in and sat down like pupils on low chairs at the tables. It was a spacious classroom with huge, Belgian-style windows. On the wall hung a huge blackboard with chalk and an eraser on its narrow ledge. On another wall was a map of the Land of Israel, with all sorts of Hebrew words that Litti didn't know. She was very nervous, but the principal's nice smile and friendly gaze reassured her. There seemed to be nothing to be afraid of here, she thought to herself.

"Mrs. Schmelzer, how can I enroll a child in the first grade who speaks only English and German? What about Hebrew? How will she manage to fit in?" the principal asked her mother.

Margalit, who very much wanted to be accepted at this beautiful school with the nice principal, stood up on a small chair and, without thinking twice, began a dramatic recitation in Hebrew:

"In kibbutz Nahalal there's no money at all
In kibbutz Ein Harod life is very, very good
And the milk from cows is pink."

After all, she had studied Hebrew with Harry Zucker, who came every morning and sang under her window.

The smile on the principal's face spread. He hugged Margalit, took her down off the chair, and informed her that she was officially accepted.

The short, slender girl with two braids and ribbons tied at their ends arrived at first grade with a new brown leather satchel on her back. At first she was received with suspicion and aloofness from her classmates, who were children of the Jerusalem "aristocracy" at that time – descendants of Sephardic Jews who had lived in the land for many generations, and so these children were full of self-confidence. For them, Litti was an immigrant girl in a plaid skirt with suspenders and tiny gold earrings with a small ruby in the center. Somehow no one had taken them from her no matter where they had been, perhaps because they didn't notice them. But the children in Litti's class noticed them, since no child wore earrings at that time. When they mocked her, Margalit tried to remove the earrings herself, but it hurt and she gave up. The children also laughed at her because she wore glasses, using it as another reason to distance her and isolate her.

"Four eyes," they teased, and she would shrivel to the side and remain silent.

"Four eyes, four eyes," the children would chant cruelly at the unusual, different-looking child.

Every day Margalit took the number 12 bus by herself to school. It traveled a long way in the direction of Mount Herzl. In the middle of the journey, in Kiryat Moshe, many children from the "bus drivers'" quarter got on. Among them were Eitan, tall and handsome; Yakov, who was always dirty and picking his nose; and Zmira – thin as a rail and buck-toothed – who later would become one of her best friends.

She already had several friends: Edna and Ruthie, who lived in her neighborhood in Romema; another one, Ruthie W., lived in a fancy house in a traffic circle that she had to cross the road to get to. Ruthie was a pretty girl who had been with her in kindergarten. Margalit used to go to play with her at her home. One day there was a power outage, and Margalit stole a doll from her friend in the darkness. She told her parents that Ruthie had given her the doll. They discovered the lie and made her return the doll and apologize.

There were also the twins, Rili and Rachel, about whom it was said that they always divided everything in two, and there was Gozal, who lived in the Makor Baruch neighborhood a bit farther away. On Saturday afternoons Margalit would go to visit her.

One day when Margalit came back from school with Ruthie and Edna, her stomach started to hurt badly. There was a big stone wall on the way. She hid behind it and, child that she was, had a bowel movement. The next day the two girls paid no attention to her. Ruthie said her mother, who was a *yekke*, called her "*schmutzikah*" ,dirty, and forbade her to play with Margalit. After a while they started to play together again: class, five stones, and other games. Once, Ruthie hit Margalit with a bucket and cut her head.

Margalit was a good student. She had a beautiful handwriting, especially with round letters. Her father would make her sit and draw the letters over and over.

"What is that? Fly poop?" he barked if the letters were too small for his liking. Thanks to his strictness, Margalit became known for her lovely handwriting, and she was later chosen to write out the Scouts Passover Haggadah on a stencil.

The first- and second-grade teacher was Remma, later a well-known opera singer. She was a tall, beautiful woman with locks of brown hair and big green eyes. Every Friday she would have welcomed the Sabbath in class. The children came to school in clean white shirts, and Remma would sing, "Rest Comes for the

Weary," and other melodic Shabbat songs. During the singing, the teacher would pass the blue JNF charity box around the room, and each child would put half a penny in it as a contribution to the redemption of the land. Margalit immediately adopted the feeling of being a pioneer, healing the ancient land.

The teacher would then read to them a chapter from the book "The Goose Shepherd," which tells the story of a girl who had a magic hammer that could heal people. Margalit immediately adopted the marvel of wonders and imagined that she was able to heal everyone.

Outside the school, the country was in turmoil. The children got the bitter taste of the events when one day their beloved teacher Remma didn't come to school and was replaced by a substitute. When she returned to class a week later, she looked very sorrowful, and was wearing a gray dress with little black drawings on it.

"Dear children," she said, "my husband Yehiam has been killed, and I'm very sad. He took part in the Night of the Bridges Operation and was fatally wounded by a bullet that pierced his chest."

Her husband, Yehiam, the son of Yosef Weitz, one of the leaders of the JNF, grew up in the Beit Hakerem neighborhood of Jerusalem. He was one of the first company instructors in the Palmach – the military force that served as the operational extension of the Haganah, the army of the upcoming Jewish state in Palestine, from 1941until 1948.

Between June 16 and 17, 1946, the Night of the Bridges Operation was carried out. It was the code name of a coordinated attack by the "Palmach" as part of the Jewish uprising movement, during which 11 bridges were attacked throughout Eretz Israel. Nine of them were blown up, one was badly damaged, and another bridge was undamaged. The success of the operation caused a temporary disruption of supply routes used by the British.

From that day on, at the Friday Sabath lesson, Remma sang the song "Two Roses" to her pupils:

"There once were two roses ...
one white, one black,
until a hand came and plucked one,
and broke the other one's heart."

Yehiam's death, on the Night of the Bridges, was just one of many that the pupils were exposed to. The British, who then ruled the country, would occasionally declare a curfew, and the children had to remain at home with their parents in the pitch dark. Sometimes they lit an oil lamp, and to dispel the terror of the curfew, would build a horse and cart with Margalit, using "Mechano," a game with red and green metal parts connected by screws. Despite the tension, her studies continued, and Margalit's excellence in school gave her confidence.

Among the highlights of the school year were preparations for the upcoming holiday of Shavuot, one of the three holidays mentioned in the Bible. It has an explicit agricultural meaning with the harvest of grain crops as well as commemorating the giving of the Torah to the People of Israel.

In ancient times, people from all over the country made a pilgrimage to the Temple in Jerusalem, bringing food and gifts for the priests doing God's work. In pre-state Israel, the leaders of the Zionist movement saw it as a symbol of the Jewish people's return to their homeland. It was celebrated by people bringing baskets of the first fruits of the harvest, accompanying this with songs and dances to recall the pilgrimage to the Temple.

Teacher Remma organized a performance for all the students. Rehearsals were held in the big outdoor schoolyard. Margalit's class prepared the dance for the event on the theme "See who comes from the field with a basket on her head." Remma divided the students into threes and taught them the dance steps. Margalit was in the trio with Rili and Rachel, and every day they rehearsed for the long-awaited show.

One day, during rehearsal, Margalit came down with a high fever and had to stay home for a whole week.

"You haven't been to the final rehearsals and you won't be able to be in the dance," said Remma, her beloved teacher. Margalit was heartbroken. She wept in secret because everyone except her was dancing and happy, so the school year ended sadly for her.

As if that weren't enough, shortly afterwards Margalit had a severe case of measles and lay in bed, helpless and feverish. Her mother put damp cloths on her body to lower her temperature while Margalit whispered, "Tata, Tata – Rubezahl."

Her father pulled up a chair by her bed, sat down and did what she expected him to do whenever she was ill: He told her the story of Rubezahl, a mythological hero in Czech-German folklore. Rubezahl was a giant who lived in a deep underground cave along with many small dwarfs who worked mining metal in the caves. The metal was transported in small trams to the entrance of the cave. Legend had it that when one of the villagers needed help, he would come to the entrance of the cave and call out, "Rubezahl! Rubezahl!" The echoing call would roll around between mountains and valleys, and then out of nowhere, the giant Rubezahl would emerge to help the person who had cried for help.

Many stories were written about him in German. Margalit preferred to preserve the memory of her father, sitting by her side, listening to his tales while holding her hand. She, in a feverish, almost hallucinatory state, savored the name "Rubezahl, Rubezahl!"

Early childhood memories can accompany us all our lives. They bring with them the marvelous sensation of heroics that stay with us always, when the real characters are long gone. The giant Rubezahl, with the capacity to help and to heal, remained etched within her heart even when she was an adult.

Chapter 36

In February of 1946, Jerusalem was covered by a blanket of snow. Margalit was in the second grade by then. She woke up one morning in the Arab house in Romema, looked through the bars on the window and saw the snow, and opened her eyes wide in amazement.

"What is that, Tata? What's all the white stuff flying in the air?" she cried.

Hearing her cry out, Miss Gertrude Noymann, their tenant, entered the room in surprise. She was a tall, slender, dark-complexioned woman. Her black hair streaked with white was gathered into a small bun at the back of her head.

"What is it?" she asked Margalit.

"Where are Mama and Papa? They're not here?" Margalit asked her in German, the language she spoke to Miss Noymann and her parents.

"You parents went to bring a baby," Gertrude retorted.

"What? From where?"

"From the hospital."

"But the stork brings babies and I didn't see any," Margalit wondered. "In the winter there are no storks here."

"This is a real baby that your parents are bringing, not the stork. Soon your Papa will come and take you to see him."

Margalit hurriedly got up and dressed. She put on a pleated, wool-lined skirt, suspenders to hold it up, and a red sweater over a white blouse. She was very excited. Her parents didn't tell her they were bringing a baby, and she was astounded. Gertrude gave her a slice of black bread with jam and made her a cup of hot tea. While she ate breakfast, her father came home looking tired, but with a big smile on his face.

"Tata, where is the baby?" Margalit jumped up impatiently.

"Is it a 'mazal tov?' Boy or girl?" Gertrude asked.

"A healthy son, thank God, and Donika too, is fine. Soon I'll take Margalit to see them."

Margalit didn't want to wait. She jumped around the room, full of excitement. In the meantime, she had received a Purim issue of her children's magazine with the story about the ten sons of the villain Haman that was read on the Purim holiday. Having no choice, she sat down and read until they left for the hospital.

Machiku had waited until the snow thawed a bit. He took Margalit's hand. They left the house and walked to the bus stop for the ride to Hadassah Hospital on Mount Scopus.

They entered a long corridor full of wailing newborns. Margalit put her hands over her ears to muffle the noise. A nurse approached and led them to a glass window in the wall. Through it they saw many babies in cribs.

Machiku surveyed the line of cribs, counting them to himself.

"Oh, there he is, your brother!" he said and pointed to a small, red, wrinkled little creature lying in a crib on wheels.

"So ugly and wrinkled, like a little monkey!" Margalit exclaimed.

"Not at all! He's beautiful and weighs a lot – four and a half kilos!"

The next encounter was accompanied by anxiety. Margalit entered the room where her mother was resting. She hurried to her bed and hugged her. Secretly she hoped that Mama would remain her mother, too, and not just be the mother of this new baby.

"He's the first child of the family born here, in Eretz Israel," her mother smiled at her. "He's what they call a 'sabra' – the symbolic cactus fruit of the country, soft inside and prickly on the outside..."

She noticed that Mama's eyes were red but didn't dare ask why she was sad if she had given birth to a sabra.

After the visit, Dad walked her to the bus stop, put her on a bus and asked the driver to drop her off at the stop near her school in the Beit Hakerem neighborhood.

Margalit arrived an hour late, at nine in the morning. The classroom door was already closed. She knocked, as was customary when you were late.

Her teacher Remma opened the door. Peeking past the teacher, Margalit saw her classmates surrounded by seminar students who had come to learn how to be teachers.

Margalit could not wait and burst out, "I have a little brother! He's a bit wrinkled, but he's a sabra. Mama is in the hospital. That's why I'm late!"

All the student teachers and Remma burst out laughing.

Tears rolled down Margalit's cheeks. Why are they laughing? He's my brother and he's a sabra.

***

Meanwhile, Machiku was sitting with Donya at the hospital.

"What'll we name him?" he asked her.

"I think we should name him after one of the grandfathers. That's the way it was always done," Donya replied.

"It's better to give him a Hebrew name," Machiku thought aloud. "Look how good it was that we gave our daughter a Hebrew name, Margalit, and now in Eretz Israel we didn't have to change it."

"But it's important that we commemorate someone from Chernowitz."

"What name are you thinking of?"

"Yossel, for your father. I never knew him, but I heard he was a devout and kindly man. It will be a continuation of the family line."

"My dear, thank you for thinking of my father," Machiku replied with emotion, "but a child is not a memorial candle, and the name Yossel will sound foreign here, from the Diaspora. Our son is the first sabra in the family. How about we call him 'Yossi?'"

From that day on, the child's name was Yossi Schmelzer.

Sometime after bringing little Yossi home, they moved into a two-room apartment with a folding door separating the rooms. The apartment was in the city center at 6 King George Street, on the fourth floor. One hundred stairs led up to the apartment. In the stairwell at every half level were huge iron windows with glass blocks that are now called "Belgian" windows. The living room also served as the master bedroom, but since there were windows all around, the apartment had a current of air from four directions. Next to the living room was a small kitchenette and from there an exit to the building's roof, almost like a penthouse.

From the roof there was a view of the entire city. The old section of Jerusalem was to the east; Nebi Samuel – the tomb of the

Prophet Samuel – was to the west; and there were three main streets that came together in a triangle: Jaffa Road, King George St., and Ben-Yehuda Street. Jaffa Road was east-west; at its center was a building with columns where they sold electrical goods, and the opulent Freeman and Bein shoe store. Southeast was Mrs. Gottlieb's tiny cosmetics shop, and at the end of the street was a public restroom leading up to Harav Kook Street. In the middle was King George V Street, named after the King of England, which crossed the city from north to south. The third was Ben–Yehuda Street, with its small jewelry stores, the Atara Café, and Zion Square.

On the third floor of the building, where the Schmelzer family lived, was also the Vardi family. They had a big bulldog named Uzi. Yossi was growing up, a cute, round-cheeked and animal-loving child. He and the dog loved each other.

One day Yossi was petting his bulldog friend, and out of playfulness the dog bit him on the jaw. Blood ran down both sides of his mouth, but the friendship remained intact. Margalit, unlike her brother, would run up the stairs out of fear whenever she encountered Uzi.

On the second floor was the Hendler family. Margalit was their guest every Saturday for prayers after lunch. There she learned to sing "Shir Hama'alot," a song of redemption, and "Tzur Mishelo," thanking God for the meal, and other blessings. Besides, she enjoyed the delicious *cholent* specially cooked in the oven since Friday and served on Shabbat at lunchtime.

Occasionally her parents went out, leaving big sister Margalit in charge of little Yossi. One day, while Yossi was still in the crawling stage, the parents went out and left him in her care. Margalit wanted to get the board games down from the top shelf of the heavy brown cabinet in the children's room. She wasn't tall enough to reach the games and resourcefully stepped up on the bottom shelf. But her weight caused the cabinet to fall forward on the floor with a tremendous crash. Miraculously, it didn't crush Yossi, who was crawling in the room at that moment.

When the parents returned home and saw the closet lying on the floor of the children's room, they were horrified and Margalit was punished.

Yossi loved animals, and after kindergarten would come to Machiku's office until Donya came to pick him up. One day he came into the office with his fist clenched.

"Guess what I have in my hand?" he asked Tova, the secretary.

"I don't know," she answered as she smiled at him.

He opened his fist and a frog jumped out of his hand and began hopping around the room. Tova was so frightened that she got up on her desk.

However, Yossi's love for animals was to Margalit's benefit. The school wanted to teach the children about nature by studying dead insects in a wooden box with a glass lid on top. Each child had to kill a cockroach, a butterfly, or some other unfortunate little insect, put pins through their bodies and stick them to the sides of the wooden box. Margalit, who was frightened of living creatures, constantly failed at this project until Yossi, her kind little brother, prepared an outstanding specimen for her that she could take to school.

Sometimes the two of them decided to drive Mr. Vardi, the neighbor on the third floor, crazy. They were up on the roof just as he stepped out onto his porch. "There's Mr. Vardi." Margalit turned to her brother. "Fill your mouth with spit and aim for his bald spot!"

The wet bomb landed smack on the neighbor's head, and he looked up at the sky.

"Hmm, raining again," he said, as the two concealed themselves and tried to keep him from hearing their laughter.

What Yossi liked most was to open Margalit's secret drawer. He would take out her diary and read excerpts of comments about her friends. When her friends told Margalit what they had heard from her brother, it was too late to take back what she had written about them.

So the two of them were always brother and sister but often not friends, as is the way with children.

Chapter 37

Everyone awoke to an agreeable morning. The sun – bright but not too hot – smiled down from the sky. It was a beautiful Israeli autumn with blossoming flowers and flocks of migratory birds winging over the houses in the city.

Margalit woke up, got dressed quickly and was ready for school in Beit Hakerem. She was now in third grade. The class's regular teacher was on maternity leave and two substitutes alternated teaching the class: a young lady teacher named Ora, and a surly man named Patkin.

Patkin was scary. He would suddenly turn red and start yelling at the students. He also wrote notes to the parents reprimanding any child who "misbehaved," and they had to sign them and send them back to him. The comments were usually about not doing homework, talking in class, or arguments among the students. Woe to anyone who was caught unaware of a tiny detail in the lesson.

Between her strict parents and the grumpy teacher, Margalit navigated in constant fear of punishment.

However, "punishment" came from an unexpected source.

She was already involved in class activities. She had girlfriends and was even chosen as the secretary of a group of friends who would do things together, including organizing get-togethers around a campfire.

That same morning, she had done all her homework and studied for the test. There was no reason to be apprehensive about anything. When she entered the classroom and put down her schoolbag, she encountered Zmira, her closest friend. When she saw her, Zmira turned her back.

"Good morning," said Margalit, who had not noticed her friend turning away. There was no response.

"Shalom, Zmira. Are you ready for the test?" Again no response.

Margalit thought Zmira must be preoccupied with the test questions and didn't think anything of her not replying to the greeting. The rest of the children entered, chatting and laughing among themselves. When they saw Margalit, they all got silent, went to the corner of the room and huddled together.

"Good morning, Hagai. Hello, Shimshon and Dan. Are you ready for the test?" Margalit approached them.

They grouped around each other in a tight circle, excluding her. Margalit felt the queasiness in her stomach creeping up and a tightness in her throat. She began to realize that the others weren't talking to her. They weren't concerned with the test or homework. They were shunning her, staying at a distance.

Tears welled up in her eyes.

"What happened? Did I do something wrong?" she asked her friend Nurit, who had just come into the classroom.

Nurit looked down and joined the group of children in the corner.

The bell rang. The teacher, Mr. Patkin, with curly grayish hair that had once been red, strutted into the classroom. He carried the class attendance book with students' names under his arm. There was silence. Everyone sat in their chairs and the test began. Margalit felt all the test material flying out of her head. She saw only black and left the test paper blank. She didn't care about the test. "Let him write me up," she thought. "Why is everyone turning their backs on me? What did I do to them?" Zmira, who was sitting next to her at the same table, slipped her a note.

"It's a boycott! You have been boycotted. No one will talk to you or let you join the games."

Margalit wanted to disappear into the floor under her desk. Boycott her? Why? She had already been accepted by the others and had forgotten about when she was a "new immigrant." She had friends, both girls and boys. Now that was gone. Everything had been for nothing. She had reverted to being the different one, alienated, who everyone laughs at and doesn't talk to. "Is it because I'm fat? Ugly, with glasses?" she thought. She couldn't bear the grief that came over her that morning. She handed in an empty test on which she hadn't answered a single question. The teacher wrote a note in her school diary. This time she wasn't even afraid of her parents.

At recess, no one approached her. She wasn't included in any game – not in five stones or class, or even tug-of-war. She stood to the side, wiping away tears so nobody would see them.

It continued in the days that followed. She was isolated from the entire class that had once been a warm haven and now had turned against her. Even her best friend wouldn't talk to her.

In the mornings she would struggle to get up, get dressed, and go to school, where all the children were hostile to her.

She would never share what she was going through with her parents; her feelings were kept inside. Most of their talks were about lessons, subjects she didn't understand and had focused on studying with Papa for exams.

One morning it all burst out. She sat on the bed and could not stop crying. The tears flooded over her like waves in the sea.

"What did I do? Why are they doing this?" she sobbed.

Her mother came to her, stunned at the unexpected surge of tears, "What happened, Margalitika?"

"They've been boycotting me in class."

"What is 'boycott?'"

"They won't talk to me or play with me, like I don't exist."

"Why do they do that?"

"I don't know. No one tells me anything. Even Zmira, my best friend, won't tell me and she doesn't talk to me either."

Her mother sat down by Margalit and stroked her head until the crying slowly subsided. That day she stayed home, full of self-pity, angry with the friends who had turned their backs on her. In particular, she was hurt by her best friend Zmira's behavior. She should have stood up for her.

The next morning Margalit left for school, her heart pounding the whole way there. What will it be like? How do I face these kids? There are lots of them and just one of me. What did I do to them? She remembered what Papa always told her, "If a big wave comes, lower your head until it passes."

But a big wave can also drown you, she thought. She didn't even try to approach any of the others and entered the class as if in mourning, her head bowed. She sat in her chair feeling unwanted, small, and invisible.

The bell rang and the pupils entered the classroom. The substitute teacher, Ora, began the lesson.

"Children," she began. "A group always has great power. The many can either build or destroy. Being together is important, but when group power is directed towards an individual in a vicious and cruel way, it can break them, completely."

All eyes were on Margalit, who shrank into herself even more. If only there were a hole in the ground, she would crawl into it. There was complete silence in the room.

"Does anyone have anything to say?"

No one raised their hand.

"All right. Either you talk and explain yourselves, or this boycott ends right now."

The first to approach Margalit at the break was Zmira. "I'm sorry, Margalit, I thought this was unfair, but I couldn't go against the whole class."

Tears welled up in Margalit's eyes. "But you were my best friend. You could've explained it to me, to them!"

"I'm just one person and there are lots of them. I was afraid that they would boycott me, too."

Bitterness came over Margalit. The group used its power for no good reason, she thought.

They sat down to play five stones. Slowly the boycott dissolved. No one ever explained to Margalit what the reason was. She was left with a sense of betrayal by her friends, sensing how much she didn't belong.

She also didn't know how the boycott suddenly ended.

It was thanks to her mother, who went to school and talked to the teacher and the teacher came to her aid. Margalit only found this out many years later.

She wondered why she didn't stand up proudly against the other children. Why did she react to their viciousness by lowering her head and crying in secret instead of fighting back and standing up for herself? Do you really have to lower your head when a high wave comes your way?

Chapter 38

Margalit was already in her pajamas when one evening Shlomko Weisbrot, whom she liked very much, came to visit. To her disappointment, this time he brought nothing for her. Instead, her parents sat down with him on the edge of the double bed and closed the folding doors between the two rooms. From the tiny slit between the doors, Margalit heard that her parents had turned on the radio, the brown one with the big buttons. Various voices came out of the radio in English, which she understood, thanks to their time in Cyprus. The parents and Shlomko didn't speak and just listened to the broadcast.

Margalit was eight and a half and very clever. Her parents didn't always explain things to her, so she lay quietly in bed in the dark, listening intently to the broadcast. She heard the names of countries read aloud, and each representative of a country in turn said either "Yes" or "No." "United States – Yes. Egypt – No," and so forth.

She was almost asleep when she heard the adults cheering loudly.

"Yes, yes! They passed it!"

She woke up completely, peeked through the slit and saw that Mom, Dad, and Shlomko were hugging each other, their faces radiating great joy. She could no longer resist, so she opened the partition between the rooms.

"What happened?" she asked, her eyes wide open. She had never seen her parents or Shlomko so gripped with joy.

"We have a state! They have recognized us as an independent state for the Jews!" her father shouted.

"Tata, what is a "state" anyway?"

Before her father could answer, her mother opened the French doors to the balcony. They all rushed outside. In the opposite corner, near the Tel- Or cinema, they saw that a crowd had begun to gather.

"We came here, to Eretz Israel, so it would become home for all Jews, and tonight they confirmed it," Papa explained to her. She saw tears in his eyes.

"What, in the middle of the night?" Margalit wondered.

Shlomko stood behind them and wrapped everyone in his big leather coat. "Look what joy is out there," he said. "What happiness!"

It was November 29, 1947. The United Nations had approved the establishment of a Jewish state in the Land of Israel. The people took to the streets en masse to celebrate and rejoice.

From their roof balcony, they watched the dancing circles and heard the words and music of the *hora*, the most popular Israeli dance:

"God will build the Galilee! God will build the Galilee!"

Until that night, Margalit had never seen people dancing in the streets – happy, rejoicing, and celebrating. From the window in Chernowitz she had heard shots and seen people falling to the ground… but *dancing*? This was new to her. Although her parents tried to explain what that joy meant, she didn't really understand. However, she, too, felt the delight and asked her parents if she could go down to the street and join in the dancing. They didn't let her, but neither did they make her go back to bed, despite the late hour.

Margalit's last thought before she fell asleep was that they at last had a home. A smile spread across her small, round face.

The next morning, big trucks rolled down the street, with Arabs shouting in frightening roars, "*Et-bak hayehud!* Slaughter the Jews! Slaughter the Jews!" The joy of the previous night had turned to terror.

That same morning, the War of Independence broke out. The street they lived on, King George, became a transit stop for military vehicles. The soldiers who paused there turned the stairwell in their building into a public urinal. Their apartment was in a strategic location, and from the French door balcony you could see everything that was happening down below. All night there was shelling and gunfire in the area, and the fourth-floor occupants were in grave danger. They couldn't get into the shelter in their building because Mr. Dankner, their neighbor and the owner of Café Allenby, had taken it over and put a ferocious dog in the doorway. There was no way they could run down four flights of stairs, be exposed to the shelling in the street, and race to the nearest available shelter, which was in the Palace Hotel at the corner of King George and Agrippas Streets. In their distress, Machiku and Donya had agreed with their neighbors from the first floor, Dr. Halevi and his wife, that on particularly difficult nights they would go down to sleep in their apartment. That way at least they would be a little more protected than on the fourth floor.

When the alarm sounded, they hurried down the stairs to their neighbors' apartment. The Halevi family laid mattresses on the floor for the Schmelzer family to sleep on.

"Tata, Tata. I'm scared," Margalit said as she clung to her father. "Did you see the fire exploding in the sky?"

"We have sandbags all around the apartment building, so they won't penetrate here," Machiku said, trying to calm her down.

"Mama, I'm afraid," Margalit whispered to Donya. She feared most of all the phosphorus bullets, fired from the direction of the old city, that pierced the darkness of the night. She lay on the mattress hugging Yossi, her little brother, so that he protected her.

She no longer remembered anything about the jackals that surrounded the tent on the Turkish coast. Those fears had faded and were replaced by new ones of the war raging around their very home. Only when the all-clear sounded and a break in the fighting prevailed, was she able to calm down a little.

Margalit took advantage of the respite in the fighting and would run across the street to Mr. Ona's –"Everything for Youngsters" store. She enjoyed reading and had a subscription to the store library. There was a long wooden bench in the store behind which stood the librarian. Opposite her was a shelf full of books with pages worn from reading. Margalit was given special permission to go past the bench and choose the books herself. Later on, she was even allowed to take out more than one.

A world of wonders opened up for her. When she read the three volumes of "Les Miserables," she imagined that she was Cosette, the daughter of Jean Valjean, the protagonist. When she got to Jules Verne's "Twenty Thousand Leagues Under the Sea" and "Around the World in Eighty Days," she fantasized that she was Passepartout operating the hot air balloon. When she read "Memories of the House of David," she could imagine hearing the wheel of torture of the Spanish Inquisition turning to extract a confession from the tortured Jews, and when she read Karl May's books, she was an avenging Native American, scalping the paleface enemy.

The books transported Margalit into a magical world where she was the protagonist, and no shelling could interfere with her illusions. She couldn't budge until she had finished reading the sad ending of "Montezuma's Daughter," "The Adventures of Tom Sawyer," who was trapped in the frightening cave, and the books about the martyrs forced to conceal their Judaism from the evil Grand Inquisitor, Torquemada.

Until the outbreak of the war, every morning Margalit would take the bus to the school in Beit Hakerem. It was cold outside, her hands froze, and on the large windows in the classroom, which were covered with the frost of a Jerusalem November, children wrote with their fingers: "A Hebrew State – Free Immigration."

During the war it was impossible to reach the school because the bus route passed through an Arab neighborhood. For that reason, all the children in the city went to the "Lemmel" girls' school, located in an Arab building that evoked a special atmosphere for its students. During recess, they would go outside, jump rope and play class or five stones. Margalit was a champion at this game, and always asked her parents to buy her more game blocks.

The mix of boys and girls at the school led to Margalit's being teased by the other children. One day when she went out for recess, children stood and sang:

> *"Danny, Danny, don't you cry*
> *You are a very handsome guy*
> *Take Margalit in marital bliss –*
> *And give her a big fat kiss!"*

She was so embarrassed. She didn't like that Danny guy at all! At that age there was still a definite divide between boys and girls.

However, this wasn't the only problem during the war. Food was hard to obtain. To help the citizens, the Israeli Government, led by David Ben-Gurion, imposed a regime of austerity in the country. In the first phase, the government introduced the rationing of food products and basic commodities, followed by clothing and footwear rationing. Allocations were set for each adult, child, and infant.

The allocations were modest. Citizens were required to personally register at grocery stores or dry goods stores in their areas of residence. To oversee the distribution of food, the government issued personal vouchers to each family, and they had to shop at their designated stores for the items listed on the vouchers. Housewives had to improvise to come up with reasonably nourishing, edible meals as varied as possible from the scant commodities they were able to obtain. Meat was not available, nor were fruits and vegetables. Therefore, the residents of Jerusalem would go out to pick *hubeza*, wild spinach, in the fields near their homes. They would crush the seeds of the plant and its leaves and make vegetable patties from it.

Due to the scarcity of products, they used substitutes, cooking tangy-tasting eggplant, using powdered eggs instead of fresh, and diluted margarine instead of butter, among other things.

Not many people had refrigerators at that time, but the Schmelzer family had an icebox. Whenever Machiku heard the iceman ringing his hand bell in the street, he would come downstairs with an elongated mesh basket. The seller would carve out a block of ice for him with a special cleaver, carry it up to the Schmelzer apartment and put it in the icebox.

Donya ate very little. She settled for a slice of white bread with some butter and a cup of coffee that wasn't from coffee beans but from roasted roots extracted from the chicory plant that served as a coffee substitute.

The main delicacies in the house were dishes made by Donya from frozen fish fillets. Margalit couldn't stand the smell of the fish and was miserable every time her mother fried it in a pan.

Once her mother tried to change the recipe. She washed the fish, ground it and made patties out of it.

"Come, Margalitika," she called her daughter. "I made chicken patties."

Margalit sniffed the plate. The patties smelled like fish, but Mama said it was chicken, so it must be. She took a bite and immediately spit it out.

"Phooey!" She stamped her foot. "That's not chicken, it's fish! I won't eat it!"

"It's good for you and it will help you grow," Donya tried to convince her.

"Won't eat it!" her rebellious daughter insisted.

Donya was furious. It was so hard to get the fish on the black market where they bought their groceries despite the rationing, just so the girl would have something nutritious.

"Go into the bathroom right now and stay there until you come out and eat!" she ordered.

Margalit went into the bathroom and her mother locked the door. She sat down on the floor and wept. It wasn't an easy confrontation between mother and daughter. However, in the house where Donya grew up there was no questioning the edicts of the parents. The only time she rebelled against them was when she went with Machiku to get married in another city and her mother, Yetti, had never forgiven her for it.

When the commotion between them subsided a little, Donya called out to Margalit, surprising her with good news.

"Come out Margalitika, this month's coupons have arrived. We're going to the shoe store." Margalit was growing, and it was necessary to buy her shoes and a sweater, but until they got their hands on the coupons, they cut the tips off Margalit's shoes with a sharp knife at the shoemaker's so she could walk in them until the welcome coupons arrived.

Margalit jumped up and left the bathroom.

"And there will be a surprise, too," Donya assured her.

Margalit accompanied her mother, curious and excited. They left the house, went past King George Street to a store on Hillel Street, and bought Margalit new, shiny, high-top brown shoes. The salesman explained how to clean them and gave them shoe polish with a pungent odor.

"What about the surprise?" Margalit asked her mother as they left the shoe store and went down the street. Her mother stopped in front of a shop window where a beautiful sweater was displayed, surrounded by woolen balls in various colors. They went inside.

"How many balls of yarn does it take to make a sweater with a zipper like the one in the window?" Donya asked the sales clerk.

The woman told Margalit to stand in front of her, took a cloth tape measure and measured her height and width.

"Eight will be enough. What color does the girl want? I'll see if I have it."

Margalit wanted her favorite blue. The sales clerk didn't have blue woolen wool, so she was content with a khaki-colored, like soldiers' uniforms. Her mother bought the eight woolen tubers and two pairs of knitting needles.

When they got home, Donya said to her, "Sit here next to me and I'll teach you how to knit. That way you'll have a new sweater that we'll have made together."

It was the first time that Margalit had done any handicrafts. Thus far, she had used a spool of yarn and woven a colorful little snake or an embroidered napkin for Shabbat. She found that she really liked doing handicrafts, and at school it was her favorite subject. One could make all kinds of beautiful things, in many shapes and colors.

"Your grandmother Yetti was an excellent embroiderer, knitter, and seamstress. Do you remember Baba Yetti's pillow that we forgot to take with us when we ran away?" Donya sighed longingly.

"Sure," Margalit replied, and the sorrow soon appeared in her eyes.

"Never mind, never mind," her mother comforted her. "Let's sit and knit together."

They sat on the bed in the living room. Donya showed her how to raise "eyes" – loops in the wool – and how to put a crochet hook inside the eyes and twist it around with the woolen thread between the knitting needles. Together they created a new sweater for Margalit.

Chapter 39

Not only bullets and mortar shells landed on Jerusalem. There were terrorist and retaliatory attacks by Arabs and the British in Israel's struggle for independence.

The echoes from these attacks were heard clearly inside the Schmelzer family's apartment, located in the city center.

Margalit remembered the muffled but powerful noise heard on February 1, 1948. The Arabs – with the help of the British – blew up the editorial offices of the "Palestine Post" newspaper on Hasolel Street in Jerusalem.

The English language newspaper's principal aim was to give the public in Eretz Israel daily information on Jews in the Diaspora and inside the country. It was also intended to provide basic knowledge of Judaism and Zionism to officials of the British Government in Palestine.

The blast killed four people and injured 30 others.

On February 22, 1948, Margalit awoke early, at six in the morning. She lay curled up, happy to remain a little longer in bed, keeping warm in the Jerusalem winter. She liked to use her imagination and think special thoughts. That morning she was calculating how many cards she had accumulated from a special series for children and had pasted in a booklet. At that time, there were many kinds of collections, such as "prizes" , shiny cardboard figures of angels and animals, or "golds" , foil paper in different shades that were used as wrappers for chocolate candies. Each prize or gold foil was pressed flat with the fingers until well stretched, and then placed between the pages of a thick book. Whoever had two "golds" of the same type could trade it with friends.

The folding door separating the children's room from the master bedroom was open. She saw her father on the edge of the double bed pulling on his elastic compression socks that reached his knees and covered the prominent veins in his legs.

Margalit knew those veins. They were thick and protruding like the bark of a tree. On top of them, her father wore khaki socks and brown shoes with laces. She saw him yawn and start to get up, when suddenly she felt a strong tremor shake her bed. This was followed by a tremendous roar, like rolling thunder.

"Donika, quick! Take Yossi and run to the stairwell!" shouted her father.

He leaped towards Margalit, pulled her up out of bed and ran, carrying her to the stairwell. She was shivering and didn't understand what was happening. They began to run down to the ground floor. Again, a tremendous boom. The glass in the Belgian windows shattered, filling the stairwell with shards. As they ran, the crackling of the shards was heard under her father's shoes. Margalit was eight and a half years old at the time and couldn't believe that her father had the strength to pick her up and carry her down to a secure area.

Ambulance sirens shrieked from up the street. People ran back and forth in panic.

"What was that? What happened?" Shouting was coming from everywhere.

Dust clouds in the air and a strong smell of burning spread reached the stairwell.

"Maybe there's a fire," said Donya. "It sounds like it was an explosion," answered Machiku.

"It's on Ben-Yehuda Street!" shouted someone who took shelter in the entrance to the building.

The noise finally subsided. Machiku, Donya, and the children slowly went back upstairs although it was difficult getting through the broken glass. Extremely cold air came in through the broken windows as they struggled up to their apartment. When they got to their floor, the sight awaiting them was ghastly. The front door had been torn off its hinges and there was enormous damage inside. The wall that separated their apartment from that of the neighbors, where Yossi's bed was, had collapsed. The bed was smashed to pieces, and various sized fragments were all over the floor.

They stood surveying the damage, scarcely able to believe their eyes. Margalit was in pajamas, barefoot and trembling; Donya was in her nightgown as pale as limestone, holding Yossi in her arms. Had it not been for Machiku's quick thinking and agility, Yossi and Margalit would most likely have been lying on the floor in the rubble.

"Good Lord!" Donya lamented. "Thank God we got away in time!"

Machiku was silent and hugged her.

"Straight from Europe in flames to a country at war," Donya added.

"Yes, but this is our homeland," Machiku added.

Donya shook her head. Yossi, the first sabra of the family, named after Grandpa Yossel, who was buried in Vienna, lay curled up in her arms. They made their way through the rubble to the tiny balcony, from where they could see the commotion below. Clouds of dust and smoke rose from Ben Yehuda Street and the demolished Orion Cinema. Ambulances with howling sirens arrived to evacuate the dead and wounded from the ruins.

Later that day, state inspectors arrived at their apartment to estimate the repairs to the stairwell windows, and they contracted workers to rebuild the collapsed walls in the apartment.

It later became known that at 6:00 a.m. that day, a convoy of three trucks escorted by a British armored vehicle had entered Ben-Yehuda Street. The convoy stopped in front of the Atlantic Hotel, and the truck drivers boarded the armored vehicle and drove away. The explosive charge weighed four hundred kilograms. It was planned by Arabs and executed by deserters from the British army who stole the vehicles. There were forty-nine dead, more than one hundred and forty wounded, including families with children, and heavy damage was done to all the buildings in the vicinity.

Many miraculous things happened to Machiku during the War of Independence for Eretz Israel. On one occasion when he was in the kitchen washing dishes, the soap fell on the floor. As he stooped to pick it up, a bullet fired from outside whistled in the air above his head. Another time, as he sat in his usual place at the head of the table, he got up to fetch a fork and a bullet pierced the back of his chair, lodging itself in the opposite wall.

However, the biggest miracle happened about a month after the Ben-Yehuda explosion.

Twice a week, Machiku would walk from his office in Beit Yahalom to the JNF management headquarters in the courtyard of the National Institutions. There he would have senior officials sign the purchase and land registration documents he had prepared.

On the morning of March 11, 1948, Machiku finished having the documents signed and set off for his office in Beit Yahalom.

A short distance from the courtyard, he bumped into Mr. Spitzer, an old acquaintance.

"How are you, Arieh? We haven't seen each other in a long time." Spitzer was glad to see Machiku, who was called "Arieh" by everyone in Israel.

"I'm fine. Running errands as usual," Machiku replied with his wide smile.

"What do you think about the hard times we're going through?"

"Well, it's not easy. We already went through war, famine, and immense distress before we came. We didn't expect the enormity of conflict and terrorist attacks we would have to go through here."

"Yes, I understand. But our goal is independence, to establish our own state."

"Unfortunately, neither the Arabs nor the British want to accept that."

"And how is the family? How are the children?"

"Striving to live and enjoy what we have."

They parted with a handshake. Machiku continued towards Beit Yahalom, and Spitzer continued walking into the courtyard of the National Institutions.

The shock wave from a huge blast reverberated off Machiku's body, throwing him down onto the sidewalk. His head hit the concrete, but he was fully conscious and suffered only minor bruises.

Again, it was a car bomb that exploded.

The Arab driver for the U.S. consulate was known to the building security guards. They suspected nothing when he parked the car in the yard and got out "for just a minute to buy cigarettes." One of the guards moved the car from blocking the middle of the yard to nearer the Keren Hayesod building. Just at that moment the bomb went off. Twelve people were killed, and forty-four were injured. Machiku got up and ran, moving through the broken glass and rubble to help the wounded, who lay screaming on the ground.

"Machiku," Donya asked when he got home, "did you hear what happened in the courtyard of the National Institutions?"

Only then did the realization sink in that he could have been the one killed instead of his friend Spitzer. "God protected me," he replied.

The conflict dragged on.

The War of Independence was in full swing. For Machiku and Donya this was a repeat of what they had already been through. They were deprived and hungry again, only this time they had two small children to feed and care for. Another difference between the two wars was the goal. This wasn't a war in the Diaspora, but one in their own country. Here, one had not only to survive, but also to live and thrive. Here, they didn't go underground and hide; everything to achieve an independent state was done openly. This difference was evident even in Donya's attitude. She occasionally sang to herself words from "*Hatikva*," the national anthem, "to be a free people in our own country."

However, the contrast between the two wars didn't obliterate the bitter memories of the previous one. One morning Machiku heard the bell of the municipal water truck. He peeked out the window and saw the truck parked by the building.

"Water, water!" the driver announced.

Machiku took the jerrycan he had prepared in advance and ran down the hundred steps from the fourth floor to street level. Water was scarce in besieged Jerusalem. There was a long line of excited people holding jerrycans and metal buckets. Machiku looked around, stricken by a horrific memory.

"Almost like in the ghetto," he said to the man in front of him in the line.

"Ghetto? What is a ghetto?" A young woman broke into the conversation. She was holding a three-year-old girl in one hand, a jerrycan in the other.

"I'm from Europe. There was war," Machiku explained.

"Yes? But really, what is a ghetto?" A young redhead joined the conversation as well.

"They don't know," thought Machiku. "But how can they not know? Didn't they know anything here in Eretz Israel?"

"When the Germans entered our city, they ordered all Jews to move to a specified enclosed area and live there, not to work or leave."

"Yes, but where did they live?"

"Their homes were confiscated by the Romanians, who were in charge of the city and cooperated with the Nazis. Anyone who had an apartment within the prescribed ghetto area was ordered to take in as many residents as possible from other areas in the city."

"Ah, he's from there," said an older woman listening to the exchange. "I've heard about people who came from there. Poor things, they're not really well."

Machiku started to respond, but just then it was his turn for the water and the conversation ended. It was more important to bring the water home than to educate those around him.

Every drop of the precious water was utilized. First, they filled a pot with water for cooking. Then some was poured into the sink for laundry and dishes. The dirty dish water was used to wash out the toilets. Only once a week could they permit themselves to bathe. They heated water in a jug on the stove, added some cold water and poured the contents over Margalit, washing her hair and body, the water flowing down from her head.

"Oh, oh, it's hot, it's burning," Margalit howled.

She apologized for the outburst after Donya dried her hair with a towel, plaited it into two braids, and tied ribbons to the ends.

Chapter 40

Jerusalem remained under siege for a long time. The road leading up to the city was dominated by Arab villagers and constantly shelled. Whenever a convoy of armored vehicles tried to break through, the Arabs shot at it and the vehicles were set on fire with the occupants inside. There was a shortage of water and food in the city, and the inhabitants were in despair. What if we lose this war? A small number of Israeli soldiers stood against the armies of seven Arab countries. Arabs stood by the fences within the borders of the country and made the sign of cutting the Jews' throats with their thumbs.

On Saturday at noon, the Voice of Israel radio station launched a new program during which listeners could request songs. There was a big demand for the iconic Yaffa Yarkoni's comforting voice performing the poet laureate Haim Gouri "*Bab El Wad*" – the Arabic name for where the battles took place on the road to Jerusalem:

Bab el Wad,

> *Remember our names for all time.*
> *Where convoys to the city broke through*
> *Our dead lie sprawled on the roadside.*

The iron skeleton, like my comrade, is mute.
Words: Haim Gouri, Tune: Shmulik Preshko, Translated
by Vivian Eden

The war seemed to go on forever.

One Saturday morning in June 1948, Margalit awoke to the sounds of singing and rejoicing coming from the street. She hurried to the balcony and couldn't believe her eyes. There were soldiers in military uniforms wearing woolen caps, happy and cheering.

"What's going on?" her mother shouted to the street below.

"We broke through to Jerusalem!" cried a young soldier. Everyone echoed him joyfully.

Donya, Machiku, and the children got dressed quickly and ran downstairs. Mr. Dankner, the owner of Café Allenby, had deemed the event important enough to open his café and offer free ice cream to everyone.

"How did you do it?" Margalit asked a soldier nearby, who was enjoying his ice cream.

"We broke through a new road that our forces paved, so we didn't have to go past the Arab villages."

"From now on, Jerusalem will receive supplies. You'll have food, and water will flow again," another soldier added. "Thank God," said Donya. "It was bad here. We were hungry and thirsty all the time."

"And dirty, too, because there wasn't enough water for a bath," Margalit added, smiling. She smiled all the time. The school's principal, David Benvenisti, even wrote in her little school diary at the end of the year "Dear Margalit, may your sweet smile always be with you."

Happy and content, the family climbed back up to their apartment. There was singing and dancing in the streets. The next day teachers had the students write an essay about the event. Margalit wrote, "Our boys broke through to Jerusalem."

Mama and Papa always spoke beautiful Hebrew. She imitated them, and so she would say "our boys," "our heroes," or "our soldiers."

Nevertheless, the joy was short-lived. The fighting continued. Fierce battles broke out in various parts of the country – in the Negev, at Latrun, everywhere. Inside Jerusalem, too, the conflict went on interminably.

One day a truck came into the street and unloaded beautiful brown and black pianos, some even shining with varnish. Margalit ran outside and shouted: "Papa, Mama, please can we buy a piano? I won't have to practice at the teacher's house. She doesn't let me play any Hebrew songs, only classical music – Mozart, Beethoven, and Debussy."

The parents went downstairs and found out that these pianos were looted from the homes of Arabs who had fled the Katamon neighborhood. Each piano was for sale at a price of 500 Lira. Machiku and Donya returned home mortified.

"Did you buy one? Did you?" Margalit shouted as she ran towards them.

"Would you want to play a piano that a poor Arab girl had to abandon when her family ran away?" her father asked her. "We don't do that. In the Bible it is written that it is forbidden to take an enemy's possessions."

For her father, it was a moral issue; for her, it was a great disappointment. Many other Jewish parents bought the looted pianos for their children – and they played them.

***

At last, the war was over.

Margalit had to part with a collection she had carefully nurtured.

Since the apartment they lived in was in a strategic location, the tiny French balcony was at the center of activity; they could see everything happening on their own street and on others nearby. The roof also made the apartment vulnerable.

However, the apartment, which was on the fourth floor, drew sniper fire from the direction of the Old City and the Sheikh Jarrah neighborhood. The "roof penthouse" adjacent to the apartment was a constant target for mortar shrapnel and bullet casings. Margalit gathered this bounty and stashed it in a cloth bag tied with a thin string. When a ceasefire was declared and residents were instructed to hand in shrapnel to police stations, it was a great loss for her. "Tata, why did we have to give them up? They were wonderful souvenirs."

"An order is an order," replied her father, a real *yekke* who wouldn't hear of any deviation from proper behavior.

"What about the bullet that went over your head when you got up from the chair after dinner, yesterday? Do we have to give that up?"

"Yes, that one, too."

"And the one that came from Sheikh Jarrah when you bent down to pick up the dish soap in the kitchen?"

"That too."

From the entire collection of souvenirs, all Margalit had left was a memory.

There was a big surprise one day when Machiku came home carrying a big, heavy package in a cardboard carton. He could barely climb the hundred steps that led to their apartment and came inside sweating and panting.

"What is it, what is it, Tata?" Margalit jumped up.

"A package from America," he gasped.

"What's in it? Who sent it?" She was enthralled.

"Judging by the weight, they sent us stones." Machiku laughed and turned to his wife. "We've got enough of our own stones in this country. I even had to pay customs for it."

Donya smiled. She and Margalit came closer. Machiku undid the twine around the package while they tried to peel off the adhesive tape strip by strip.

Grandma Yetti had two brothers, Sammy and Aaron, who had fled Vienna to America. They had heard about the economic hardship of new immigrants in Palestine and decided to send Leon and Donya a package to aid them.

Machiku and Donya finally managed to unpack the carton. Inside were shiny fabrics, pairs of shoes and some cans. Donya went through the pile of clothes, picking up each item one by one.

The first thing she grabbed was a silk dress with shiny red suspenders.

"Oh well, this will be fine for going down King George Street in the Purim parade," she joked.

Margalit put the dress over her mother's chest and they both burst out laughing.

Next was a dress skirt of see-through gauze. Margalit measured it against herself. It reached down to the floor. From among the shoes, she found a pair of high heels, and she made a show for her parents as if she were a nightclub dancer.

Then came the best one of all.

"Black and white patent leather men's shoes!" exclaimed Machiku. "Who am I, Charlie Chaplin?"

He put on his shoes and began to imitate the funny walk of the famous comedian, who he had seen in silent films before the War of Independence at the Studio Cinema in Jerusalem.

After they stopped laughing, they decided to look at what was in the cans their relatives had sent. Machiku got out his amazing Swiss Army knife and opened one of them.

A cloudy white mass was revealed.

"What is it, God help us?" Donya stared at Machiku.

Before he could answer, Yossi stuck his finger in the can and licked it. "Mmm ... sweet, delicious," he said.

"Unbelievable," Machiku replied to Donya. "They sent us sweet, condensed milk."

They each stuck their fingers in the can for a taste of the sweetness.

"Well, at least for that it was worth carrying the carton all the way up here," laughed Machiku.

"I wonder what they were thinking there in New York," Donya pondered. "We should wear these clown clothes, dance around in fancy shoes licking condensed milk off our fingers?"

They all laughed, but Machiku suddenly became serious, realizing the irony of their situation. The kind uncles had sent their poor relatives second-hand clothing they wouldn't even wear there.

"They had good intentions," Donya said to soothe his distress.

They pushed the package underneath the bed and went back to the reality of their austere lives in the shadow of war.

Chapter 41

The activity that Donya was involved in wasn't enough to satisfy her after so many years of not doing anything outside the home. "I should give more," she thought. She contacted WIZO in Jerusalem, and they referred a few young women to her who had immigrated to Israel after the Holocaust. None of their families had survived. A place for them to live was arranged at Beit Hachalutzot in Jerusalem. With Donya's help, the girls were sent for vocational training to help them rebuild their lives.

Bruria was one such girl, young, delicate, and graceful, with curly hair and brown eyes. When they met, Bruria hardly spoke a word, not about her past life or what had happened to her family. The warmth coming from Donya, who had herself known suffering, managed to melt Bruria's heart.

"Let's think about what you can study and have a skill to earn a living from," said Donya on one of Bruria's visits to the Schmelzers' apartment. They sat at the makeshift table in the living room. Donya poured her a cup of sweet compote with plums, apple slices, and pudding powder. The dish was a treat for the girl, who didn't have much to eat. She smiled gratefully and said shyly, "I would like to be a nurse."

"That's great," the overjoyed Donya told her. "It's a wonderful profession. There will always be a need for nurses here, where there is constant unrest and attacks on the Jews. It is also a vocation for the soul – giving to others as much as possible. I think you'll love it."

Donya contacted WIZO, where, as always, they helped by getting her into nursing school with a modest scholarship. Bruria continued her visits to Donya.

The nursing school experience enabled her to open up to others. She began to talk enthusiastically about her studies, friendships, the people she met, and how interesting it was to carry out the tasks she was given at the hospital.

By the time the War of Independence had broken out, Bruria had almost completed her training. It was hard for her to get time off for visits, but whenever she could, she sat down with Donya and Machiku and told them about the wounded she was treating. Many injured soldiers were brought to the hospital and it was sad that some of them had no families. The moment they had arrived in Israel they were taken into the army and sent to the front lines. These young men were so very lonely. The heart ached for them. There was no one who came to visit, and no one to encourage them, to help them recover.

One day Bruria arrived and she and Donya went out on the improvised "penthouse" balcony. Her eyes lowered, her face flushed, she said to Donya: "I've become acquainted with one of the wounded soldiers. We want to get married, but there is no way we can."

"But that's terrific," Donya exclaimed. "I'm so happy for you. Family and children are the most wonderful thing in the world." For a moment her mind drifted back to her wedding in Bucharest, alone with Machiku, without friends or family.

She would help Bruria and her heart's desire. They would marry at their home and she and Machiku would be the sponsors. She'll make sure that it's a joyous occasion, and prayed that Bruria had found a loving husband, someone who would care for Bruria the way Machiku cared for her.

"But we have no place to live. He cannot be in Beit Hechalutz; it's only for women."

"Don't worry. We'll help you as if you were our own daughter."

"His name is Yaakov, and he's an orphan. He's still in the army, but before that, he drove for the Egged Bus Company."

Bruria managed to bring Yaakov to meet the Schmelzers, and Donya decided to organize the event.

"We can set up the *chuppah* , thewedding canopy, outside on the roof. We'll get the refreshments donated from cafés here on the street, and the Army rabbi will come and perform the ceremony," Donya enthused.

She mobilized all her organizational skills for the wedding. The only obstacle was the ongoing fighting.

Then on June 1, a cease-fire was declared. It was just before Margalit's birthday.

On a pleasant summer afternoon, the tiny apartment was filled with soldiers in uniform and wool caps and some of Bruria's friends from Beit Hachalutzot. Rabbi Shlomo Goren, later chief rabbi of the IDF , came and performed the ceremony.

Margalit remembered this wedding for many years. She remembered the joy of life amid the grueling war and the exceedingly intimate blessings for the newlyweds that made the young soldiers burst out laughing – although at the time she didn't understand why.

Chapter 42

After the war, Donya began a steady job. This was another step towards shedding the image of the new immigrant.

As the children grew older, the need for Donya's constant care diminished. She was left with time on her hands and decided to seek work outside the home. She found a position at a government project to enhance children's nutrition. She first served as chief assistant and then put in charge of the budget and organization of nutrition in school kitchens. They traveled around the country, mainly to development towns where there were hungry children who weren't even familiar with noodles or bread. They succeeded in getting contributions of food products such as milk powder, egg powder, and fish fillets, from various organizations.

"Machiku," she would say, her eyes sparkling with joy, "I took part in setting up a cocoa project."

"What, some kind of factory? Who built it?"

"It's not an industrial building. It is just a 'project.' Every day at ten o'clock the children receive a roll and a cup of cocoa in school."

"Where do you do it?"

"We've set up one hundred and fifty kitchens around the country and trained nutrition teachers to work in them. We also receive surplus food and assistance from the Hadassah Women's Organization."

"I'm glad, and very proud of you," Machiku told her. He had not forgotten the times when he had fed her, sure that he would lose her. Now they took pride in their work, their creativity, and the shared overcoming of obstacles and difficulties.

For the next ten years Donya worked on the nutrition project and did much to build it up.

Later on, Donya received an offer from Zalman Shazar, Israel's first Minister of Education, to work as head of the ministry's culture budget, supervised by Yitzhak Navon.

Navon initiated a project to alleviate ignorance and illiteracy among new immigrants. He often told how he had taught his own mother to read and write. It was extremely important for him to contribute in this way to the advancement of the country's citizens. In school, groups of adults attended classes after regular school hours, taught by specially trained young women soldiers.

Donya then moved on to set up an organization to aid writers and artists.

From every manager she served under, the diligent, sharp-witted Donya learned new things. She devoted herself to her work and saw it as a mission. A highpoint was when a new project, "Art for the People", was initiated Its goal was enriching the cultural lives of adults and children throughout the country via theatrical performances for them.

"It's important for me not to dwell on the past and be filled with hate as a result of what we went through. Not to forget, but neither to allow the Holocaust to stop us from fully living our lives. Instead, I engage in giving to others. For me, it's like water to quench the thirst," Donya told Machiku.

Machiku nodded, knowing exactly how she felt. He saw before him the young Donya who had come into his office. With her determination and seriousness, she made her way into his heart and is the mother of his children. He loved and treasured her very much.

Chapter 43

The letter telling him of his mother's death reached Machiku many months after it occurred. The Iron Curtain had hindered such correspondence and only then did he learn what had happened.

"We need to move to Romania," Bubbi told his wife Clara one day in mid-1946.

"But we're in Romania, in Chernowitz."

"Our city is tossed from hand to hand like in a card game. Each time there are fewer cards left in the deck. In the post-war arrangements, Chernowitz has been annexed to Ukraine, so we have an option either to move to Romania proper or stay in Chernowitz under Ukrainian rule."

"How much longer will we have to move back and forth like this?" Clara complained.

"We're lucky the Soviets are back. I heard that in February, when the Germans were still here, they had planned to exterminate all the Jews left in the city."

Clara shuddered at the thought but found it difficult to have to leave her home again.

"The Soviets are already here, so why not just remain? I have no desire to pick up and move again."

"I want to go to Bucharest, the capital. There are a lot more options there."

"What about my sisters and their families?" Clara asked.

"We'll take them with us."

Neither of them had yet mentioned Mammu Regina. Bubbi organized everything. He was big and strong, and a wealthy man. After being appointed bank manager, he amassed a lot of gold and hid it in a secret place. He then sent his daughter, Ruth, to Bucharest, wearing a big, heavy coat with a huge amount of cash hidden in its lining. Who would check inside the coat of a twenty-year-old beauty with big green eyes and velvet skin? The family, he decided, would follow.

Only then did he talk about it with his mother.

"Mama," Bubbi said to Mammu Regina, "I have to tell you something." She was used to the sound of his thunderous voice and his decisions of all kinds, but didn't anticipate what he was going to tell her this time. "We're leaving Chernowitz and moving to Bucharest."

"How can I leave my home and all my memories and go somewhere new?" his mother replied, startled.

"You won't have to move," Bubbi said quietly. "My sister Lottie will stay with you in our apartment."

Regina looked at him sadly, tears in her eyes. At her age, she didn't cry easily, although she had suffered numerous calamities over the years.

"Do you mean to leave me here alone with all the violence and harsh Ukrainian regime? We have seen enough of the murders, robberies, and rapes they committed here."

"They won't bother you," Bubbi tried to convince her, "I'll leave you money and see to it that you have plenty of food."

"But Lottie can't take care of me. She herself needs support with her disabled son."

"I don't want to argue about it," Bubbi declared. "We're moving, and you'll be fine."

Regina knew Bubbi well. If he had decided on something, nothing would change his mind. Children, she thought to herself, should take care of themselves and their own children. It's painful, but it's the way of the world. She was smart and experienced, yet her aching heart affected her proud demeanor. But she would say nothing, nor would she whine to her son like some poor servant.

Bubbi, Clara, and their children left the house, and it emptied out all at once. A strange silence prevailed. After years of living in overcrowding and noise in her house adjacent to the ghetto, which she had generously offered to family and strangers, the silence was deafening. She had no appetite, but wandering through the empty rooms, she thought she heard the voice of Litti, her granddaughter. Maybe it's just her imagination?

She was cold, and there was no one to bring in wood from the yard and light the fireplace for her. Had there been someone, she would have discovered that the wood was no longer there.

Over time, Lottie, her son Yoji, and her husband, Izu, emptied the food storage Bubbi had left for her. One day Lottie came to her with news of her own.

"Mother," she told her, "we're leaving. We'll stay in the village and from there we'll try to get permits to travel to Palestine."

Regina had expected this to happen and didn't say a word. "My God," she thought. "You have forsaken me here. Now no one will know when I take my last breath." She thought of Machiku. She didn't even know what had happened to him. Is he alive? What about Donya and Litti? Did they ever reach Palestine? She had no news from there. She didn't even know whether to sit *shiva* or not. These days she spoke often only to God, Machiku, and with Yossel, her late husband, whom she had not addressed in a long time. All day she wandered in and out of the empty rooms, awaiting redemption.

when he received news of Mammu's death, Machiku sat shiva. He pictured her with the white hair gathered back, wearing the long floral print dress she loved, and her warm eyes looking up at him adoringly. An indescribable sorrow engulfed him.

"What could you have done?" Donya said, feeling his pain. She loved her smart, sensitive, generous mother-in-law so much that she saw her as a second mother. "You had to go. If not, we wouldn't be alive today."

"I'll never forgive Bubbi," Machiku blurted out, his face grim. "How could he leave an old woman alone in a huge, cold, damp house without food and no way to light the fireplace? Or maybe he thought the gold coins he left her would keep her alive?"

"Are you angry with Bubbi or with yourself?" Donya dared to ask.

"Of course I'm angry with myself. I was the first to run away. In my heart I knew I would never see her again, that I would be leaving her in a family of selfish, hard-hearted people. They would always take care of themselves first."

"What choice did you have? You had to protect me and your daughter. You knew that otherwise sooner or later we would be killed and our bodies thrown into the Prut River like so many others."

"Donika, it's a millstone around my neck. At night I see Mammu lying huddled in bed, alone, deserted. I'll never forgive Bubbi. Couldn't he have arranged a safe place for her? Maybe take her with the rest of his wife's family? Or even stay there with her?"

"I, too, am very sad about Regina's death," Donya lamented, leaning softly on him, wiping away her tears.

"My dear Mammu, I would not wish such an end even to my enemies. A person has rights in this life. She was a noble woman, always looking to help others and give to those in need. In the end she was left with no one to close her eyes and say *"kaddish"* ,the prayer for the death of a close relative.

"You don't know what the circumstances were. Maybe Bubbi had no other choice. If you could forgive him, maybe you could also forgive yourself."

However, it was very difficult for Machiku to forgive his brother for such an affront to their mother, especially since he believed that Bubbi did indeed have a choice.

Chapter 44

They were granted a bit of comfort when the Iron Curtain began to open and Donya's mother, Grandma Yetti, immigrated to Israel. The day before her ship arrived at Haifa Port, everyone went to sleep at the house of Lottie and Cousin Harry, whose father and Yetti's husband were brothers. Mama, Papa, Margalit, and Yossi lay down to sleep broadside on the cousins' double bed, a funny experience.

Machiku and Donya had not seen Grandma Yetti since fleeing Chernowitz eight years earlier, and they were very excited. Grandma Yetti was born in the town of Buczacz in Galicia, where she had been a friend of the author Shmuel Yosef Czaczkes, later the Nobel Prize laureate Shai Agnon.

She was the only surviving parent, the only family member who could tell them what had happened in Chernowitz after they left.

Margalit didn't remember her, just as she didn't recall anything she went through until the age of six. She remembered only "Baba Yetti's pillow," but her parents' excitement affected her, too.

In the morning, the whole family hurried to the port. A large ship docked in the harbor and a gangway was lowered. A tiny woman with white hair pulled back in a bun slowly descended. She wore heavy stockings. One foot was in a cast and she used a cane. Margalit approached her and was greeted with a pair of blue-gray eyes set in a kindly, wrinkled face.

Grandma Yetti had come alone. When they asked her what had happened to Grandpa Hersch Zvi, she told them that from the overwhelming joy at receiving their permit to immigrate, he had a heart attack and died on the eve of the *Simchat Torah* holiday,Donya froze, not only from the news of her father's death, but because of its haunting date.Every year on Simchat Torah, the Schmelzer family had gone to the Yeshurun Synagogue in Jerusalem for the dancing and singing around the Torah in a circle. It was always a happy occasion marking the end of the cyclical reading of the Torah and the beginning of a new cycle. In Israel, on the eve of Simchat Torah that year, Donya lay in bed and told Margalit that she wasn't in the mood to go to synagogue for the festivities. She sent her alone with Machiku. She could not have known that her father died that very evening, but she seemed to sense it. The connection to our parents is always with us, even if we're not conscious of it.

The whole family returned to Jerusalem with Grandma Yetti. Yossi, Margalit, and Grandma were in one room, the parents in the other. At night they would close the folding doors between the rooms.

Grandma had brought with her a crate that contained treasures, including "Baba Yetti's pillow" in all its splendor, and a strawberry-colored embroidered duvet, like the ones made for brides. In its lining coins were sewn as a portent of future wealth. And there were also photographs. Margalit saw, for the first time, what she looked like as a baby; what her grandparents looked like when they were in Chernowitz; her parents on their wedding day; and her again, a few days before the escape from Chernowitz.

When she arrived in Israel, Yetti resumed her embroidery. She bought thread and yarn in various colors and made tapestries that were works of art similar to those seen only in the palaces of European kings.

Margalit and her grandmother soon got to know each other well. Yetti spoke Yiddish to her and Margalit answered in German.

Gradually, Margalit learned Yiddish from her; she had always loved languages, so she learned quickly.

There was a library of Yiddish books in Jerusalem, and Grandma sent her to take out books for her. When Margalit was already comfortable in Yiddish, she would let her read books from the library. Margalit loved historical novels. She read about "Rabbi Shmil from Córdoba," one of the outstanding sages of the Golden Age of the Jews in Spain, and the wonderful tales of Sholem Aleichem, whose works were translated into Hebrew, entranced her. Nevertheless, nothing could compare to the juiciness of the Yiddish images. For example, instead of "Don't interfere with arguing couples," Sholem Aleichem wrote, "Jewish rabbi: Never get into bed between man and wife."

After she finished a book, Grandma would talk with her about it, about love and Judaism and the relationship between them. Her grandmother, on her own, would sit by the window and read from *Tz'enah Ur'enah*, known as the "Woman's Bible" for her generation.

The Schmelzer's home was a traditional Jewish home, but Grandma Yetti was stricter than her children on the rules of *kashrut* , what you are permitted to eat, and the separation of dairy and meat. For example, on the tin plates they used, she etched on the back the letter 'D' for dairy, and 'M' for meat dishes.

On Friday evenings, Margalit would accompany her grandmother to the *Oneg Shabbat* reception at the Yeshurun Synagogue. She loved this Jewish tradition. Grandma taught her the meanings of the prayers, and the melodies she sang to her were sealed within her heart.

On Saturday mornings, Grandma's footsteps would be heard on her way to the synagogue wearing the high-top shoes she had brushed thoroughly on Friday. She would wear a fancy floral dress and a hat bought from Ms. Horowitz, the well-known Jerusalem milliner.

During the High Holy Days of Rosh Hashanah and Yom Kippur, Margalit would sit in the women's section of the synagogue next to her mother and grandmother. The synagogue was large and built with stadium seating, tiered rows of benches. When the cantor was in a hurry to get through the service, some of the women would lose their place in the *siddur*, the prayer book. Grandma Yetti would dispatch Margalit from siddur to siddur to show the worshipers where they were in the prayers. Margalit secretly called herself "Grandma's Assistant."

And thus, a special relationship was woven between the only surviving grandparent, her granddaughter Margalit, and her grandson Yossi.

Chapter 45

Margalit experienced an important breakthrough when her acting talent was discovered. While in Cyprus, she had learned to recite texts dramatically. When the teacher discovered this, she occasionally let her read aloud to the class. Her friends admired her precise pronunciation and clear, pleasing voice.

Over time, one of the teachers at the school organized a troupe that performed every Friday at the assembly in the school's large playground. The children lined up according to class. They would begin by singing the morning anthem, followed by calisthenics to the accompaniment of "The Port Song – In the Distance Ships Are Sailing." It was a good, healthy way to start the day.

At the end of the gymnastic exercises, the school troupe would perform.

Margalit was no longer the immigrant girl in the eyes of her friends. Her participation in the troupe improved her social status, and her dramatic talent became something she cherished all her life. She loved these performances more than anything. On Fridays they would read the Torah portion of the week, combining it with a Zionist song of the day:

In the mountains the sun is blazing
In the valley still shines the dew.
What more can we give you than this,
A Homeland we love so true.
Words: Natan Alterman, Tune: Daniel Sambursky,
Translated by the author

***

There were special presentations on the holidays. The most elaborate of these was the ceremony for Shavuot. In preparation, the students would arrive at school early so as not to be roasted in the scorching sun.

In the agricultural settlements and in the *kibbutzim* they brought products sown and harvested there. In cities like Jerusalem, the "first fruits" were purchased at the Mahane Yehuda open-air market and placed in straw baskets.

The entertainment troupe got up on the roof of the school building. Yehoram Gaon, later an iconic national singer, dressed in white as the High Priest, would turn to his 'flock' and ask, "Children of Israel, have you brought the first fruits?"

And the crowd would answer, "We have, we have! We labored hard, from the rock and the flint."

Then Yehoram would raise his hands to the heavens and sing in his warm, soothing voice, "Look upon us from Your sanctuary on High, and bless Thy People Israel."

Margalit loved these ceremonies so much that she was prepared to get up at six in the morning and rehearse for hours in the hot sun.

One day, the school troupe was invited to perform on Shavuot before all the school children of Jerusalem. The presentation took place on Shavuot in the courtyard of the National Institutions in Jerusalem, the JNF and Keren Hayesod.

Papa, who was now called Arieh, still worked for the JNF as a clerk in the legal department and could not have asked for a more fitting holiday gift from his daughter. Despite his rich experience as a lawyer, he couldn't practice law in Israel, as he didn't have a license. The red carpet he had hoped for from the JNF leadership came down to a job as a clerk. Still, he appreciated his good fortune in being able to make a living and never complained.

The troupe's Shavuot performance was in the courtyard outside the main office where the JNF, the enterprise of his life, was located. He invited Mama, now called Yehudit, to join him in one of the offices. They both stood at the window and watched the scene below. In the yard were scores of children dressed in white with wreaths on their heads and carrying baskets of fruits and vegetables. The troupe, led by the "High Priest" as in the days of the Temple, stood on the roof of the building. Margalit proclaimed:

With baskets on our shoulders, our heads adorned with
wreaths,
We come with first fruits from the corners of the land.
Words: Levin Kipnis, Tune: Yedidyah Admon, Translated
by the author

The school children answered in song:

From Judea and Samaria,
From the valleys and Galilee,
Make way, make way, we bear first fruits
Hup, hup, with flute and drum.

The children didn't understand what they were singing. Weren't
these baskets from the local market filled with the best produce
of the land? Papa Arieh-Leon and Mama Donya-Judith stood
embracing at the second-floor window.

"Donika, we're here, in our homeland," said Machiku.

"Yes, the ancestral Promised Land," Donya said as she snuggled
up to him.

Epilogue
Three Graves

Grandfather Yossel's Grave

My grandfather Yossel fled to Vienna during World War I, died there, and was buried in the Great Cemetery of Vienna. In 1985 my mother made me this offer:

"I'm inviting you for a trip to Germany and Austria where I can show you the culture of the world I grew up in."

"Mama," I told her, "I can't. A hidden fear engulfs me." Until then, I had not set foot in Germany.

"We'll take Eli, your husband, too," she pleaded.

A week passed but the fear remained inside, oppressive.

"You know what?" she said at the end of the week. "I'll invite the granddaughters, too, and we'll all go on a tour throughout Europe."

At that proposition, I could no longer resist.

The whole family set off. Grandmother Yehudit, Eli and me, and our three girls: fifteen-year-old Osnat, and the twins, Gili and Liat, then ten and a half.

We had a wonderful trip to Europe. We visited museums and saw paintings and sculptures in Italy. At the end of each museum tour, we adults felt like we were falling off our feet. As for the girls, who were already exhibiting artistic tendencies that only got stronger with time, they asked if we could start the tour all over again.

In Switzerland, we heard yodeling, ate fondue on shared family prongs, and climbed high mountains. We almost forgot the important stops we wanted to reach: Germany and Austria. Then came the moment – crossing the border between Switzerland and Germany, near the Schaffhausen Falls.

As we approached the border checkpoint, I felt a trickle of cold sweat running down my back. A German soldier came out of the booth.

"Everyone out of the vehicle, please," he ordered in German.

I didn't mind receiving reparation payments from Germany, nor did I mind speaking German to my parents at home. However, hearing the well-known order in this place, even if said politely, brought up an old, inner terror. I got out of the car, my legs shaking, and I handed him our papers. The policeman examined them and allowed us to continue on our way.

We drove to Munich. On the way, we wanted to visit the Dachau Concentration Camp. At the time, Waze didn't yet exist, so we pulled over to the side of the road. I got out of the car and stopped an older man. I didn't want to ask about the road to the concentration camp, so I asked cautiously, "Excuse me, sir. Do you know how we get from here to the Dachau Museum?"

The man's face reddened as if I had offended him.

"It is not a museum. It is a concentration camp!" he shouted in German. That was my first experience on German soil with a German.

It was the girls' first encounter with a Holocaust museum. There were no huts, objects, or gas chambers, but my children examined every photograph, every caption, and my heart went out to them. "What are they?" I wondered. Second or third generation of Holocaust survivors?" I have no answer even today. The important thing is that they're first-generation sabras.

From there we continued to Vienna. For my mother, Vienna was a place she had known well since her youth. She was nostalgic for the culture, music, and films of the famous Empress Sisi. Such nostalgia dwells in the hearts of all Chernowitz natives who grew up in the Austro-Hungarian culture of the previous century.

At first, we went to the huge cemetery of Vienna. We wanted to go to Grandfather Yossel's grave, which I had never seen. However, we had no landmark. It was raining hard. The place, a forest of evergreen trees and gravestones in various shapes, some magnificent, some in ruin, was enormous.

Mother walked without a map, without knowing what block or plot the grave was in, going where her legs carried her. Suddenly she stopped.

"It's here," she said.

We looked around. The graves were blocked from view by dense vegetation among thick trees.

"What's here, Mama?"

"Yossel's grave," she said, and began to make her way through the foliage, clearing away dry twigs and thick roots from the walkway.

We came upon a tall gray tombstone. On it, in blurry script, was written in Hebrew, Yiddish and German:

The rest of a pious innocent man
God's Commandments always in his heart
Head of Talmud Torah
In the city of Chernowitz
The Teacher Yosef Berav Zeev Schmelzer
Was gathered to his people on the Tenth day of Shevat, the
Hebrew year
May his soul rest in peace
JOSEL SCHMELZER
Aus Cernowitz
Geborn yahre 1840
Gestorbn 10 Feb 1917

Yossel was my grandfather. I had not known much about him, but I thought it was a great privilege for me as an Israeli to stand in this foreign land and connect the roots of the trees in the forest to the roots of my family.

Grandma Regina's Grave

For years I had heard the stories about my Grandma Regina: my father's great love for her and about the fabled city of Chernowitz, which was like Vienna. There they had both lived together peacefully for many years. However, I didn't think that I would ever visit it. Yet as part of my work at the Open University, I was sent to train Open University instructors how to teach the courses in the Soviet Union. I went twice, going from city to city, conducting workshops on how to be a good tutor. On a planned third visit, I had an incomprehensible longing and went on condition that I would be able to visit my hometown, Chernowitz.

It wasn't easy getting there. I had to take a ten-hour taxi ride on poor roads until I stood at the gates of "Little Vienna" – Chernowitz. As the taxi advanced down the main street of the city, I was astonished. The houses with the sculptures still stood – gray, peeling, neglected. Entire streets were only half-paved, and sewage flowed in the gutters. The town square was empty and no bells rang in my heart at being there. All the marvelous stories were as nothing. I felt an emptiness envelop me. I hired a very old person who was there during the war and after, even under the Communist regime. He took me to all the places connected with my family's history, such as Turkish Street, where the ghetto began, where Regina had her home and my parents' apartment on General Mircescu Street.

"Would you like to go in?" my guide asked me.

I nodded.

We went up to the third floor and he knocked on the door. A Gentile Russian woman opened the door. He explained to her in Russian who I was. I burst into tears and she stroked my head.

"Malyshka, Malyshka," she said, calling me a little girl in Russian.

I tried to imagine where my room had been, where the living room was, but nothing came to mind.

That evening I called my mother in Israel. "I was in our apartment in Chernowitz today."

Silence. I could hear her breathing.

"And did you go down to the basement, where Papa hid our money?"

"No, Mama. It's probably not there anymore."

The next day we toured the town square. The opera house stood desolate, empty and neglected, but signs of yesteryear remained. The Great Synagogue, where Yossel prayed, and where the cantor was none other than the renowned Joseph Schmidt, had been turned into a movie theater. In a remote corner of the hall was a small metal plaque:

"Cantor Joseph Schmidt prayed here."

I closed my eyes and tried to imagine the singing of the Yom Kippur prayer "*Kol Nidrei*" by Grandpa Yossel, Papa Machiku, and the boys. I heard nothing.

Opposite the synagogue was the small terrace where Hersch and Yetti stood when Dad came to ask them for Mama's hand. "Herrengasse" Street was, according to their stories, the most magnificent street in Chernowitz. The carriages passing by, the women in luxury clothing, the cafés – everything was gone. A world that is no more. Only the village women still sit on the street corners selling eggs, milk, and flowers as before. Everything is there, but as if in another world.

We went to the town hall, where I searched for the record of Grandma Regina's death. The clerk opened a massive ledger, and there, in handwriting, appeared the line:

Regina Schmeltzer. Died - June 1946

I asked the guide to take me to the cemetery. We came to a place with many crooked or shattered tombstones and dry vegetation. There was no attendant there, and without one, we could not have found her grave. To my great disappointment, we left without seeing it.

The Chernowitz of my early childhood is a world that is no more; if it survives, it is only in my imagination.

When I returned to Israel, I told my mother about the trip. She emitted a deep sigh. "Chernowitz was a world of culture, books, theater, and a picture-perfect life. We never went back," she added.

Later, many years after my visit to the city, the opportunity arose to close a circle. The "Next Generations" organization, in which I am active, planned a trip to Ukraine. Only after I was assured that we would pass through Chernowitz did I sign up for the trip.

"This time I have to go to the cemetery and find Regina's grave," I said to myself. "Whatever it costs, I'll put up a tombstone for her." I prepared everything in advance. I got a guide who came with a listing that he swore was original. We arrived at the cemetery. Everything seemed tidier than the last time. Maybe we entered from a different gate. Maybe they had spruced it up. We walked among high and low tombstones until we came to an arid plot of ground between two tombstones.

"This is here," said the guide. "Here's the map I made at City Hall. The official stamp is here."

I looked left and right, not sure that was the case. However, the guide stepped aside to give me privacy, and I wrapped my head in a scarf. Now I was closer to the age Regina was when Papa left. I wanted to light a memorial candle, only there was nowhere to put it. The place was full of weeds that could have caught fire. So, I put the candle on the stone of a neighboring grave and said two prayers – *Kaddish* and *El Malei Rachamim* – Merciful God."

I wondered if Papa's God, the *Kadosh Baruch Hu* (the Holy One, Blessed Be He) would hear my prayer, the prayer of a woman.

I wasn't able to erect a tombstone for my grandmother this time either, but I thought of the great love my mother and father had for their parents and the family they raised in Palestine-Eretz Israel. That is the best tombstone. A tombstone of construction, continuity, and hope.

Grandma Yetti's Grave

Grandma Yetti experienced what Regina and Yossel did not. She was privileged to immigrate and live in the State of Israel. She was fortunate to see the fulfillment of the Zionist dream in all its aspects. She was lucky enough to see her grandchildren grow up in this land and give them everything she could in the way of culture, poetry, and faith.

She lived until three weeks after my wedding. She couldn't come to the ceremony. She lay in bed, saw me in my white wedding dress, raised her hands to her eldest granddaughter, and recited a blessing.

When we returned from our honeymoon, she was already very ill. She waited to die so she could say goodbye to us. I wasn't allowed to go to the funeral "because 'children' do not go to the cemetery." My parents are also buried in the same cemetery in Givat Shaul in Jerusalem, a place of peace and serenity, in the midst of slender cypress trees. Everything there is neat and well maintained.

Yetti's grave is in Block C, Section 7. On her tombstone is engraved the name of Grandfather Hersch Zvi, who had not been privileged to immigrate to Israel, and the name of her grandson, Nathan-Norbert. He perished on the way to the camps in Transnistria, Romania, to where his family was deported during the war.

When I light the memorial candle, I tell Grandma about the new branch, the tribe – the Ganor clan: Eli, our three daughters, and the grandchildren. I also tell her that our escape gave life, a new life.

Epilogue
Living in "Eretz"

Papa Machiku

Papa adapted to life in the Land of Israel and never complained about anything. He always told people how we came to Palestine "wearing only a bathing suit." I never ventured to ask how they weren't shivering from cold when they arrived, since it was Purim and raining hard. It was of course a figure of speech that meant "We had nothing." Papa no longer dreamed of his work for society and the homeland being recognized, but he fulfilled his dream of becoming a full-fledged lawyer in the Land of Israel. While I studied for my matriculation exams, he studied for his law certification exams. On one festive sunny day, he showed up at home wearing a black courtroom gown and holding a lawyer and notary certificate in his hands. He bought all the volumes of the "Laws in Israel" series and ordered a suitable stamp for his new status. However, he believed that there was no longer any point in opening an office as a self-employed person, so he continued working at the JNF until he retired.

The opportunity to pursue his profession came his way when the Germans decided to give reparations to Holocaust survivors. People came to him for help filling out the forms in German and sending them to the relevant institutions. He refused to take a fee for his work. Even when he was in financial distress, he always made sure to give to others and not demand anything for himself. One day a woman survivor from Chernowitz arrived at our home with a huge cardboard box. Papa had succeeded in getting reparations for her and had refused to accept a fee. She bought him a fine set of dinnerware and coffee cups with saucers made by the well-known Rosenthal Company. My parents bequeathed the set to me and my brother Yossi. To this day, we don't use it. Each of us tries to persuade the other to keep it. So as not to quarrel about it, we take turns, alternating the coffee set and dishes set, all still unused.

Mama Donya

The home phone rang.

"Can I speak to Yehudit?"

"Who is this?"

"I'm calling from the Ministry of Education and Culture."

Yehudit is the Hebrew name of my mother, Ida-Donya.

She came to the phone. "Hello. Who's calling?"

"Yehudit, this is the director of the Art Festival. We need six million lira. Otherwise, this year the festival won't be able to take place."

"Yossi," she said to her boss, "don't worry. I'll find you the six million. The festival must go on."

I, who was then fifteen, heard the call and wondered how she could have six million pounds while I had to work all summer at a camp to buy myself a nice winter coat.

At the start of their joint journey as a couple, a division of roles was established between Donya and Machiku. He was the responsible adult, supportive and in charge. She, so many years younger than he, was to be protected from life's hardships. She was willing to follow him wherever he went, to leave her family and be together with him through all the vicissitudes of life.

She always insisted on doing what was important in order to get what she wanted. Her main goal was to be with him – an admired figure, an adult, a boss, and an intellectual. If he was to be strong, she must support him and give him center stage. He had the most significant role as the "anchor." Thus she managed to maintain a strong marriage for so many years. He didn't yield his strength, but she did and was often ill and needed his support. After they arrived in Israel, she began to realize she needed to get better and take an active part in life. This feeling within her came and went in secret, beneath the surface of their life together. She may not have been aware of it.

When Yossi the sabra son was old enough, she went to work outside the home. She got a job as a bookkeeper with the government's department of nutrition. I remember how they would sit side by side, Papa guiding her as she learned more and more. She later became the budget director in the Ministry of Education's Culture Division. As part of her job, she worked with the finest Ministers of Education: Shazar, Yigal Allon, and Navon. They would call her by phone to consult with her about the funds they needed to raise.

She was frail and needy until my father's death, and only afterward did she reveal herself in full force. We thought she wouldn't survive without him, but after almost forty years of marriage, her personality fully burst forth. She became a creative leader who contributes to others as much as she can. Only when he was no longer there to cast a huge shadow of protection did her true strength of character emerge. She increased her activity in the B'nai B'rith organization and established a club in his memory in the "Gilo" neighborhood of new immigrants in Jerusalem. There she served as the organizer of cultural programs and bazaars for the needy. The organizers would set up tables and people would put piles of clothes on them for donation. She made sure to mark them all. Some were sold for the benefit of new immigrants, and some were donated. For long hours, she would sit with an old typewriter and fill in forms for the new immigrants who came from Russia and were eligible for German reparations. All this, of course, was without payment.

At age ninety she still rode the bus from Katamon to Gilo – not in a taxi so as not to spend B'nai B'rith funds for personal use. She loved her granddaughters with all her heart. She supported them, listened to them, and accompanied them as they matured.

When she told them of Machiku's surprising marriage proposal they asked her, "Grandma, did he kiss you after he asked for your hand?"

"There was no such thing in those days," she replied emphatically.

And I...

As an adult and mother, I participated in a workshop organized by "Next Generations of Holocaust and Heroism." In the workshop, second-generation Holocaust survivors learned to tell the stories of their parents and their own experiences growing up in a family of survivors. We were a group of about thirty men and women. Already at the first meeting, each of us had to tell their story briefly. When my turn came, this is what I said:

"When the Russians entered the city of Chernowitz, the parents fled with their little girl to the forest and hid until the storm subsided."

"Where is your sister today?" asked the group facilitator.

"I don't have a sister."

"Then who is the little girl in the story?"

No sound came out of my throat. My heart pounded so hard that I was sure everyone could hear it. "I'm the girl," I finally replied.

There was silence. They all looked at me, stunned.

It was a turning point in my life. Following the fundamental question asked by the facilitator, I was struck by the recognition that I am a first-generation Holocaust survivor, not second-generation as I had perceived myself until then. I was there, even if I remembered nothing about it until I was six, apart from what my parents told me. I always saw myself as a second-generation child. One of my daughters had even tried to tell me in the past that I was a Holocaust survivor, and I had rejected the idea. In my eyes, I had all the signs of a daughter to parents who went through the Holocaust.

Mom has always been anxious for my brother and me. "Take a sweater to the dance," she would insist on Independence Day Eve, even if it was hot. "Be home before eleven and make sure someone escorts you to the door."

"Mama, it lasts until midnight. No one will want to accompany me," I protested.

But then I discovered that Papa had hid on the corner of the street leading from the building where my Scout troop met. He followed me from a distance so he wouldn't embarrass me in front of my friends.

Once, I sat up all night and cried until my parents broke down and agreed to let me attend an overnight Scout camp, working on a kibbutz.

In other words, in my eyes, the second generation was one that grew up in homes full of anxiety and behavior as if in the Diaspora. Every time Mama came to a parents' meeting at school, I would be ashamed of her floral dress, her hairstyle and the rolling "R" when she spoke Hebrew that revealed her origin.

However, we weren't considered "real" Holocaust survivors. We were just "Holocaust- light" – type B – because we had not been in the extermination camps. We had only spent almost three years in hiding and on the roads, from the day the Russians entered Chernowitz until 1944, when we arrived in Palestine.

So what are we? Holocaust survivors or not?

In first grade, I was considered a new immigrant. I had pierced ears; I felt inferior to the children from the pure Sephardic families. These families had been rooted in Israel for many generations, and I attended the Beit Hakerem School in Jerusalem with their offspring.

The turning point in my social standing began only after my teacher Remma Samsonov recognized my recitation and performance qualities and recruited me for the school entertainment troupe that performed on holidays and festivals in many venues, in school and at other places.

The change in my concept about my own place in the Holocaust came only after the workshop. It was there that I understood and recognized my being part of the first generation. I have since learned that there is also a special title for people like me: "baby survivors." Yet I continued to feel that I also belonged to the second generation, a kind of mixed package.

Consequently, I, too, began to see in myself signs of the first generation: In the theater, for example, I always had to sit on the aisle, subconsciously prepared in case I had to run away. I always have a piece of bread in my bag, and a sweater near me.

My personal turning point brought me to the realization that these stories must be told and passed down from generation to generation.

Today I organize and lead workshops for the "Next Generations" so that people can learn how to tell their own stories and their families' Holocaust stories.

Step by step, through study and then attending a writing workshop, I acquired the capacity to look at myself as a child, with empathy and compassion, as well as at my parents, who did their best to stay alive.

It is impossible to know how the events I went through as a child affected me. I don't remember anything until the age of six. I've even tried to remember through hypnosis, but nothing brought back my memory. However, psychology says that a child's body remembers, and the body speaks as if it had words. To this day, my hair curls up at the sound of chickens squawking, even while watching TV or reading something about chicken coops.

I have never forgotten the eyes of the jackals. The specific memory of their gathering around the tent, or emitting blood-curdling howls, is gone, but my fear of them remains. Every animal that reminds me of jackals scares me, especially cats. To me, their howling is very similar to that of the jackals, as are their eyes and teeth.

I cannot go into water without feeling great fear, real horror. In my dreams, I walk into the sea, and waves that get higher and higher swallow me up.

The Next Generations

Machiku and Donya have been gone for many years. The generation they brought has grown and developed. My brother Yossi took a Hebrew last name – Ari – which is short for our father's name, Arieh. He specialized in the field of health and became a key figure in that field at the Phoenix Insurance Company.

I married Eli Ganor. We had three daughters: Osnat, and the twins, Gili and Liat. Four grandchildren were born to the family: Shalev and Yuval to Osnat, Daniel and Yael to Gili. Liat is a proud, loving aunt to her nephews and is devoted to them. Sometimes I think how proud my parents would be to help raise these great-grandchildren. Each one is beautiful in their own way, and each one grows and develops in their unique way. The chain goes on. And in the words of the Zionist lullaby "There Where the Cedars Grow," that my mother used to sing to me:

> *"Even though cruel hands expel me,*
> *And I wander from place to place,*
> *My heart is forever in Zion.*
> *I turn east to the sun, my eyes burn with pain*
> *My prayers go out to the hallowed shore*
> *Where God will bring me once more."*

Acknowledgments

This story has been in my heart for many years and had not been written. I thank everyone who helped me bring it into the world. I grew up with some of the stories and filled in many details from sources I had; the rest I completed through my imagination. Many questions remain unanswered. When it was still possible, I didn't ask, and today – there is no one to ask.

My dear parents, thanks to you I am here in Israel today. You believed we would arrive, and you had faith that good would prevail, despite the myriad difficulties along the way. You instilled this belief in me as well.

My beloved daughters, Osnat, Gili, and Liat, and my maturing grandchildren, Shalev, Daniel, Yuval, and Yael, served as my inspiration and my goal: to leave this story of the family's past so that it will not be forgotten.

To all those who encouraged me to write and accompanied me along the way, I am deeply grateful.

Ilan Sheinfeld, author, editor, gifted teacher, and writing workshop facilitator – you opened the door to the world of literary writing, accompanying me patiently and professionally in the process of searching for the path from the beginning, sentence after sentence, character after character, until the creative forces found their way and broke out. Finally, you also edited my book with your characteristic skill. Thanks to you, even today, at my advanced age, the melody goes on.

My dear friends, partners in the writing group – Hanochi, Galia, Ricky, Lanka, Yael, and Etti – you have been a source of encouragement, love, and feedback. Together we wrote and supported each other. We shared secrets and became a family. Together we rejoiced with those of us who already brought out a book – and there are more to come.

Dr. Rachel Shifron, Adlerian Psychologist: The beginning was when I saw your husband Gadi's book, which tells about your life, and I didn't think I could do that. You were there for me in the writing process – guiding, encouraging, reading, and illuminating the road to the heart and the past.

Jungian psychoanalyst Esti Li-Dar, group facilitator and storyteller: I met you many years ago at the Next Generations' "How to Tell the Story" workshops. You imbued in me your spirit with your way of telling a story to bring the full experience and emotion of someone who grew up in the home of parents who came from "there."

My dear friend Yael Yotam who lives in France: We met when we both wrote our doctoral dissertations. You listened with interest to my story of the escape, and since then you have encouraged me to tell it. You tried to help with your insight and creativity, and you told me again and again how important the story is and how worthwhile it is to tell it.

Yossi Ari, the first sabra in the family and my beloved brother: You were there for our parents and Grandma Yetti. You traveled with our parents and saw our father find his father Yossel's grave in the huge cemetery in Vienna. You enriched the stories, and thanks to you I filled in important things that I didn't know about at all.

Zeev Milch, a dear, close friend: You had a listening ear and I turned to you whenever I got lost in the literature and historical background of the period. You read my first draft and your comments helped light the way in my writing.

Professor Zvi Yavetz (Harry Zucker), my first Hebrew teacher in Cyprus, later a noted historian and one of the founders of Tel Aviv University, filled in many gaps about Chernowitz and our time spent in Cyprus. He continued to call me Litika and we remained in contact until he passed away in 2013.

When his book about Chernowitz was published, he gave me a copy, with this dedication:

> To Litika and Eli,
> *This time not a book about Rome*
> *But a simple story about my childhood*
> *In the city you fled from in 1942.*
> *With deepest affection,*
> Zvi Yavetz

My cousins – Bubbi's children, Ruth Figel and Yoji Schmelzer. Since you were adults when you left Chernowitz, you recalled many details about the city, the family, and the war. You contributed your memories and your sentiments, and I am grateful to you.

Yuvali Cohen-Ganor, my 11-year-old grandson asked me, "Grandma, who do you want to read this book? Children? Adults?" When I replied, "Everyone," you suggested the Hebrew name of the book, "Escape to Life," which I immediately agreed to.

Gili Van Amen Ganor, my daughter: When I was looking to "dress" my book in a cover, you undertook the task with understanding and creativity and faithfully drew what I saw in my imagination.

Sources

Schmelzer, L. (1942). *A handwritten diary (in German) about the period from August 1942, recounting 49 days on the beach in Karataş, Turkey.* Located in the Zionist Archives.

Schmelzer, L. (1970). *A detailed interview on the period of the Russians in Chernowitz (1940-1941),* submitted to the Institute for Diaspora Jewry, The Hebrew University, Jerusalem.

Schmelzer, M. (2004). *"Beyond the Future: Stories My Father Told Me."* (self-published).

Yavetz, Z. (2007). *"My Chernowitz,"* Kinneret, Zmora-Bitan Publishers Ltd., Israel 2007.

"Geschichte Der Juden in Der Bukowina" (1958). EDT. In German, vol. 1-2.

Our World, Tel Aviv, Israel[1]

---

1. Dr. Leon Schmelzer was among the writers and served as a member of the publishing committee. The volumes were written in Israel, but deal with events and opinions that originate many decades back. For me this was an important lesson in the history of Zionism as it developed in Bukovina. It included important personalities in its history, and leading figures from my family who influenced the events. There I saw for the first time a photograph of my paternal grandfather Yossel, whom I never got to know, and another photograph of Dr. Chaim Weizmann during his visit to Bukovina.